THE CONFESSION OF
PIERS GAVESTON

THE CONFESSION OF PIERS GAVESTON

a novel
by
Brandy Purdy

iUniverse, Inc.
New York Lincoln Shanghai

The Confession of Piers Gaveston

Copyright © 2007 by Brandy Purdy

iUniverse books may be ordered through booksellers or by contacting:

iUniverse
2021 Pine Lake Road, Suite 100
Lincoln, NE 68512
www.iuniverse.com
1-800-Authors (1-800-288-4677)

Because of the dynamic nature of the Internet, any Web addresses or links contained in this book may have changed since publication and may no longer be valid.

Certain characters in this work are historical figures, and certain events portrayed did take place. However, this is a work of fiction. All of the other characters, names, and events as well as all places, incidents, organizations, and dialogue in this novel are either the products of the author's imagination or are used fictitiously.

ISBN: 978-0-595-45523-2 (pbk)
ISBN: 978-0-595-89832-9 (ebk)

Printed in the United States of America

What greater bliss can hap to Gaveston
Than to live and be the favorite of a king?

—from *Edward II* by Christopher Marlowe

THE BEGINNING:
THE BURNING

In every candle flame, in every torch, camp and bon fire, I see her face. Every time I stretch out my hands to the hearth's welcoming warmth, I see her writhing in agony amongst the flames: blackened, burnt, and bald, her beautiful long black hair all gone, eaten up by the hungry flames. And I hear the rattle of the heavy chains binding her firmly against the stake.

Her eyes alone—so deep a brown they appear black, just like mine—remain the same, human still, amidst the ruins of a beauty the flames would render monstrous. The fire, and those who condemned her to this fate, have stripped her of everything else—her dignity, her liberty, her property, her life. They have also deprived two young children—a boy of seven and a newborn girl—of their mother. But "Justice must be done," "Thou shall not suffer a witch to live," her judges sanctimoniously declare.

Though twenty years have come and gone, her eyes haunt me still. Awake or dreaming, I see them, pain-filled and beseeching, rimmed in red and overflowing with tears, as they turn to me, silently conveying a message heart-heavy with a mother's love and regret that she will not be there to care for me and see me to manhood grown.

I hold her gaze, and it is as if we two are alone, and my ears are deaf and my eyes blind to the boorish Gascon peasants and French soldiers that surround us. Even though my nursemaid, Agnes, is there, her hand upon my shoulder, I neither hear nor heed her tearful, urgent pleas that we leave this accursed place. In this moment only my mother and I exist, everything else is as nothing, and time has stopped.

Even should I be cursed with eternal life, forgetfulness would never find me. The memory is seared into my mind just as surely as if it had been branded there. Indeed, my body *is* branded. I carry the mark of that day upon my hands in the form of scars from when I, a foolish and hysterical child, tried to pull her from the flames.

Even now I am haunted by the laughter of those who watched as I yelped and leapt back, reeling, nearly fainting from the blistering intensity of the pain radiating from my palms. I *hated* myself then; defeated by the least little lick of the flames, when she stood powerless and trapped within their midst. And, most of all, I hated them—that merry, mocking crowd, cavorting round the bonfire like May Day revelers while my mother burned!

How many of them had come to her for healing herbs, salves, and specially brewed teas to help ease their aches and pains, to have their wounds dressed, their bones set, and their children brought into the world? How many of them had found their way, in tears and dire need, to our door? My mother, Claremunda of Marcia, was as kind and wise as she was beautiful, and her heart and door were *always* open to those in need; no one was *ever* turned away. And now they dubbed her "Satan's handmaiden" and cast her into "the purifying power of flame!" Hypocrites! My heart screamed.

Nowadays those who gaze upon my hands say the scars are the Devil's Mark, left upon my flesh when Satan's crimson-eyed night-black hellhounds reared their ugly heads to lick Piers Gaveston's hands the night he swore his allegiance to the Dark Lord. I make no attempt to hide them. I wear gloves only in winter and when I ride. All other times, I flaunt them, decking them with a glittering array of rings, especially rubies which I adore above all gems. Even though they ceased to pain me long ago, Edward, His Most Christian Majesty King Edward II by the Grace of God, (or Nedikins as he prefers me to call him in our most intimate moments), covers them with kisses and soothing lotions as if they still festered and throbbed. But the truth is, no lotion, no matter how cool or sweet smelling, can soothe away the pain of seeing the person you love best in the world being burned alive before your very eyes while you stand by, small, helpless, and alone, surrounded by those who do naught but laugh and cheer.

No sooner had I leapt back from the fire's agonizing kiss than I was swept up, high into the air, by the village priest. "*Thou shall not suffer a witch to live!*" his voice thundered as he held me above the dancing flames and I felt the soles of my red leather shoes scorch. Choking and nauseous from the scent of smoke, and her dear burning flesh, he drew me back, and a tearful sigh escaped me, for I had grown so slick with sweat I feared I would slip from his grasp and fall straight into the flames. He turned me round to face him and I remember thinking what a crime it was to entrust a man with such soulless eyes with the salvation of men's souls. "*Thou shall not suffer a witch to live!*" he repeated, shaking me hard. "Remember that, Piers Gaveston, witch's brat!" With that he cast me aside, flinging me from him as if I were some stinking bit of offal that offended his nose and eyes. I struck the ground so hard that my shoulder was jarred from its socket and the breath knocked from my lungs.

Before I could regain my breath or wits and summon strength enough to scream the curses that raged within my heart, Agnes snatched me up and fled as fast as her legs could carry her. From over her shoulder I had my last glimpse of my mother. The chains had stopped rattling. She was still now; her head sagged forward, like a flower grown too heavy for its stem.

This is how my story begins. Of course I was born like everyone else, but it was the day my mother died that changed forever the course of my life; a life, like hers, that is also likely to end in murder.

Thus here I sit in gloomy, windswept Scarborough Castle, perched high upon the cliffs above a raging sea, awaiting Edward's return with reinforcements—by which I mean a miracle—while Pembroke's army bays for my blood. Or is that but a delusion wrought by the crashing waves and the wind whistling through the cold stone walls?

Our provisions, like our numbers, are few; few would rally to the cause of the most hated man in England. And with every day that passes that number shrinks as yet more of my supporters slink away into the night.

The time to surrender draws nigh. I will not see this siege drawn out until all are skeletons and starving. But not yet, not while a slender hope remains that Edward may return in time, even though that hope has no more substance than a cobweb, I will cling to it for just a little while longer. Soon, I will do what needs to be done, soon; but not yet. For now I shall while away the anxious hours with this little book Edward gave me.

The covers are gold, embossed with vibrant emeralds and peerless pearls, but the pages are blank, a clean creamy field of vellum that awaits my words. When he gave it to me, Edward said that the words I would fill it with would far eclipse the value of the gems outside, though I daresay he intended that I should immortalize our love in poetry or pen laments to dying swans.

Poor Nedikins, I fear the value he places upon both me and my words will plummet when he reads this; *if* he reads this. Whether this book will ever reach him, I do not know. But, if it does, and should it survive that encounter, it will be in a *very* battered state. You see, I know Edward very well. For twelve years I have been the center of his world. Verily, I can see him now as he reads the revelations I shall soon set down. Pearls and emeralds will fly as he bashes this book against the wall, or flings it onto the floor and leaps and stomps upon it, screaming: *"How could you do this to me?"* Like as not, he will end by throwing it in the fire then burn his fingers snatching it out again. He may even set his tunic afire beating out the flames. But be that as it may, I am determined to set down the truth about my life since no one else can do it for me.

Edward is blinded by desire, to him I am perfection. His behavior does naught to belie the rumors that I have bewitched him. In England they say there are two kings: Edward who reigns, and Gaveston who rules. And to my child-bride Meg, so sweet and trusting, I have been too much a stranger. Agnes and Dragon, who know all, can neither read nor write. Others know fragments of the story, but not the whole, and by everyone else I am despised.

Mayhap even now, when I have only just begun, it is already too late to set the story straight. My infamy, I fear, is too well entrenched. Whenever they tell the story of Edward's reign I will always be the villain and Edward, the poor, weak-willed, pliant king who fell under my spell, the golden victim of a dark enchantment. There are *two* sides to every coin, but when the bards and chroniclers, the men who write the histories, tell this story will anyone remember that?

People say so many things: facts, falsehoods, and fanciful marriages betwixt the two, but nothing is ever exactly as it seems. Whatever I am—good or bad, wrong or wronged, guilty or not—*please* do not condemn me unheard. As the end of my life draws nigh, please allow me to have my say; withhold your judgment for just a little while ...

A Companion Fit
For A Prince

I lost everything the day my mother died. No one can ever know how much it hurts to wind the clock of memory back to the days before ... before she died, before I became infamous and notorious, a harlot in masculine form, the most hated man in England, and the beloved bedfellow of a feckless, addle-pated king, the object of an obsession that nearly sank the ship of state and tore the land asunder.

I was born in Gascony, in the year 1284, and before they burned my mother a castle was our home. It was crafted of golden stone, with a large rose garden, fish ponds, and an orchard that yielded apples, cherries, and pears. And behind the kitchen there was an herb garden, with a sundial at its center, where I used to sit and play with my spaniel while my mother and Agnes gathered the ingredients for their remedies.

After her marriage, my mother had borne three sons in quick succession, my brothers Arnaud, Raimond, and Guillaume. My father, Arnaud de Gaveston, was overwhelmed by his good fortune. Not only had the need for an heir been more than amply met, but he had been blessed with this trio of hale and hearty sons who favored him in both appearance and demeanor, while I was entirely my mother's child. Where they were tall, big-boned, and sturdy, my slenderness and middling height gave the deceptive appearance of delicacy, a fallacy that, in years to come, would cause many to think me an unworthy opponent in the tiltyard and battle. So I, being in a sense superfluous, was left entirely to my mother, to ease her loneliness, and be both a comfort and companion to her. And I could not have been happier! For the first seven years of my life, I was cherished and adored!

By any standards, my mother was a remarkable woman, not only beautiful but wise. In this world where women are regarded as ignorant chattels little better than cattle and are prized only for their beauty, childbearing abilities, dowries, and housewifely skills, her learning set her apart. And it was my good fortune to inherit her quick mind. She taught me languages and poetry, songs and stories of romance, fables, history, and heroes, and to dance, play upon the lute and harp, and to write a graceful hand, and she insisted that I acquire a firm grasp of mathematics.

And having, at that time, no daughter to pass her secrets on to, she initiated me into her ancient religion. She taught me to love and revere the goodness and light that is the Lady, the Goddess, men worshipped long before the Christ came. And she taught me never to fear death and told me all about the Isle of Apples where our souls sail away to when we die. But we were ever mindful of the Law and the Church's persecution of our kind—they called us Witches—and for safety's sake, we donned the masks of proper Christians. Mass we seldom missed, we dutifully confessed our sins, and a chaplain was always a part of our household. Together, with Agnes and our little coven, we performed rituals and spells, to honor the Lady and ask Her to protect us and bless all of our endeavors, and grant us health, happiness, and a bountiful harvest, or to bring the rains when a drought threatened. And with the herbs that are Her gift to us, we healed the sick and eased the pain of those in the throes of suffering, dying, or laboring to bring a new life into the world. And four times a year we came together to celebrate the change of seasons. But curses we *never* did speak, nor harm a man or hex his crops or beasts!

I saw my father so rarely he was almost a stranger to me. And I knew my brothers little better. They were soldiers all, their allegiance sworn to the English King Edward I, and the business of war often took them away. I was always uneasy in their company, to my child's eyes they seemed so big and brawny, always laughing and passing a flagon of wine between them. Their coarse jests, lusty boasts, and heated brawls both bewildered and repulsed me. When they deigned to notice me at all, it was only to make me the butt of one of their jests. Indeed, they would never really notice me until I became Edward's Favorite, then they would come scurrying to court, drunken, surly, and avaricious, and I often had occasion to wish them at the bottom of the sea, they did so plague and vex me.

But on the whole, mine was a very happy childhood. Until the night every-thing fell apart and shattered, and I learned, at the tender age of seven, what frag-ile, precious things love, happiness, contentment, and security are; no matter how much you treasure them, they can all be taken from you—stolen, destroyed, or irretrievably lost—within an instant. And when all your hopes and happiness hang upon one single person and you lose them ... it is like having your heart ripped out of your chest while it still pulses, beats, and bleeds. The pain is inde-scribable, and you *long* for death, but it doesn't come, and you have no choice but to suture the wound closed as best you can and go on with a life that has lost all or most of its meaning. And though you would do *anything* to get them back, there is *nothing* you can do, the hopelessness and despair, the desperation and sense of failure, are like a quartet of the keenest, sharpest daggers embedded deep within your heart. And you learn to fear love even as you crave it; to put up walls around your heart even as you long for someone to come along and tear them down, because you know what it is to lose everything that matters, and if it hap-pened once, it *can* happen again; there is no pain worse, and the fear never goes away.

I was sleeping in my mother's bed the night the French soldiers came for her. I remember the sharp splintering of wood as they bashed the doors in, startling us from a sound sleep, and my spaniel's outraged barking. With rough hands, they dragged her from the bed in her night-shift with her abundant black hair flowing wild about her face and down her back, like a cloak, all the way to her knees.

The village priest was there, a tall, black-clad figure, hovering ominously behind the soldiers. I can still see his cold, dead eyes of the palest icy blue, and grim, thin-lipped mouth. His white hair, still thick despite his years, was cut round, as though someone had placed a bowl upside down upon his head. He was the last to leave. He lingered in the doorway, glaring at me, as I sat cowering in the bed, frozen by fear, hugging the rose satin coverlet tight against my chest.

My spaniel growled and lunged at his ankle. Calmly, with no shadow of emo-tion flickering across his pale face, he dealt my pet a savage kick before he turned his back and left the room, his black robes billowing out behind him. Only then could I move. I sprang out of bed and sped down the stairs, just in time to see my mother being dragged outside.

Agnes ran to her and tried to drape a cloak about her shoulders, for it was a cold night and she was clad only in her shift and bare feet, but the soldiers shoved her aside. "Take care, old woman, lest we come back for you!" they cautioned.

At the *very* moment my mother's feet crossed the threshold, there was a deaf-ening crash of thunder and the sky opened up, lightning flashed fit to blind, and the rain came down in torrents. The soldiers jumped and trembled and their hands flew up to form the sign of the cross.

"*Witch!*" the priest snarled. "Such tricks will avail you naught!" His hand shot out to slap her. "*Take her!* Those whose faith in the Lord is strong need never fear *her* power!"

They shackled her with heavy chains, and, as they led her away, the howling wind carried her voice back into the castle, sending me her love and imploring Agnes to take care of her children.

I would have followed her, but Agnes held me back. She carried me back upstairs, stroking my hair and murmuring soothing words as I lay my head upon her shoulder and wept. She tried to calm and distract me by having me help her tend my poor spaniel, who had suffered a broken leg, but I could tell her fear was as great as mine. There was a quaver in her voice and her hands shook.

I never saw my mother again before the burning, and for years afterwards I lived in terror that the French soldiers, or others like them, would make good their threat to take Agnes. Many a year would pass before I could sleep through the night without suffering nightmares that made me wake up screaming.

When I left the village of Guienne that terrible day I was without a penny or a home. Were it not for Agnes and our devoted manservant Dragon, I would have been an orphan as well. My father was beyond reach, having offered himself as a hostage to the French King on Edward I's behalf—an action he would undertake thrice before prison conditions fatally undermined his health—and my brothers were also with the army. And what lands and manors we had not lost through my father's ardent espousal of the English King's cause, were confiscated upon my mother's death, for the Law states that the property of a condemned witch is forfeit, and my mother was a wealthy woman in her own right, having inherited much from her late father.

We sheltered in the forest near the castle that had been our home. Agnes, who is never without her leather satchel that brims with herbs, specially prepared salves, bandages, and almost everything else a healer requires, maneuvered my shoulder back into its socket and applied a poultice of comfrey root and honey to my hands while Dragon held my baby sister.

Dragon, I should now explain, is so named because of an ailment of the skin that lends the appearance of scales, and a wild, ferocious countenance that conceals a heart both tender and true. He roamed the roads as a vagabond, an outcast who likened his life to that of a leper, until the day he met my mother. Her kindness, coupled with her skill with herbs, eased his suffering, thus winning her his lifelong loyalty. He would have lain down his life to save her. The French soldiers beat him brutally when he tried, and he lay senseless and bloody in the muck where they had thrown him while she burned. For the rest of his life Dragon would bear the scars of that day, just like me. The beating left him with a dragging limp and a deep, furrowed gash in his left cheek that savagely twisted the side of his mouth and garbled his speech. Never again a clear word would he speak, and greater still would be the horror of those who looked upon his face.

Of Amy, the babe my mother was nursing when the hammer of Justice came crashing down on our contented little world, I can hardly bear to write.

Unlike most great ladies, my mother would not have a wet-nurse, she would feed each child born of her body on true mother's milk instead of that which flowed from the breasts of a hired stranger. After the burning no one would take pity, no one would suckle the witch's babe. Under cover of darkness, Dragon stole milk from cows and goats, but Amy would accept neither. She screamed in hunger and protest until she could scream no more, then she whimpered.

Dragon dug a tiny grave at the foot of an ancient apple tree, and by the light of the moon that is the sacred symbol of the Lady, I laid her tenderly in the earth as if it were a cradle. "Go to the Isle of Apples, little sister," I softly whispered. "Eat of the magic fruit and become eternal." Agnes sprinkled apple blossoms over her tiny corpse and Dragon filled in the grave.

It is far too painful to fully delve into the years that followed. No doubt it will surprise many that the King's pampered and petted minion has experienced all the ugliness and brutality of poverty firsthand. I, who sit at Edward's side and preside over lavish banquets, have lived on nature's fruit and watery gruel. And I, the flaunting, preening peacock in gaudy multihued satins, silks, and velvets, have gone barefoot dressed in patched and threadbare homespun hand-me-downs.

After the Church's "purifying flames" consumed my mother, I roamed about Gascony being passed fast and frequently betwixt my kin. All of them had mouths enough of their own to feed without the added burden of a growing lad with a broken heart and burned hands, a limping, sad-eyed spaniel, an aging nursemaid rightly reputed to be a witch, and a grotesquely disfigured manservant whose looks never failed to produce a shudder and hastily averted eyes.

It was all very painful and bewildering, this sudden plunge into poverty and grudgingly given charity. None of my kin felt any affection for me, and they never let me forget the debt of gratitude I owed them for succoring "The Witch's Brat." And years later, when I became the King's Favorite, they were quick to call in that debt, and I was quick to pay; I wanted them and the unpleasant memories to go away.

Someday, I vowed, I would be the center of someone's world again. I would rise like a phoenix from the ashes of poverty, and love and riches would again be mine! I have since learned that the life of every person is like a book of lessons, and here I will give you one from mine: Be careful what you wish for lest you get it; Time may reveal it to be more than you bargained for. There is *always* a price to be paid. No wish is ever granted free and gratis; somehow, someway, someday we *always* pay, and it is often our misfortune to discover that the price is far too great, but by then it is too late.

All those years until I was of an age to join my father and brothers in the army, I struggled not to slip into common, lowborn ways. Heedless of the ridicule it earned me, I fought to retain the courtly manners my mother taught me. As I toiled for my bread and board, and left one relative who did not want me to go to another and then another, I recited poetry and stories, I sang, did sums, and set myself exercises in Latin, French, English, and Italian grammar. Sometimes I even augmented our meager funds by working as a scribe and writing letters for those who could not. In the marketplaces of the villages we visited Agnes sold love potions, charms, and remedies, while I plied my pen for pennies, and Dragon took whatever work he could find. Sometimes we stole if our circumstances were dire. We did what was required and sacrificed our morals to survive.

When I reached the proper age, I went to Flanders to join my father and brothers in the English King's army.

Agnes accompanied me, and neither of us cared a mite about the other men's jests that I was the only soldier they had ever known who brought his nurse with him on campaign. Cooks, wives, and harlots they could well understand, but a nursemaid for a grown man unencumbered by children? "Mark me; I have set a new fashion!" I declared and went on my merry way. Agnes has always been the constant in my life, the only one who truly *knows* and loves *me*, and I would not have been parted from her for the world, nor she from me.

I acquitted myself well and seemed to have a natural aptitude for soldiering. Though by no means was it easy! On the contrary, the training was arduous and grueling, more rigorous than anything I had ever known. Everyday, when I returned to my tent at sunset, I was hobbling like an old woman, so sore I could hardly move. I spent hours soaking in my copper bathtub in water just as hot as I could stand, endeavoring to drive the soreness out. And afterwards, when I gingerly lowered myself onto my cot, it was not fragrant oils Agnes rubbed into my skin, but strong liniment. Every part of my body ached, especially my arms, shoulders, back, and thighs. From dawn till dusk I was learning to wield the weapons of war, the crossbow, broadsword, mace, lance, and shield, to move in a suit of heavy, clanking armor and chain-mail, and to fight on solid ground and astride a horse.

One evening, when I lay sleeping upon my cot, still on my stomach after my massage, my naked body glistening with, and reeking of, liniment, the captain who had charge of my training came into my tent. I started awake at the touch of his hand upon my back. He bade me to remain as I was. He had a proposition for me. We both knew I had the makings of a great soldier, I was making excellent progress, and there was no reason why I should not advance further and faster. His hand roved downward, over the small of my back, and lingered meaningfully upon my bottom. The decision was mine to make, he said, his fingers questing, I could suffer the slow and agonizing repetition of these same exercises day after day for a *very* long time, or I might progress at a swifter pace, as my quick mastery of each successive skill warranted.

It was obvious what he wanted, and his hands parting my thighs made it even more so. I protested that I was weary to the bone and ached all over.

"Then a little more soreness won't matter; will it?" he asked.

I said I supposed not and let him do as he liked while I lay like a corpse beneath him, though he seemed not to mind, and afterwards departed my tent with a smile after flipping a penny onto my back. Alone once again, I lay there feeling empty and cold inside, and missing my spaniel; she had died of old age the year before. It was at such times that I always missed her most.

He was by no means my first; far from it in fact. I'd had lovers before, both male and female. For me sex is money, sex is power, sex is *survival!*

I lost my virtue early. It was stolen from me in the most violent, ugly, and terrifying manner imaginable, as part of a secret bargain struck between my uncle— a most unscrupulous innkeeper—and the lodger who occupied the best room.

Greedy for the coins proffered him; my uncle sold me without a care or remorse. I was nine years old at the time. After I recovered, I would have no more of *family charity*. And so a boy-harlot I became. It was my idea entirely; no one forced or persuaded me. Agnes was horrified and wept when she found out what I had done and begged me to desist. "Do not walk this path, Piers!" she pleaded, but I had already decided. I know it all sounds rather cold and calculating, and far too weighty a decision for such a young child to make, but sometimes the truth is like that, and I was already old beyond my years. My rapist had opened my eyes to my allure, and my value. The Goddess gifted me with *great* beauty, the kind that inspires awe and takes the beholder's breath away, and as a male and a child I was doubly forbidden. Sodomy, like witchcraft, can lead straight to the stake and—if you believe in that sort of thing—an eternity of hellfire afterwards.

And I, with my dark, precocious, come-hither eyes and knowing smile, was temptation personified, and the coins came pouring in.

It was easy. All I had to do was smile, take off my clothes, think of the coins and the food, shelter, shoes and clothing they would buy, and pretend that their kisses and caresses did not leave me feeling numb, empty, and cold inside. And soon the words "pleasure" and "pretense" became one inside my mind, and upon the bedsheets I became a most accomplished play-actor. My body quickly learned the rules of the game, and how to deliver what was expected, but I never felt the spark of passion. But I didn't care. Now horses carried us on our travels, we were garbed and shod in nothing but the finest, and we dined upon the best fare the innkeepers and my patrons could provide. They gave me jewels and furs, some even claimed to love me, but to them my heart was a locked door. One gentleman swore I was worth my weight in gold and sat me naked upon a scale then, true to his words, counted out the coins accordingly. He squandered his entire fortune upon me. I heard he died in an almshouse two years later, damned and disgraced, disowned by his family, without a penny to his name. He did not heed my warning: "Loving me is expensive." He said I was worth it. Did he still think so at the end, I wonder?

As for the captain who had his way with me, well I soon had *my* way with him! And I made it clear that my favors do not come so cheaply! I was *never* a penny whore; at nine I was worth more than nine whores put together, and at fourteen my value certainly hadn't fallen! And when my horse was killed beneath me in battle I had a new black charger with four white feet worth three times the value of any other horse in the King's army and a squire to attend to my new horse, armor, and weaponry. It was the captain's decision, made when he found me weeping outside the King's tent, waiting to report my rape.

I continued to serve in the English army, soldiering and playing harlot whenever time and chance permitted. Then, while in Scotland on one of his many campaigns, King Edward singled me out for an unprecedented honor—I was to join the household of the Prince of Wales in the hope that I might prove a good influence on that flighty, feckless young man.

Young Edward, it seemed, was altogether lacking in the masculine attributes and princely dignity that his father considered essential for a future king. Military pursuits made the Prince yawn and roll his eyes in boredom, and he habitually fell asleep at tournaments, though he enjoyed hunting and riding to a certain extent. He loved pageantry and display, to stage theatricals, and to keep low company, consorting with the likes of ditch-diggers and bargemen. And he liked nothing better than to scamper up a ladder and thatch a cottage roof, or spend a day digging ditches, trimming hedges, or rowing in the fens. To his mind, there were no pleasures greater.

In my person, the King explained, were embodied all the best qualities of a refined gentleman and a seasoned soldier; courtier and warrior perfectly balanced, each in just the right measure. I was neither too rugged and coarse, nor too delicate and effete despite my middling height and willow-slender build. If I were to become the Prince's companion, it was hoped that, in time, he might come to emulate me. There are many who say now in hindsight—myself included—that it was the *worst* mistake Edward Longshanks ever made!

The year was 1300, a new century and a new beginning for me, when Agnes, Dragon, and I arrived at Langley, the Prince's country manor in Hertfordshire. I was sixteen, the same age as Prince Edward himself. My memories of that day are so keen it might have happened yesterday!

The Great Hall where the Prince was to receive me was the most splendid I had ever seen. Its walls were painted in cheerful shades of red and yellow, decorated with bright, colorful shields and a mural of jousting knights. Musicians in the Prince's blue and gold livery played in the gallery overhead, filling the air with the pleasing harmony of fife, lute, tabor, and harp. And sweet-scented rushes cushioned the stone floor. Sumptuously arrayed nobles, haughty and aloof, ranged themselves in two rows leading to the royal dais and eyed me with interest and suspicion.

I was dressed humbly, but well, in a red wool tunic with black silk hose and soft, high, black leather boots. A black leather belt cinched my waist, because I must have something to hang my sword and purse from, and at the same time served to further accentuate my slenderness. My black wool cloak was fastened at the shoulder with my most precious possession, the brooch that had been my mother's favorite—a silver crescent moon paved with sparkling diamond chips; it was the only thing of hers I had been able to save. My black hair was freshly washed and trimmed to chin-length, and, unlike most men, I disdained to wear a beard or moustache and kept my face clean-shaven instead—the better to invite caresses I've found. Besides, a beard might detract from my mouth—sensual, arrogant, and inviting all at the same time, the kind of mouth that makes people either want to kiss me or slap me, though some find it exceedingly difficult to decide between the two.

Verily, I know this dwelling upon my appearance gives the impression of vanity, nor will I plead "not guilty" to such a charge, but as I write this I do not know what roads this memoir will travel down, whether it will be tossed contemptuously into the fire by one of my enemies, rendered unreadable by Edward's copiously flowing tears, or preserved and passed down through the centuries. If the latter be the case, then it might be of interest to future generations to know my outer appearance as well as the inner workings of my mind. Myself, when I read a story, I always like to be able to picture the characters, and maybe you do as well.

I confess I was *terrified* as I approached the dais where the Prince sat, or rather lolled, under a gold-fringed canopy, yawning and sleepy-eyed, in a throne-like chair. But I hid it well; by this time I had already become adept at concealing my emotions, hiding them behind a shield of false confidence, flippancy, and nonchalance.

And what of the Prince himself? Edward was a toweringly tall buttercup blonde with cornflower blue eyes and a fresh-faced complexion that radiated life, innocence, and good health. He was richly clad in a celestial blue satin tunic embroidered with gold and yellow roses, blue silk hose, and shoes with absurdly long points at the toes adorned with gold embroidery and large yellow silk rosettes. A circlet of gold crowned his blonde hair, worn long with the ends curling up. He slouched there half-asleep, with a white greyhound dozing at his feet, and his Fool seated on the steps, his head level with the Prince's knees. Yet the moment his languid blue eyes lighted upon me it was as if he had been doused with ice water, he sat up so quick and alert!

"Piers Gaveston, Your Grace," his chamberlain announced as I knelt before him.

The Prince gestured for me to rise even as he struggled to his feet, stumbling over the greyhound and his ridiculous shoes, reaching out a hand to steady himself against the jester's head, causing the little gold bells on the Fool's motley-colored cap to jingle. He righted himself and tripped his way down the steps, nearly falling into me.

Instinctively, I reached out to steady him, and he stood there before me, regarding me with the most sheepish and endearing grin that went, like an arrow, straight to my heart. Then he began to speak.

"I … I am … Prince … Prince …"

As though any introduction was required! Not a soul was present who did not know who he was, yet his own name seemed to have escaped his mind!

"*Edward!*" his sister Mary, a frequent visitor to the court despite her nun's vows, hissed, helpful and bemused.

"Edward … Prince Edward," he nodded, though I had the distinct impression that had she said Edmund or Clarence he would have introduced himself as such and never noticed the mistake.

The Fool, however, was not one to bite his tongue and spoke the words that were in all our minds:

"Forsooth, Prince Edward, one would think you had just been introduced to some comely damsel instead of a lad!"

We all laughed then, even the Prince, though the roses in his cheeks bloomed brighter still.

The greyhound was sniffing round my boots and, to give the Prince time to compose himself, I asked: "May I?" indicating that I wished to pet the dog.

"*Anything!*" he breathed. "*You* may do *anything* you like!"

"Thank you, My Lord," I smiled, "I love dogs."

"Then you shall have a puppy!" Edward, ever generous, declared. "I have written to my sister Elizabeth requesting that she send her white greyhound to mate with mine, for I ... I have a great ... *Desire* ..." the word seemed to stick in his throat as his eyes gazed deep into mine. "... to have some puppies from them, and you shall have one!"

"Thank you, My Lord," I answered. "For your kindness I am most grateful."

Court etiquette required that I kneel and bow my head to give evidence of my humble gratitude, but the Prince put out his hands to stay me.

"Nay, my friend, do not bow to me!" And then, to the consternation of all, *he embraced me!*

It was then, I think, that the first seeds of hatred were sown against me. They saw I had a sort of power over him. Courtiers are natural born schemers, they are raised on suspicions and crafty machinations calculated to secure royal favor, and they knew at once that a serious rival had entered the field. And, it is an ugly truth that must be said, the English are notoriously hostile to foreigners, and the Gascon lilt in my voice rendered me a moving target for their barbed and well-aimed insults.

After this brief introduction to the Prince, my servants and I were escorted to my chamber. I was weary from my journey and flopped gratefully onto the feather bed, and Dragon came to tug off my boots.

"Snakes and apples, how perfectly apt!" I remarked as I admired the heavy white satin bed curtains richly embroidered with emerald green serpents and apples of ruby red. "Do you think it is an omen, Agnes?" I teased. Looking round, I saw that the whole room was an allegory of temptation, the carvings, tapestries, hangings, and bedclothes all told the tale of Eve being tempted by the serpent in the Garden of Eden.

"Need you even ask, my dear?" she chuckled knowingly.

"Nay," I smiled and lay back happily, stretching my arms above my head, "I needn't."

"You made quite an impression, Child!" she crowed with her green eyes twinkling.

"I *always* do!" I answered, with laughter in my eyes and bubbling from my lips.

Yet there was a strange sensation in my stomach, not unpleasant or painful at all, but distinctly peculiar, and like nothing I had ever felt before. It was a bit like the gentle fluttering of a butterfly's wings or a cat rubbing soft against bare ankles, but even these are poor comparisons. I then pictured Prince Edward's smile, so endearing, eager, childlike, and sincere, and realized that more than one person had left the Great Hall charmed.

COURTSHIP

And so I became the Prince's Favorite, his constant companion, always at his side. We rode together to hawks and hounds, and made merry with music, minstrels, and masques, and rolled the dice till the candles burned out. We romped together, swam, wrestled, and regaled each other with songs, jests, and stories, and played at archery, bowls, bandy-ball, and Hoodman Blind. And I *did* try to interest Edward in swordplay and jousting, I really did, but he was *hopeless* in the tiltyard! It was only when I competed in tournaments that he managed to stay awake.

It was inevitable that I should rouse the jealousy of the nobly born boys who coveted the Prince's favor. They were contemptuous of me, these titled lads with lands and monies to inherit, each one accompanied by a retinue of servants and governed over by a pompous eagle-eyed tutor. "The Gascon," "The Landless Foreigner," "The Nobody," they called me. Their taunting condescension rankled me, but I would never let them see how much they hurt me. Instead, arrogance became my armor and vanity my shield. My tongue was my sword, ever ready with a jest, double-edged; witty on one side, cutting on the other. Yet behind these weapons lurked a sad and lonely boy. And in this, Edward and I were twins.

His had been a lonely childhood, with his father, whom he both respected and feared, so often away waging war on the French, Irish, Welsh, and the endlessly bothersome Scots. And, before she died, his mother, Eleanor of Castile, frequently accompanied the King on his campaigns. His sisters, with the exception of the worldly nun Mary, were married off to forge dynastic alliances. And his brothers were either dead or too young to be suitable companions for him. His life had been spent in splendid isolation, surrounded by servants and sycophants who hoped to find favor in the next reign.

I pitied him, but I held back from telling him about myself. It was not because mystery captivates; my life is not a pretty story, and I feared that if he knew the truth he would despise me. Now, when it is too late, I realize that this was a mistake. My silence allowed Edward to sculpt me to fit his dreams, and by these illusions I also became trapped.

We complemented each other well, despite our differences; we used to say that I was the moon to his sun. And, when we were alone, I tended to forget that my friend would someday be the King of England. It may be presumptuous of me to say this about a royal personage, but Edward was like a brother to me, and I loved him as such. When I was with him during those happy days at Langley, it was as if the years of my childhood that I lost had been blissfully restored to me, only my mother's loving presence was lacking.

It was not long, however, before a subtle change began to steal like a shadow across our friendship. There were times when I would catch him watching me in a shy yet amorous way. I would emerge dripping, naked, from a swim in the River Gade or look up from a game of cards and find his eyes upon me. Each time he would blush and turn away, crimson-faced, to waylay whoever happened to be nearest and engage them in conversation, his voice stammering and high, while his fingers tugged at the neck of his tunic as if it fit too tight. When we talked he would lean forward in such rapt attention, drinking in my Gascon lilt, that he would topple off the edge of his chair. Other times his eyes would be so intent upon me that he would neglect to watch where he walked and would fall over the furniture or stroll straight into a fish pond.

One day he boldly inquired of me: "Did you hear music when we first met?"

"Yes, My Lord," I answered, "your musicians were playing in the gallery overhead, and quite well too, if you will permit me to add."

"Oh yes!" he exclaimed, grinning sheepishly as a flaming scarlet blush suffused his cheeks. Poor Edward, he had forgotten that there had actually been musicians present that day!

Another time, he sought me out in the meadow where I lay under the light of a full moon.

"Piers," he ventured shyly, "I see you do this often; you steal away to lie beneath the moon. Please tell me why, it worries me; I have heard it said that the moonlight brings madness!"

"The moon is sacred to the Lady, the Goddess," I explained, "it is Her symbol, and in its light I worship Her and by Her I am blessed. And it also brings me peace."

Edward gazed back at me, nervous and bewildered.

"I am a witch," I confided, "as was my mother before me."

"*A Witch!*" Edward gasped. "Piers, you must not *say* such a thing, let alone *be* such a thing! You could be burned!"

"I *was* burned." I sat up on my knees and showed him my hands, extending them palms upward to display the scars, ugly, rough, and red.

Of course, he had noticed them before, but had always refrained from asking how the injury had happened lest it cause me embarrassment or pain.

It was then that I told him about the day they burned my mother.

"Do they hurt?" he asked softly as his fingertips traced lightly over my scars.

"Only in my memory," I said, starting at the sudden feel of water splashing down onto my palms.

It was the first time anyone had ever wept for "The Witch's Brat." Looking back now, I think it was then that I fell in love with him.

Most people will say, and no doubt many will believe, that the sly Gascon saw a chance and seized it. And, given my history, I cannot blame them. But they are mistaken. You have only my word for it, and you may choose not to believe me, but it is the truth, I swear, I loved Edward before he gave me a single jewel, castle, or sinecure. The day I met him, the lock upon my heart was fatally weakened, and when his tears fell upon my hands the hasp broke and I let him in.

At Christmas, in the cold of winter, our affection grew warmer. It was a night of feasting and revelry, games, dancing, and drinking, and Edward had indulged—nay *overindulged*—in them all. Indeed, he had upon a dare eaten an entire marzipan Nativity scene all by himself and I fully expected the royal physician to be roused out of bed to tend him during the night.

He found me alone in a small chamber to which I had withdrawn for a moment's solitude, leaning against the stone windowsill, gazing out at the snow-blanketed land, glowing brightly beneath the moon's silvery light.

He eyed me appraisingly over the golden rim of the goblet he raised to his lips, admiring my slender, lithesome body luxuriously sheathed in a tunic of wine velvet and matching hose that fit me like a second skin.

Boldly, I met his gaze and held it until, blushing, he looked away and busied himself with the now empty goblet, setting it down upon the nearest table, knocking it over, and fumbling to right it again.

Then, grinning apologetically, he turned back to me and explained: "I've drunk so much wine tonight that you're beginning to look attractive to me."

"Only *just* beginning?" I teased, arching my brows.

He lurched towards me, stumbling and swaying.

"What would you do if I kissed you?" he asked.

I tilted my head from side to side, pretending to consider the question.

"This," I said simply and reached up to cup the back of his neck in my hand and draw his mouth down to mine.

I kissed him full upon the lips. His mouth tasted of wassail and marzipan. Poor Edward, he was too startled to respond, so our first kiss was entirely one-sided.

When I stepped back, arching my brows in a silent "Well?", Edward toppled to the floor, cushioned by the spice-strewn rushes, overwhelmed, let us say, by drink, for if I claim my charms as the cause, you—whoever you are that read this—will most likely dismiss me as a shameless braggart, conceited, and more than a little in love with myself, if you have not done so already. Therefore, let us say that the wine went straight to poor Nedikins' head.

I left him lying in a heap of gold-trimmed red velvet, senseless, with his limbs sprawled every which way.

I lingered for a moment in the doorway and looked back over my shoulder.

"Goodnight, my Prince!" I whispered.

CONQUEST

And then the unexpected happened, and I was as astounded as if fish had suddenly fallen from the sky; it was not *I* who seduced Edward—*he seduced me!*

It was one of those nights when I am condemned to relive my mother's death in my dreams. I cried out and started awake with my face bathed in tears. Edward heard my cry and came to me, a candle held aloft, casting a golden glow about his anxious face. All tender concern, he eased the velvet robe from his shoulders and slipped into bed beside me, his arms reaching out to hold and comfort me.

I would not have him see my tears and turned quickly onto my side, so that I lay with my back to him. Undaunted, he curled around me, nestling close, and I could feel his linen nightshirt and the strong body beneath it against my naked skin. He murmured soothing words against my neck. A frisson coursed along my spine and I leaned back gratefully into the curve of his body. Soon my lids grew heavy and I drifted into a light, delicious sleep. I felt as if I were floating in warm water. Then the caresses changed and I came fully awake at the feel of Edward's lips grazing my shoulder and his hand roving over my hip to curl round my manhood. I stiffened; in more ways than one.

"*I cannot fight it anymore!*" Edward moaned, his breath hot against my neck. "I want, I *need*, to love you!"

"And I need to be loved," I said and surrendered, for me it was as simple as that.

A wonderful warmth came to replace the coldness and fill up the emptiness that had been so long inside me. For the first time, I knew passion and surrendered to it gladly.

I awoke smiling the next morning, blushing like a virgin at the memory of the night's pleasures. Edward! My mind was awhirl with thoughts of him. "Edward loves me!" my heart sang. Like a well-contented cat, I stretched and rolled over to look at the pillow on which his head had lain. And in that instant the smile died upon my lips. My heart lurched, and I felt as if I had been kicked in the stomach. There, pinned upon the pillow, was a clasp of rubies set in gold as gleaming bright as Edward's hair. I fell back, heavy as a stone, and lay flat, staring up at the canopy.

"Do you mean to mock me?" I demanded of the snakes and apples embroidered overhead. Did the green silk serpents hiss "Be careful what you wish for lest you get it!"? How cruel of them to remind me when it was already too late! I felt hot and cold at the same time, and I had to close my eyes against the dizziness, and the snakes and apples that had seemingly begun to writhe.

This sparkling clasp pinned upon the pillowslip, was it payment for services rendered? Had I misjudged the situation entirely? By allowing Edward to become my lover had I lost what I valued most of all—my friend?

Agnes came in a little while later and I hastily composed myself. This really would not do! All these maudlin thoughts about love when finding a costly piece of jewelry pinned to one's pillow is far from an unpleasant way to start the day!

"I enjoyed myself royally!" I announced.

"Oh Child, I'm so happy for you!" Then, she must have sensed something. Her brow furrowed and she reached out and gently tilted my chin up so I would meet her eyes. "You *are* happy; aren't you, Child?"

"Of course I am!" I smiled.

Before she could question me further, Edward came bounding in with his fearsome, shaggy-haired wolfhounds. His face wreathed in smiles, he announced that he had come to roust "the lazybones" out of bed as it was far too fine a day to remain inside.

"Come along, Piers!" he urged, "you're lazing away the best part of the day!"

"Very well, My Lord," I smiled, stretching and yawning once more, "for you I shall make the effort!" And I kicked the covers down around my feet.

"*Piers!*" Edward gasped as he sprang forward to quickly draw them back up, covering me to the chin. "Sleep has befuddled your brain; *Dame Agnes is present!*" he added, darting a meaningful glance towards where she stood beside the fireplace heating water in a small cauldron for my morning ablutions.

"Of course she is! Agnes sees me to bed every night and comes to me every morning when I wake!"

At my words, his frown deepened.

"Forsooth, Edward, it would be ridiculous for me to suddenly be struck shy before Agnes now! Had she a gold coin for every time she has seen me thus she would be the richest woman in the land and live in a palace with a diamond spangled ceiling and ermine carpets! Is that not so, Agnes?"

"Aye, Child," she nodded, "and emeralds on the walls!"

"In fact," I continued, "her eyes were the first to see me; she acted as midwife when I was born!"

"Well you are no longer an infant!" Edward informed me. "You are seventeen now, and certain parts of you are considerably larger!"

"Every part of me is larger than it was when I was born, Edward," I quipped, "including my eyelashes."

Edward clenched his fists and, as his face turned an alarming shade of red, screamed: "*The whole world can gaze upon your eyelashes to their heart's content, but as for the rest of you ...*"

"Peace, Edward!" I laughed. "Do not court apoplexy over a trifle!"

"*A trifle!*" he shouted. "*A trifle!* You account *this* a *trifle?*"

"I do!" I sat up and rebelliously kicked the covers to the floor then stood, gloriously nude, and shook back my hair. "And if you continue to shout and glower at me like a thundercloud then I shall keep to my room all day!"

"Well ..." Edward began, relenting slightly.

With a satisfied nod I withdrew behind the ornately carved screen to attend the call of nature. A moment later I peeked round the side and flashed him my most beguiling smile.

"You may bring me my basin of hot water if you like, Nedikins," I offered, employing the love-name by which he had asked me to call him.

How quickly he rushed to comply! Agnes had to caution him to go slowly lest he spill it. He stood beside me, rapt and worshipful, watching my every move. Suddenly he took the washcloth from me, absently flinging it over his shoulder, over the top of the screen, and maneuvered me so that my back was against the wall. He put his hands on my shoulders and, with an insistent pressure, pushed me down onto my knees.

"Do what you did last night, Perrot," he said, using the love-name he had given me. "Show me that such bliss does not exist only in the realm of dreams!" As he spoke, he hitched up his tunic and fumbled with his hose.

"Edward ..." I began hesitantly.

"*Please* Perrot!" He grasped the back of my head and urged it forward.

"*I live only to serve you, my Prince!*" I said tartly and did what he desired.

Edward did not notice my lack of enthusiasm. He got what he wanted and was happy, for him it was as simple as that. But it did not end there. On the contrary, I was to discover that Edward's newly awakened sensuality was on a par with gluttony. Had he craved food the way he did my body he would have been too immense to move!

Clad in my riding clothes with my face clean-shaven, I hastily ate two spoonfuls of porridge, washed down with a sip of breakfast ale, while Edward looked on impatiently.

"Child, you really must eat more than that!" Agnes protested when I stood up and Edward instantly seized my hand, ready to rush me out the door.

I smiled and came back to take the little oatmeal cake, seasoned with cinnamon and raisins, from the tray. I kissed her cheek and then, settling my plumed cap at a rakish tilt, let Edward lead me to the stables.

Peasants paused to respectfully doff their caps as we flew past, racing across the countryside, with the sheep scattering and bleating before us. It was exhilarating to feel the wind in my hair and the power and speed of my night-black steed, and soon all worrisome thoughts fled, seemingly blown out by the clean country air, and I began to truly enjoy myself.

"I win!" Edward announced, reining in his chestnut stallion and leaping from the saddle.

"I did not know we were racing, My Lord," I said as I dismounted, "I do not recall your uttering a challenge."

"It matters not," Edward said breathlessly, his arm going round my waist as he guided me beneath the spreading branches of a massive oak tree. "Now it is time for me to claim my prize!" He dropped to his knees and pulled me down beside him. "Take down your hose, Piers! Never mind," he gasped, grappling with my clothes when I did not instantly comply, "I'll do it for you!"

It was a performance that would be repeated several times before the day was done.

When I returned to my chamber Agnes gave a cry of alarm at my bedraggled appearance. "Sweetheart, what happened to you? Did you take a tumble from your horse?"

I certainly looked as if I had. I was all rumpled, muddy, and grass-stained.

"Nay, from Edward!" I said tartly, tossing aside my cap and sinking down onto the bed. "And more than one; this day I have been tumbled aplenty! And I like it not!" I tugged off my leather boots and flung them at the wall.

"Tell me," she said gently, sitting down beside me.

"It is different now! *He* is different now! He cannot keep his hands from me! He says: 'Why talk at all when there are so many much more interesting uses for our mouths and tongues?'! I've had lovers before who were very ardent, but none so voracious as Edward! And if I make my annoyance known he accounts it just a trifle to be smoothed over with kisses! He is not the same sweet boy who wept over my scarred hands, now he is Lust incarnate! And I want him as he was before! That is the Edward I love, not this lusty glutton!" I let my head sink onto her shoulder in despair.

"Indeed, my love, it *has* gone sour!" Agnes lamented. "I am so sorry, Child, I never thought ... He is smitten, to be sure, but ..." she shook her head, sighed, and stroked my hair. "Perhaps there is cause to hope; you were Prince Edward's first, were you not?"

"Yes," I nodded.

"I thought as much. I would have wagered my last coin that he was a virgin. He's not as worldly as you are, my sweet, it's all very new to him, and, at the moment, it's all he craves. But in time ... mayhap he will settle and be his old self again?"

"Verily, I hope so!" I cried.

There are few things in life that are said to be everlasting, and hope is reckoned to be one of them, but now, as I write these words, I have long since abandoned it. Edward never did get his fill of me, when last I saw him he was as ardent and insatiable as ever, a glutton feasting at the banquet of my body.

Perhaps it was naïve of me, but I honestly did not know what a transfiguring effect the sexual act can have upon a friendship. It changes *everything*, like night to day or white to black. Still, I determined to make the best of things.

And yet every morning when I awoke to find a new present pinned upon my pillow—the star sapphire of Saint Dunstan, a magnificent table diamond, a brooch of balas rubies, a black cameo set in a nest of glittering dark garnets, a pair of peridot rings, one set in silver and the other in gold, and countless more—I suffered the same sadness all over again. Disappointment and discontent became my constant companions and, try as I might, never could I elude them.

Compact of
Brotherhood

Shortly after we became lovers, Edward decided that we should be wed.

I greeted this solemn pronouncement with raised eyebrows. "Surely it cannot have escaped Your Grace's attention that we are both men?"

Ever impractical, Edward decided we would not let this stop us.

And soon we were standing before the tapestry of a unicorn being captured by a virgin, in the room adjoining Edward's bedchamber, being joined in holy wedlock, or "a compact of brotherhood" as Edward would ever afterwards describe it. Edward was solemn and joyful in celestial blue and rose silk, babbling on about the sacredness of the occasion, while I, in spring green and scarlet satin, was trying very hard not to laugh.

The ceremony was performed by a fat monk with greedy fingers, eager for the bulging purse of gold Edward offered him. I believe Edward found the fellow in a tavern, the redness of his nose, slurred speech, and weaving walk seemed to indicate a fondness for strong drink, indeed I smelled it upon his breath as he hiccoughed his way through the service.

As he slipped the ring—set with the biggest ruby I had ever seen—upon my finger, where it remains to this day, Edward said: "Before the eyes of the world, let it be known that I adopt you, Piers Gaveston, my beloved Perrot, as my brother. But in truth, before the eyes of God, we are as surely and truly bound as husband and wife. I hereby take and acknowledge you as my own, tonight, tomorrow, always and forever, and beyond life itself."

As I told Edward at the time, letting it be known will not make it be believed.

Afterwards, when we were alone together in Edward's enormous bed, I lay idly twisting my hand, watching my ruby sparkle and flash in the candlelight.

"Verily, it looks just like a candied cherry!" I exclaimed. And Edward explained that it was indeed known as "La Cerise" or "The Cherry" because of this resemblance.

And then he raised his head from my chest and, with a besotted smile, asked: "Do you love me?"

"Yes," I, in all sincerity, answered, and then I turned the question back on him. "Do *you* love *me?*"

"How could anyone *not* love you?" he demanded, sitting up and shaking back his love-tousled hair. "You are the living God of Beauty, you are perfection personified, your every gesture gives new meaning to the word grace ..."

He said much more, but at that point I stopped listening. There was that sinking feeling in my stomach again!

"Edward," I interrupted his rapturous recitation of my charms, "how much did you say this ruby is worth?"

"£1,000 my love!" he answered proudly.

I nodded and forced a smile. We must all learn to live with our disappointments.

ALL HALLOW'S EVE

On October 31st—All Hallow's Eve—Edward and I set aside our finery and donned simple clothes and went out to mingle with the commonfolk on the village green. We joined hands and danced round the bonfire, lighting up the dark night, to keep the evil spirits at bay on this special night when the veil between the worlds is thin and the souls of the dead are free to wander as they will.

We ate our fill of roast suckling pig, and merry serving maids made certain our tankards of apple beer were never empty. Edward bobbed for apples and joined in the old game of tossing the peelings over the shoulder to see who one's husband or wife would be. It is said that they will land in the shape of the first letter of that person's name. And for those who did not know their letters he deciphered them, drawing squeals of delight or dismay from the maidens who surrounded him.

And we eagerly sat down at the trestle table to have our share of sweet, creamy apple crowdie. It was a moment of high excitement that everyone looked forward to. Baked within the crowdie were a pair each of coins, marbles, rings, and beads. According to tradition, whoever found the coins would be rich, the rings would soon marry, the beads withdraw from the world to take holy orders, and the marbles would lead a cold and lonely life. How I laughed at the expression upon Edward's face when he found both a ring *and* a coin in his crowdie, while I received a marble. Verily, whoever baked it did not stir the mixture very well to have so many tokens found so close together! Those around us heartily clapped Edward upon the back in congratulations and shook their heads and sighed to condole with me. Even as Edward scoffed and assured me that I would never be cold or lonely as long as his life endured, I laughed and joined my voice with the others informing him that "the crowdie never lies!" And then I pulled him from the bench and we ran back to join the dancers round the bonfire.

But Edward's pleasure was short-lived and he drew back nervously when a woman came forth robed in green with a crown of dried flowers upon her unbound hair to represent the Goddess, hand-in-hand with her consort, the brown robed and antlered Horned God. Though the Church, in its persistent attempts to purge this night of its pagan taint, would have us believe they are only a lad and lass from the village costumed to represent summer's end and autumn's start, I am not deceived.

Edward's lips trembled and he turned and fled when he saw me kneel reverently before them.

I found him cowering amongst the trees, darting anxious glances back at the bonfire, no doubt imagining the dancers were lascivious, cavorting demons even though he knew them to be nothing but good and simple country folk.

"You should not have brought me here tonight, Piers!" he cried. "Now I will surely go to Hell!"

"If you do it will be a Hell of your own making," I shrugged, nonchalantly taking a bite of the apple I held.

"I take it that you do not believe in Hell," he frowned.

"Certainly not! It is nothing but a horror story the Church tells to frighten its children into submission! All that nonsense about poppets with pins stuck in them, dark rituals with black candles and inverted crosses, and the Lord's Prayer recited backwards, sacrifices of virgins and babies, and familiars in the form of giant, sinister toads and black cats suckled on blood from the Witch's Mark! It would all be very amusing if innocent people didn't have to die because of it! Stories like that feed people's fears, Edward! Witchcraft, as you think of it, is born of the mating of superstition and fear and is completely foreign to the Lady's loyal adherents. The truth is infinitely more beautiful and, to most minds, boring."

"What do you believe then?" he asked, curiosity overcoming his fear.

"That when we die we sail away to the Isle of Apples and there eat of the magic fruit and become eternal." I took another bite from my apple then offered it to him.

"When you speak of these things, I almost forget my fears!" He accepted the apple and took a bite. "I almost forget that I saw you kneel before that horned devil!"

"That was no devil, Ned!" I laughed incredulously. "The Horned God is the consort of the Lady! He is the lord of the woodlands and of the hunt, that is the reason he sports antlers; there is no deviltry in it! He is born at the winter solstice, unites with the Lady at Beltane—what you call May Day—and dies at summer's end—Samhain; All Hallow's Eve. It is life renewing itself, a circle that goes round and round with no end and no beginning, and it is *beautiful!* He is the sun to Her moon, as you are to me," I said, reaching out to stroke his golden hair. "But come, do not be afraid, Nedikins, I am with you, and tonight is a night for dancing, feasting, and love." I took his hand and led him deeper into the shadows.

Events Leading Up To
My Banishment

From the start we have been too open and indiscreet. In the beginning, I *did* try. I urged that we keep our love behind locked doors, but Edward has such an open and honest nature; he does not know the meaning of the word "discreet" and has no desire to learn.

It was when we accompanied his father to Scotland in 1303 that these concerns first began to weigh so heavily upon my mind. It was a burden, I soon learned, that Edward was not inclined to share with me.

When one thinks of a soldier's tent "cramped" and "small" are the words that generally come first to mind. But a prince of the blood must have something more palatial, a portable palace in miniature, replete with fine furnishings and a feather bed.

As Edward's companion of choice, and a mere knight in rank, etiquette required that I sleep on a pallet at the foot of his bed to be within ready call should he require anything during the night—besides the knight himself, of course. That first night, as I prepared to lie down upon my pallet, Edward sat up in bed and gave a howl of protest.

"*No!* I will not have you sleeping at the foot of my bed like a dog!" He patted the empty space beside him.

"Nedikins, we are in a tent. Here the walls are not stone or wood. And see," I pointed to the entrance flap, "there is no door that we might lock. Be patient, wait until we can be assured of privacy; this brief respite will only make us enjoy it more!" Again, I started to lie down, but Edward would not be dissuaded.

"*No!* If you do not get into bed with me I shall get out of bed and pass the night with you on the floor! Now be sensible, Piers," he pleaded, patting the mattress again, "and come to bed!"

I knew full well that to acquiesce would be flying in the face of sensibility, but I gave in; I was tired and not inclined to argue. But while Edward slumbered peacefully, I passed a very nervous night, keenly aware of every sound, fearing someone, especially the King, might enter and catch us lying entwined and naked.

Later, when we were back at Langley, we were involved in a foolish escapade. We trespassed on Walter Langton's land and poached his deer. Rather than apologize, Edward assumed an air of princely pomposity and answered his father's Treasurer and longtime friend with great arrogance and disrespect. My laughter only encouraged him and made matters worse. It was not one of our shining moments.

As punishment, Edward was deprived of my company and his allowance. But meek acceptance was not for him, oh no, he must bombard everyone whose opinion might hold sway—his stepmother, sisters, and even the despised Walter Langton—who, in Edward's mind, was entirely to blame—with a barrage of groveling letters beseeching them to use whatever influence they possessed to persuade the King to reinstate me. And he managed to obtain funds from some obliging friends and courtiers and proceeded to follow his father about the countryside hoping to be forgiven, he even sent him two barrels of sturgeon as a conciliatory gift. To me he sent dozens of despondent letters in which he poured out his heart, penned maudlin poetry, and agonized over what I was doing in London and who I was doing it with. He implored me to have my meals sent up to my room instead of taking them in the Common Room of the inn or at taverns lest I be seen and desired.

Poor Edward! Had he but known! Being seen and desired was how I lived! I frequented the bathhouses and taverns, and I had many patrons among the wealthy merchant class. There was a Flemish mercer, famous for his tapestries, who had me stay an hour with him every afternoon save Sundays. And a goldsmith's widow, a sad-eyed woman with graying hair, who only craved a little tenderness, which I was happy to provide in the rented room where we met twice a week. And a careworn banker with a bald head as smooth as an egg that he would have me stroke while I sat on his lap and he told me all his woes. And I was not staying at an inn at all, but with my tailor with whom I had a mutually beneficial arrangement—I got lots of beautiful clothes and he got me. Apparently he preferred my warm and pliant body to cold hard coins. And there are people who say I have no head for business!

After two months the King forgave Edward and allowed me to return to him. Edward was ecstatic, though suspicious about how small my London expenditures had been, and how I happened to return with more money and clothes than I left with, but I have my ways of distracting him and he soon forgot all about it. But it was not the end of our troubles, and soon disquieting rumors about the true nature of our relationship led the King to visit us at Langley.

His father's presence wrought no change in Edward's behavior. I cannot count the times I had to whisper a reminder that we were within the King's sight and those keen eyes did not miss much. Time after time I saw them fix, a stern, steely-blue gaze, upon us as Edward flung his arms about me, leaned in so close to whisper in my ear that his lips grazed my flesh, or pressed his thigh against mine when he sat down beside me.

It was inevitable that a confrontation should take place.

One afternoon when I sat alone on the hearth-side settle staring morosely into the flames, a book lying forgotten on my lap, Edward came bounding in like some great rambunctious puppy, panting and pink-cheeked from vigorous exercise. He flung himself down beside me and his arms went round my neck. His lips were pressed to mine when his father walked in.

He was upon us in two strides, seizing Edward by his embroidered collar and pulling him off me. I watched in horror as he flung him aside and Edward slammed face first into the wall. His fingers caught at the tapestry as he fell, taking it down with him.

"*Stand up!*" he ordered. I obeyed while Edward coughed and writhed upon the floor, endeavoring to extricate himself from the heavy, musty folds of the tapestry in which he had become entangled.

"Piers Gaveston, you have failed me grievously!" roared the gray-bearded Hammer of the Scots, glaring down at me from his great height, like Zeus upon a thundercloud poised to hurl a lightning bolt to strike me dead. "It is not often that I make a mistake regarding a man's character, but there is something about you I did not notice on the battlefield; you exude a certain sensuality which," he darted a meaningful glance at his son, his head just now emerging from beneath the tapestry which still lay, like a turtle's shell, heavy upon his back, "you have clearly used to your advantage. This is what comes from entrusting a poor, landless foreigner with the welfare of the Prince! Take yourself back to Gascony, and do not return if you value your life!"

By now Edward had managed to crawl out from underneath the tapestry and was hugging his father's ankles, washing the dust from his boots with his tears, and begging him not to take me from him.

"Remove yourself from my sight!" the King thundered as he jerked one foot free and dealt his son a savage kick.

Edward yelped in pain, his arms going up to shield his head from the onslaught of blows that followed. It was not a sight I cared to see and I fled hastily, wincing at every yelp and blow that followed me.

Later Edward came to me, all battered and bruised, with both eyes blackened, and his lip crusted with blood where his father's boot had split it. He lay on my bed with his head in my lap and wept while I cleansed his face.

I could not believe it, but he had gone so far as to compound his folly by asking permission to give me Ponthieu, which he had inherited upon his mother's death. With its revenues, I would no longer be poor or landless, and I would be styled the Count of Ponthieu.

Poor Edward, he showed me the place on his head where his father had ripped out a handful of his hair.

"Can you not do something, Piers?" he sobbed.

"Such as?" I asked, stroking his hair.

"Well you *are* a witch," he lowered his voice to a whisper, "and I have heard it said that a wax poppet fashioned in the likeness of one's enemy with some clippings of his hair and nails ..."

"*Edward!*" I thrust him from me. "I know nothing of such things! That was not the way of my mother's witchcraft, nor is it mine! And even if I did possess such knowledge *never* would I use it! Do no harm, lest it come back to you threefold!"

I rang for my servants and bade them pack my things, while Edward continued to weep inconsolably upon my bed.

"I cannot live without you!" he sobbed, then raised his head to look at me. "Can you live without me, Piers?"

When I did not answer he wept all the more. But what could I say? To say "no" would be a lie, but to say "yes, just not as well," seemed brutally frank and unkind.

The next day I kept to my chamber. It was known all about that I was banished, and I did not care to face the mocking eyes of the court.

I lay in bed, staring up at the canopy, pondering my fate, then inspiration blessed me. I would go and throw myself upon the mercy of the King! It would be difficult. I would be required to perform a delicate balancing act in which I must stay on good terms with both the current king and the future one.

"Agnes! Dragon! Make haste!" I cried when they came rushing in. "Dress me entirely in white! I am going to see the King and I must look as heart-sore as the most wretched penitent! Where's that prayer book Edward gave me? Not that one, rubies are far too tempestuous for a time like this! The white one with the pearls on it!"

"Well?" I asked when at last I stood before the big silver mirror Edward had given me, arrayed all in white with the little white pearl-embellished prayer book clasped demurely in my hands. "Do I look suitably repentant?"

"Can you manage a few tears, Child?" Agnes asked. "Nay, do not tax yourself, my sweet; I'll get an onion from the kitchen."

"Mayhap a rosary would be a becoming touch?" Dragon suggested. "Have you a white one?"

"Of course!" I cried, scrambling for my jewel coffers. "Edward gives me a new one every Sunday, I must have one in every color and stone known to man!" I sat down on the window-seat and spent several tense and tiresome moments untangling a multitude of multihued strands of rosary beads until I found the white pearl one with the silver crucifix dangling from it.

"What is it you mean to do, Child?" Agnes asked when she returned with the onion.

"I shall tell him the truth," I confidently declared, "but not the whole of it; there are certain details I would not bore him with."

"Aye," Agnes agreed, "the King is a busy man and should not be bothered with trifles."

And that is what I did. After all, Edward *did* come to my bed. And he was *very* insistent, and ardent. I was overcome. A nightmare had disturbed my sleep and left me feeling vulnerable. It was all so new and unexpected! I had never been seduced by a prince before!

"And if you will pardon my bluntness in saying so, Sire, but while I would not offend you for the world, nor would I offend your successor either."

And knowing that I had lost his goodwill made my heart ache unbearably. I could offer nothing but my most humble and heartfelt apologies, though I knew they would not suffice; *nothing* could excuse the great and grievous wrong I had unwittingly committed.

When I was too overcome with tears to speak, the King laid a hand upon my shoulder and bade me take heart, he knew now that I was not to blame and lamented that he had been so harsh with me. The terms of my banishment would be mitigated somewhat and distinctly in my favor. I would be allowed to remain in England for another two months, until the tournament season ended, so that I might have the chance to take a few more prizes. He knew that tournaments contributed much to my coffers, the prizes being great and including the like of money, horses, armor, weaponry, and gems. And I was to have a pension of £100 per annum. And now that he understood the circumstances, he could find no fault with my behavior, and actually apologized for his son being the cause of so much distress to me! He removed me not as a punishment, he bade me understand, but for my own sake. "I see now that it was folly to entrust the Prince with such a treasure!" he fumed as he paced furiously before me. "I have thrown a pearl before a swine!"

Yes, I know, I am shameless!

As I went out the door I heard him bellowing at his chamberlain to send for Prince Edward and quickened my steps in consequence. Edward was going to be *furious!*

"Quick!" I cried as I dashed into my room. "I must change!" I began wrenching my white pearl and lace trimmed tunic up over my head. "My cornflower blue tunic! And the hose and shoes to match! *Hurry!* Edward will be here soon and he is certain to be in a beastly temper!"

How right I was! He burst into my bedchamber, his face cherry-red with rage, and found me primping before my mirror as if I hadn't a care in the world.

"What kept you?" I pouted. "I've been waiting for you *all* day!"

"Including the hour you spent pouring lies into my father's ears?" he demanded as he towered over me, pulses pounding, fists clenched tight at his sides and quaking as he struggled to resist the urge to strangle me.

"Oh that?" I shrugged, turning away from him to rummage through the jewel box Agnes held for me. "Is it even necessary for me to explain?"

"By God's teeth, I should say it is! You told him …"

"Oh Nedikins!" Eyes brimming with tears, I turned to face him. "Have you so little faith in me? Is it not obvious that I did what I did for us? Do you not see? If he thinks me an evil influence, that I corrupted you, he will *never* let me come back to you; and think how unhappy poor Perrot will be without his Nedikins! But, if he sees me as the victim, there is hope that we shall be together again before many months have passed, once he is persuaded that you will mend your ways and take no more boys into your bed."

"My darling, how could I *ever* have doubted you?" Edward, instantly mollified, sighed as he reached for me.

"Verily, I do not know," I said sulkily, "but you did! Nay, touch me not!" I laid a hand upon his chest and shoved him lightly, and most unconvincingly, away. "I am angry with you! You haven't said a word about my new tunic, and I had it made special just to please you! Observe the color, it is cornflower blue, the exact same shade as your eyes; I like having your eyes upon me."

"It is beautiful," he said. "Forgive me if I did not notice it before, it was only because its wearer is so beautiful that beholding him blinds me to all else." He reached for me again and this time I relented and let him embrace me. "Will you dismiss your servants now?"

"I think I had better," I said and gestured for them to depart, which they did with knowing smiles.

"How could I ever have doubted anyone so beautiful?" Edward sighed. "Ah, Piers, I am a fool!"

I was tempted to say: "Yes, you are!" but I held my tongue.

Can he *really* not know that beauty and sincerity do not go hand-in-hand and having one is no guarantee of the other?

THREE MONTHS APART

"One moment without you is like one thousand years!" Edward, signing himself "Lovelorn Ned," wrote in one of the many ardent letters he bombarded me with.

Instead of back to Gascony, I had gone to Ponthieu, not as its master, but to spend my exile in princely fashion at his estate of Crécy. Edward had seen me off at Dover, deluging me with tears and gifts, and a quartet of guards, ostensibly to keep me safe, but really to serve as Edward's spies.

I missed him, yet a part of me welcomed the separation. I was two-and-twenty and had been some six years constantly in Edward's company. I needed to feel free again; to be able to move without Edward's arms instantly reaching out for me.

While we were apart, Edward wept, gnawed his nails until they bled, spent sleepless nights tossing restlessly upon his bed, and had his physician apply leeches to his temples, but nothing could keep him from brooding about my fidelity, or lack thereof. I daresay he had just cause to doubt me. While I have always been faithful to Edward in my fashion, like fashion I am hardly ever constant. And yet it was Edward who, upon pages so blotted by tears I could hardly read them, confessed that he had been untrue and begged for my forgiveness.

Poor Nedikins, it seems that in my absence the King had assigned a new tutor to him and the brothels of London became their schoolroom. Maude Makejoy, a lewd strumpet from the stews of London, was hired to dance naked before him and then teach him the *proper* ways of carnal love. Poor Edward! At last, to appease his fearsome father, and put an end to these tawdry and loathsome excursions, he took a lady of the court as his mistress and her womb soon quickened with his son. Nine months later, Edward had the boy christened Adam then did his best to forget all about him and banished the lady to a convent. But the old King was pleased, although he did not live to see this baseborn grandson; Edward had proven himself capable of siring offspring and that was all that mattered.

Of course, I readily forgave him; in my eyes there was nothing to forgive. I knew that Edward would be king one day and to fulfill his destiny he must marry and beget heirs to assure the succession. So why should I weep when he only did what was required?

Three months later a messenger in royal livery came galloping through the gates.

"Hie you to London, my dearest love, as fast as sea and horses can carry thee!" Edward implored dramatically. "My father is deceased and I am now King, though it is you who rules my heart, and I need you here beside me."

I arrived in London a week later to find myself created Earl of Cornwall and engaged to marry Edward's niece, neither of which I had been expecting.

REUNION

For our reunion I wanted intimacy without ceremony. We would sup alone on roast chicken, freshly baked bread slathered with honey and sweet butter, and fruit, I decided, and I issued orders that the servers should withdraw after setting the table.

After my bath, Agnes massaged me with perfumed oils, and I donned a magnificent swirl-patterned tunic of silver and sapphire blue and hose of dark blue silk embellished with exquisite silver embroidery. Sapphires and diamonds twinkled all over me, even on the long narrow, tapering toes of my fashionable pointy shoes.

As I stood before my mirror, Agnes and Dragon assured me that Edward was certain to be enthralled. And he was! He came to me with open arms and would have led me straight to bed, but I made him wait.

We sat down to dine and the servers hastily withdrew, leaving us alone at last.

"I missed you," I said softly, reaching across the table to lay my hand lightly over his.

"Did you?" Edward asked, tilting the silver goblet in his hand as if he were a prospective buyer scrutinizing the workmanship. "Who is Lord Roderic of Spain? And why did you give him a silver cup?"

"As a remembrance; he was my guest for a fortnight and I greatly enjoyed his company."

"I see," Edward nodded gravely, "and did he enjoy yours?"

"Verily, I do believe he did!"

"*Did you sleep with him?*" Edward slammed the goblet down with such force that the red wine sloshed out to stain his cuffs and drench his fingers.

"Sleep?" I decided to take him literally. "No, Nedikins, of course not!"

And I did not lie! Lord Roderic of Spain was a man who understood the meaning of discretion, and he was always careful to leave my bed after our business was concluded lest he fall asleep and the morning light, and the servants, find him there. Our affair was conducted with great dignity and decorum. We were discreet even though Edward's spies obviously found out. But that is what they were paid to do, and it is a very poor spy indeed who fails to discover something. So Edward got his money's worth, as did Lord Roderic, and they both had me to thank!

"You are certain?" Edward queried doubtfully. "You did not sleep with Lord Roderic?"

"Edward," I answered irritably, "if it will make you happy, I shall swear upon the Bible that I was wide awake every moment I spent with Lord Roderic!"

"Oh Perrot!" he sighed as all his suspicions and fears melted away. "You would do *that* for *me?*"

"Yes, of course I would!" I said brightly.

Tears welled up in his eyes, and dearest Nedikins was too overcome to speak. And I decided it would be best for all concerned if we went to bed without delay, *before* he thought to ask me about the night the Bishop of Durham came to dinner and ended up staying for breakfast.

An Earldom And
A Wife

And so it began, the deluge, the embarrassment of riches that Edward wantonly and recklessly showered upon me almost daily—money, jewels, clothes, horses, titles, castles, wardships, levies, licenses, tariffs, and lands. Edward gave *everything* to me, and by doing so he made his nobles, the great families that are the backbone of England, despise me as an usurper, an upstart, and a thief.

They likened me to a foul and poisonous mushroom flourishing overnight upon a dung-heap. And, in truth, I cannot fault them for saying it; Edward's largesse and my rapid rise lent credence to this impression. Everyone conveniently forgot that I was wellborn and that my father had given his life and sacrificed his fortune in the service of Edward's father, but everyone remembered that my mother had been burned as a witch. And the fact that I was born in Gascony certainly did not help matters. We Gascons have a reputation little better than gypsies, nigh all Englishmen think us lazy, shiftless, lying, quarrelsome, braggarts; wastrels, drunkards, troublemakers, and thieves, flamboyant in both dress and manner, good for nothing, and dishonest to the core.

They also hated me for my saucy wit. To them I am irreverent and brazen. I parry their insults with jests and witticisms and these are taken up and repeated by others and have the tendency to stick like the most tenacious mud. I sometimes think my tongue is my own worst enemy. I am apt to forget that I do not enjoy the immunity of the official Court Fool who, like a good shepherd tending his flock, may freely mock his betters to ward them away from the sin of pride. I have a terrible habit of speaking without pausing to consider first the consequences.

And of course, there was the matter of sodomy, the vilest sin in society's eyes. Edward made no attempt to conceal his passion for me; he flaunted it openly. It is one of those truths that society prefers to leave unsaid, but such affairs betwixt men are commonplace, though they are most often conducted in secrecy and shame, shrouded in the fear of discovery, public condemnation, and eternal damnation. Sodomy may be a burning offense, but we live in a world of men where women are relegated to hearth and home. Men spend months together in long, arduous military campaigns where women are not always readily available to satisfy their carnal needs. For some it is an act of nature, for others it is a mere necessity, but as long as the men involved comport themselves discreetly and fulfill their obligations to family and society, nothing is ever said, and to their amours all eyes feign blindness. But Edward would not let them pretend, he reveled in his love for me; he wanted everyone to know and see.

Soon it was being said that I was the true power behind the throne. Verily, it is a bitter jest! I am Edward's "Principal Provider of Entertainment" and entertainment is *all* he expects of me. I often think that between the two of us I am the only one who realizes that I have a brain. Edward greets my attempts to discuss serious matters with laughter and an indulgent smile. He laughs, kisses me, pats me on the hand or knee, and tells me that such matters are not for one as beautiful as me. Statecraft, science, and philosophy, he says, will wither my beauty, line my brow, and make my poor head ache. "Just be beautiful, Piers," he says, "do not tax yourself talking of taxes!"

But it was Edward's gift of the earldom of Cornwall that, more than anything else, turned the nobility against me. The elevation of a commoner—or a whore to put it bluntly—to such a degree was unprecedented.

Leading the pack were the earls of Warwick, Lancaster, Pembroke, and Lincoln, or "The Black Dog," "The Buffoon," "Joseph the Jew," and "Burstbelly," as I mischievously dubbed them at a banquet one night to amuse Edward. Sad to say, the good earls are sorely lacking in humor, for which I did respectfully don mourning the next day, and even as I write this, they *still* have not forgiven me for those naughty, but apt, little nicknames.

They opposed my being made earl for two reasons. Firstly, I am a landless foreigner, an upstart unworthy of even the smallest of the honors Edward has given me. And secondly, Cornwall, with its lucrative tin mines and lavish income of £4,000 per annum, has always been in royal hands.

Nedikins foresaw their objections and before I even set foot in London had, to his mind at least, resolved all the difficulties.

If Cornwall must be in royal hands, then royal I must become, hence my betrothal to his niece, Margaret de Clare, a sweet young maiden of thirteen. To Edward it was as simple as that. But the peers of the realm were appalled. The King's niece was too lofty a match to be thrown away on a Gascon nobody! To which Edward replied I was no longer a nobody as he had just created me Earl of Cornwall. As for my being a Gascon, well there was nothing anyone could do about that!

As you can surely see, we are going round in circles: I am married to Margaret to make me worthy of the earldom, and made Earl of Cornwall to make me worthy of Margaret.

Furthermore, Edward decreed that henceforth none should address or refer to me as Piers Gaveston ever again, I was to be known *only* as the Earl of Cornwall, and for anyone to disregard this edict would be a sure way of incurring his displeasure. Poor Edward, he doesn't realize it, but no one gives a fig whether he is displeased, and what little respect his subjects have for him dwindles daily; in Scotland they boast that they fear the old king's bones more than they do his living heir! As for myself, I could not possibly care less whether they call me Earl of Cornwall or not, there are far worse things they can, have, and do, call me than Piers Gaveston, and, after all, it *is* my name!

Edward also chose to exact vengeance upon Walter Langton whose tattling tongue had led to my temporary banishment. He dismissed him from his post as Treasurer, sent him in chains to the Tower of London, and confiscated all his goods and treasures and gave them to me. Naturally, everyone thought I was behind it.

It was at this time that our quarrels began in earnest and I realized that our joyous, carefree days were done.

"Do you not see, Edward?" I railed, pacing back and forth before his desk where he sat signing papers, or trying to; I fear my body garbed in black silk fantastically embroidered with scarlet was proving too much of a distraction for him. "They say I *use* you, and those who hear them *believe!*"

"Use me then, my darling!" Edward cried magnanimously. "I don't care!"

"*But I do!* Edward, try to understand; your generosity exceeds all reason and makes me appear what everyone thinks me—a Gascon upstart, a leech feasting on the blood of England! No commoner has ever been raised up so high and quickly! They say I am forgetful of my place!"

"Your place is right here with me!" Edward smiled, sat back in his chair, and patted his thigh. "And don't you dare forget it or I shall be very cross indeed!"

"This is no jesting matter!" I persisted. "The most powerful men in the realm have sworn themselves my enemies! Warwick swears to make my death his life's work! And your cousin Tom of Lancaster thinks I have stolen his destiny; the life that should have been his! Before you elevated me, he was second only to you in wealth and lands and thought it his right, his due, by both prominence and blood, to be the man who sits closest to you as your most trusted advisor, and now he has been bumped down to third because of me!"

"Oh a pox on Cousin Tom!" Edward rolled his eyes. "I would not trust him to tell me what shoes to put on in the morning! But this is all nonsense! Do not be absurd, Perrot, no one hates you! How could they hate anyone so beautiful?"

"Apparently it poses no difficulty for them! Do not sweep aside my concerns, Edward, as if I were some simpleton who thinks the earth made of marzipan! I speak as I find! And must you always go on about how beautiful I am? Do you not know that there is more to me than just a pretty face?"

"Of course there is, my darling!" Edward smiled indulgently. "You have an exquisite body as well as a beautiful face!"

Seething with fury, I turned on my heel and stormed from the room with Edward hot on my heels, wondering what he could have possibly said to upset me.

"I am fluent in four languages, Edward, I write an elegant hand, I have an excellent grasp of mathematics, and," I added, just before I slammed the door in his face and shot the bolt, "Lord Roderic taught me a smattering of Spanish; he said I have a very quick and agile mind!"

"*He did!*" Edward gasped. "These wily Spaniards will say *anything* to get what they desire! Surely you were not deceived? Were you? Piers! Answer me!" He pounded insistently upon the door. "Piers! I am the King and I command you to open this door! Piers! Do you hear me? Piers! Ouch! This door is damnably thick! Piers! Do not make me summon men-at-arms with a battering ram!"

Agnes was sewing by the fire and she looked up questioningly when I came in, kicked off my shoes, and threw myself onto the bed.

Blanche, my precious white greyhound, raised her sleek head and regarded me from her basket where she lay on a cushion of red velvet that perfectly matched the ruby collar glittering round her fair neck. I whistled to her and she came bounding up onto the bed to burrow into my arms and lick my face.

"A lover's quarrel, Child?" Agnes inquired, setting aside her sewing and coming to sit beside me.

"A quarrel, yes, but whether love has anything to do with it I really cannot say!" I raised my voice so Edward would be sure to hear me. "Nay," I added softly, shaking my head, "I *can* say. I *know* I love him, but ... time and familiarity have not restored him to his former self. Now that he is King he dotes and fawns on me and showers me with gifts that make everyone despise me! Before he came to my bed I felt loved, now I feel bought. With the others it didn't matter, that was business, I rendered a service and was paid well for it, but I don't want to feel that way with Edward. Before Edward I felt nothing, now I feel *too* much. I should have known better than to open my heart, but he pried it open; he was so sweet and sincere, so open and trusting, so childlike and innocent in his ways; I could not help but love him! But when innocence is lost it is gone forever and what takes root in its place isn't always good or pretty. Edward lacks insight, I've known that from the start, he never sees past surfaces, he takes everyone and everything at face value, and when he discovered lust through my body, he forgot everything except carnal pleasure and what his eyes see. I often think that, to him, I have ceased to exist as a person and have become instead only a favored and beautiful bauble he wants to have about him all the time, as if I were a chain of gold or a diamond ring possessing neither feelings nor soul, only a beguiling sparkle that fascinates and pleases the eye! I often wonder what would happen if I became disfigured, through accident or disease. I am a trained soldier and I compete often in tournaments. Accidents happen; men are wounded in battle, I have seen it with my own eyes. Would he still love me then or would he cast me aside in disgust? And someday, I *will* be old." Blanche nuzzled my neck and whimpered to be petted. "At least you will always love me, Blanche, no matter what I look like," I said, hugging her.

"So will I, Child! Piers," Agnes reached out and tilted my chin up so I would meet her eyes, "you *do* know that?"

"That is the *one* thing I have *never* doubted!" I assured her, and, taking her hand from beneath my chin, I kissed the palm.

"And he loves you too, Child," she continued, "but his eyes are easily dazzled. But, if you are truly unhappy, there is no reason we cannot leave and seek our fortune elsewhere. You are my own precious child—I could not love you more if I had given birth to you—and I would not see you miserable for the world! And this is *not* the life you should have had!"

"But I have made the best of it," I smiled and gently tucked a stray wisp of gray hair back inside her wimple, "and I shall continue to do so. What other lover could keep me even half as well as the King of England? Experience has made me rich, and *this* is my crowning achievement! Do not worry for my sake, Agnes, I will be fine."

Edward's banging took on a renewed vengeance.

"Piers! Open this door! Christ's Blood, my hands will be bruised black and blue from knocking!"

"Well said, Nedikins!" I shouted. "No one could resist a plea as tender and loving as that!"

Edward fell silent for a moment then called sweetly: "Perrot! *Please* open the door; it is your Nedikins who loves and wants to see you!"

I stood up, stepped into my shoes, and snatched up my hat—a soft black velvet cap with a jaunty red plume—and snapped my fingers for Blanche. I lingered a moment beside the door to take a deep breath and brace myself before I unlocked and opened it.

Edward greeted me with open arms and a broad smile. And around him, to both left and right, a large audience of curious and appalled courtiers and servants had gathered.

"I am taking Blanche out for a run in the garden," I announced, shunning his embrace. "The performance is over!" I added for the benefit of our audience. "Pass the cap, why don't you?" I suggested tartly, taking my cap off and thrusting it at Edward. And, without a backward glance, I sauntered briskly down the corridor.

When I returned to my room I found my cap lying on the bed. Edward had filled it with gold coins. And there was a note: "If I visit you tonight will you be sweet to me?"

An hour in the palace gardens romping with Blanche had cooled my temper and I laughed merrily and rang the bell to summon a pageboy. By this point in my life, I was surrounded by so many pageboys that I felt like I was shepherd to a flock of green and yellow sheep. Edward chooses them for me himself; he thinks it a *grand* sight to see them wait upon me. All of them are little green-eyed blonde-haired boys clad in my green and yellow livery, the better to contrast my black hair and dark eyes. He chooses them then is consumed with worry that I might succumb to the temptation to take these golden-haired lads to bed. It is a wonder, Agnes says, that jealousy hasn't gnawed holes in his stomach. Actually, there is no foundation for his fears; they do not tempt me at all, I have *never* lusted after children's flesh. But I don't tell Nedikins that; I refuse to give him the satisfaction or the peace of mind.

"Go to the King," I bade my page, "and tell him that if he visits me tonight I will be sweet to him."

Ignoring all objections, including my own, Edward decided I must have the grandest wedding England had ever seen.

We spent hours arguing about my wedding clothes, shouting and nearly coming to blows amongst swathes of velvet, satin, silk, taffeta, and lace.

Edward would have me arrayed in celestial blue silk.

"You will look *heavenly!*" he enthused, draping the costly sky-colored silk about my shoulders.

"A heavenly fool, you mean! It is the color of purity and therefore best left to virgins and brides! This marriage is mockery enough without my very garb making a joke of me! Nay, take it away!" I thrust it aside. "Send it to Meg for her marriage gown if you like, but I will not have it! Methinks I shall wear this sea green satin embroidered with vermilion instead," I announced, draping it round me and turning to consult my mirror. "Do you not think it fine, Nedikins? The delicacy of the green with the fire of the red!"

"Ah!" Edward sighed, clasping his hands and looking fit to swoon. "None shall be more beautiful than you!"

"Ungallant!" I charged. "What of the bride?"

"*None!*" he emphatically declared.

And soon I found myself standing before the church doors with Edward at my side watching the bridal procession wend its way towards us.

"I love weddings," Edward whispered. "Oh Perrot, don't you wish it were ours?"

"*No!*" I answered sulkily. "I grow weary of these foolish spectacles! I wish that this one were done rather than just begun!"

But even then my bride was drawing near, a slender girl garbed in celestial blue silk and flowing red-gold hair crowned with gilded rosemary. Sweet music surrounded her, played by fair-haired boys in white silk with colored ribbons streaming from their sleeves, and maidens gowned in white, their hair unbound beneath floral wreaths, bearing the bride-cakes on gilded trays. Then Edward was descending the steps to take Meg's hand. He bent to place a chaste kiss upon her softly blushing cheek then led her to me and placed her hand in mine.

Not a word of my vows do I remember speaking. It was like there was a fearsome black crow inside my head cawing over and over again: "This is a mistake! This is a mistake!" And then the Bishop joined us, binding our hands together with a length of white silk, to show that we were now one.

Our guests, gathered round the church steps, began to cheer, and Edward, veering wildly betwixt shrill laughter and heartrending sobs, stepped forward to pour silver coins over our heads as Meg and I shared our first kiss.

Our hands were unbound and the crowd surged forth to congratulate us.

I looked at Edward with tears pouring down his face and decided he should be even sorrier before the day was out. I fished a silver coin from where it had caught in my jewel-encrusted belt and slowly raised it to my lips and bit it.

"*Silver!*" I said petulantly. "Am I not worth gold?"

"Not on your wedding day!" Edward sobbed.

"Ah, well," I shrugged, "there is always the wedding *night!*" And I stepped past him to take my bride's arm and escort her inside the church for the wedding mass.

Gloomy and teary-eyed, Edward sat beside me at the feast that followed, and grew even more so when I refused to quarrel with him on the grounds that it was all his doing. He was my sovereign lord, and I a loyal servant of the Crown, and he bade me marry the lady; did he honestly expect me to disobey a royal command? And though the great trestle table fairly groaned beneath the bounteous array, and music, laughter, and revelry surrounded us, Edward and I could do nothing but drink and carry on our taut and taunting flirtation while our plates remained untouched and those around us wondered what was wrong.

"Nay Nedikins," I taunted sweetly, "what's done is done! You have made your bed and will have to lie in it, whether it pleases you or not, and you must do so alone. Tonight," I directed a meaningful glance at my bride, "duty takes me elsewhere!"

Edward grasped my hand so tightly a bruise would be blossoming there by morning. With a quaver in his voice and his eyes full of tears, he begged me to tell him that I loved him still and nothing would ever change that.

I offered him my most beguiling smile and stood up from the table and, leaning down close, bade him follow me. He did, and I gave him every assurance that my feelings had not altered.

Edward returned to the table with a dreamy and contented smile and was delighted to discover that he had suddenly acquired a hearty appetite.

The feast dragged on for what seemed like hours as I watched the seemingly endless procession of dishes parade past my eyes. There was a roast peacock so skillfully re-dressed in its gaudy plumage that I would not have been surprised if it had suddenly begun to screech and flap its wings, a pair of calves heads, one silvered and the other gilded, elaborate subtleties, allegories pertaining to matrimony sculpted of sugar and marzipan, wobbly jellies of red, yellow, and green, and all manner of meat pies, fish, fowl, and game, soups by the score, and cakes, pies, and custards too numerous to name.

Edward and the servers tried to tempt me, but I felt as if cold stones were lodged within my heart and belly, and I could do nothing but shake my head and drink cup after cup of hippocras, hoping vainly that the warm spiced wine would melt the uneasy coldness inside. And still that crow inside my head kept cawing: "This is a mistake! This is a mistake!" and I prayed the hippocras would silence him or drown out his cries.

Then it was time for the eagerly awaited ritual of the bride-cakes. Custom dictated that every guest bring a small, round, flat cake adorned with currants, honey, fruit, or nuts, and stack them as high as they could upon a table. The bride and groom must stand, face to face with the table of cakes between them and lean forward and kiss. If the cakes remain in place the marriage will be happy, fruitful, and prosperous, but if they topple the very opposite will come to pass. Need I even tell you that they toppled?

Edward was at my side in an instant declaiming like a hero of legend: "Nay, my beloved Perrot, do not fear! By my life, you shall be happy and prosper, I swear!"

At his words Meg smiled and ventured to ask shyly: "And shall we have many children, Uncle Edward?"

Edward could not answer, so I smiled and confidently asserted *"Dozens!"* and kept smiling even as Edward stamped his foot down hard upon mine to show how much he disliked my answer.

Nearby stood Warwick, Lancaster, and Lincoln.

"Generally I do not hold with superstition," The Black Dog growled, stroking his long black beard strewn and matted with bread crumbs and sour cherry sauce, "but this is one time when I think it will prove correct."

Burstbelly nodded and grunted his agreement but could not offer further comment as his mouth was crammed full of cake.

"Aye," The Buffoon nodded, preening in his pink and orange striped taffeta and stroking his little pointy gold beard. "Do you think The Gascon even knows what to do with a woman?"

"Poor lass, she might as well have stayed in the convent and took vows," Warwick answered, "for all the good this marriage will do her. Methinks being the bride of Gaveston and a bride of Christ are not so dissimilar; either way she will spend her days sequestered in the country with her maidenhead unbreached and nothing to do but ply her needle and pray!"

Hearing their words, I had the most amusing idea for a jest and my eyes eagerly sought Aymer de Valence, the Earl of Pembroke, the wisest and most esteemed of Edward's councilors.

I found him standing near a window-seat, looking very distinguished in deep green velvet. His gray-speckled black hair was newly cropped and the style suited him well. Indeed, I thought him a most elegant figure, so tall and trim, and far too serious, and it was neither the first nor the last time that I found myself lamenting that he stood with Warwick, Lancaster, and Lincoln as my enemy. He is such a solemn man and guards his smiles and laughter like a miser, and this I have taken as a challenge. Someday I will make the Earl of Pembroke smile at me!

"My Lord of Pembroke!" I rushed up to him and laid my hand upon his sleeve. "You are a married man!"

"Yes, Gaveston," he nodded indulgently, condescendingly, as if he were speaking to a simpleton or a small child, "as you well know, I am a married man, and yonder is my lady-wife," he indicated a lovely silver-haired woman gowned in gray satin. "Why do you not go and talk to her? She finds you charming and amusing."

"Unlike you!" I pouted. "But this is something I cannot discuss with your lady-wife; if I tried you might challenge me to a duel! Lean down a little, you are too tall!"

"Oh very well!" he frowned. "But do stop stroking my sleeve as if it were your pet!"

He obliged me and leaned down and I whispered into his ear: "When I am alone with my wife what am I to do?"

"Good heavens!" Pembroke straightened abruptly. "You mean you do not know? Gaveston, this is most ... awkward! Can you not ask His Majesty? Given the close nature of your ... ahmm ... friendship, I should think it would be best if ..."

"Nay," I shook my head adamantly, "for he is jealous and will not tell me!"

"Well your brothers then?" Pembroke suggested.

"Guillaume is drunk under the banquet table reciting love poems to Edward's wolfhounds. And I dare not ask Arnaud and Raimond; they would laugh at me for the rest of my life!"

"Yes, yes, I ... I see what you mean," Pembroke nodded commiseratively, "to be sure, your brothers are most disagreeable fellows! Very well then, let us sit down," he indicated the window-seat, "and I shall do my best to ... enlighten you."

Poor Pembroke was so agitated that I didn't have the heart to go through with it. "Nay, My Lord, you need not! I like you too well to embarrass you further! Rest assured that in all matters pertaining to the bedchamber I am *exceedingly* well versed! I sought your advice only in jest."

"Now, really, Gaveston!" Pembroke fumed. "This is *intolerable!* You have placed me in a most awkward position!"

"Well, My Lord," I ventured with a mischievous smile as I pressed my thigh against his, "if you find this position awkward there are others we might try!"

Angry and incredulous, Pembroke rounded on me. "Are you *flirting* with me, Gaveston?"

"Yes, of course I am!" I said brightly. "Has it *really* taken you this long to figure that out?"

A perfect picture of indignation, Pembroke leapt to his feet. "I grow weary of your jests, Gaveston! Forsooth, you are a brazen knave, unnatural and audacious! You should be ashamed of yourself! *This is your wedding day!*"

"You misunderstand, My Lord, this is no jest! And if you object to today, there is always tomorrow, or the day after. As for my wife, she need never know, nor yours either," I added, standing up and laying my hand upon his sleeve again. "The Italians say: 'Caress only your enemies,' so I thought we might try and see if there is truly merit in that phrase. But you are not interested, I think, and my heart *grieves* for it!"

Pembroke just glowered at me. "Indeed, I am most decidedly *not* interested! Hush this unseemly prattle now, and take your hand off my sleeve; His Majesty approaches!"

"Ah, Edward!" I cried as I spun round to greet him. "Condole with me, my dearest friend! The Earl of Pembroke refuses to make love to me!"

"*Well I should hope so!*" Edward exclaimed. "God's blood, bones, and teeth, Piers, I cannot let you out of my sight for a moment! Thank you, My Lord, once again you have proven yourself to be a man of great wisdom," he nodded to Pembroke as he began to lead me determinedly away. "Come, Perrot, and leave the Earl of Pembroke in peace!"

"As you like," I shrugged. "Well, My Lord," I smiled as I turned back to Pembroke, "we shall have to continue this conversation another time!"

"*God preserve me from such a fate!*" Pembroke staunchly declared.

As Edward led me away, I turned and winked at Pembroke. But he just glowered at me and repeated his assertion that I was a "brazen knave!"

Soon it was time to see the bride and groom put to bed to the tune of much ribaldry and laughter. Only a choice few would be allowed at first into the bridal chamber so, to appease the crowd, Meg stood upon the threshold while her sister Eleanor knelt and reached up beneath her bridal gown to untie her garters.

It is accounted a sign of good fortune to catch the bride's garters. If caught by someone unwed, they will marry within a year, and if a man gives the garter he catches to his lady-love and she accepts it their love shall last forever.

The first landed on the head of whey-faced Hugh Despenser, even then talking statecraft with his pompous father—the sly old goat! His perpetually ink-stained fingers twitched the trailing blue silk from his dull cheese-colored hair with unconcealed annoyance as he continued his conversation.

Lancaster caught the second one and turned instantly to present it to his lovely wife Alice with whom, despite her complete and contemptuous indifference, he was passionately in love. Alice just glared at him then turned away with her nose haughty-high in the air, leaving him holding the garter and turning scarlet with embarrassment.

Once the garters were thrown, Meg and I were escorted into the bridal chamber. A gaggle of giggling ladies surrounded Meg on one side of the chamber while a group of bawdy-witted men surrounded me on the other and helped us to undress.

After the fine white linen nightshirt was slipped over my head Edward stepped forward and grasped my shoulders. "*You are mine!*" he said and kissed me hard upon the mouth. "Lest you forget!" he added as he reluctantly released me. It was fortunate indeed that we were thickly screened from the ladies' sight, though they did wonder why all had of a sudden gone quiet.

When Meg stood in her shift and I in my nightshirt, each on opposite sides of the bed, the door was thrown wide and the Bishop led the other guests inside. He blessed the bed with holy water and then, to much laughter and encouragement, we climbed in. The Bride's Cup was brought forth, filled with a warm, strengthening caudle of wine, milk, egg yolks, cinnamon, and sugar, and we must each drink from it, passing it between us. "Drink it to the dregs, you will need all the strength it can give you!" someone in the crowd shouted.

Only Edward stood apart, as silent and sullen as a monk. He was in a Hell of his own making and not even all his tears could douse the flames!

As the merry company filed out after drinking one last toast to us, Edward followed with leaden steps and tear-blinded eyes, causing Meg to marvel: "I never knew Uncle Edward to be so maudlin at a wedding before, by his manner one would think it was a funeral instead!"

I could not help myself, I threw back my head and laughed and laughed, and once I started, I just could not stop! I laughed until my sides ached and I was gasping for breath and tears ran down my face.

Meg drew back and cowered nervously with the covers pulled all the way up to her chin, no doubt thinking that she had married a madman. And Edward turned round and stared at me as if I had completely lost my wits, but that only made me laugh more. From the corridor my brother Guillaume wondered what had been in that caudle and bade a servant fetch him some if it would make him even half so merry.

At last, my laughter subsided. I held Edward's gaze, licked my lips, and proceeded to taunt him further by lifting my nightshirt over my head.

"I *always* sleep as nature made me!"

Poor Edward, he became so flustered that he bumped into a table, sending golden cups clattering to the floor and rolling every which way.

When I saw the look on his face, so hurt and bewildered, I instantly regretted my teasing. I wanted to jump out of bed and run to him, take him in my arms, and assure him that all would be well. But I didn't dare. Meg was there and I could sense her unease. Edward would just have to wait. I would make amends later, I promised, and hoped the look I gave him conveyed as much.

With a woebegone countenance and sagging shoulders, Edward departed our bridal chamber. I knew then I would have to go to him, even if it was my wedding night.

A long and awkward silence followed. Meg tensed when I reached out to take her hand. "All's well, sweeting," I said gently, "you need never fear me; I promise I will always be kind to you."

I settled myself comfortably against the pillows and arranged the bedclothes to my liking. If truth be known, I prefer to sleep alone, though I often let Blanche sleep with me, especially during thunderstorms as they always frighten her. I suppose it is because the bedchamber has been the stage upon which I have earned my bread and butter for so long that I welcome the chance to lie solitary with no performance expected of me.

"It's all right, sweetheart. We needn't do anything tonight. We can wait until you are ready."

"No, I ..." Meg blushed and lowered her eyes, "I want to."

I kept my amusement and surprise to myself and drew her gently into my arms.

She really is a pretty child; even though as I write this she is approaching eighteen, I still think of her as a child. At thirteen she had a gawky, coltish body, all legs, tall and too thin, but her amber eyes and wavy waist-length red-gold hair were beautiful, and I found the spray of freckles across her nose delightful.

I let her lie with her head upon my chest and grow calm listening to my heart-beat while I stroked her hair. I was very gentle with her. Indeed, I could not be otherwise. Her shyness touched something deep inside me, and to this day I recall the trembling timidity of her little hands that had not yet learned how to caress, and the curiosity that vied with her modesty. I held her close and kissed away the tears that came with the sharp pain that broke the barrier betwixt maiden and womanhood.

Afterwards, she surprised me by confessing that she had long been in love with me.

"I remember the first time I saw you," she blushingly confided. "I was seven or eight years old, and I had come to Langley for a visit. I was walking in the orchard with my nurse when I saw you. I had never seen anyone so beautiful and I doubted for a moment that you were of this world. I nearly asked my nurse if you were one of the Faerie Folk. You were all in green and had a white puppy with you. You were wrestling with Uncle Edward under an apple tree. My nurse took my hand and insisted that we turn back; she said we had walked enough for one day. Do you still wrestle with Uncle Edward?"

"Constantly!" I bit my lip to suppress the laughter that threatened to bubble forth.

Later, when Meg was sleeping soundly and the night was still, I stole softly from our bridal bed, found my robe, and went to Edward. And oh what a state I found him in! He was upon me in an instant, regaling me with the horrors of the agonizing hours he had passed without me, how he had wept and rolled upon his bed in hellish torment, biting his nails until they bled, and tearing at his hair, trying yet unable to banish the visions of me doing my husbandly duty with Meg. He was just about to send for the royal physician and have him bring his leeches!

"*How could you do this to me?*" he wailed.

"But Nedikins," I said sweetly, "it was *you* who did this to *me*, and to Meg; we both know she deserves better!"

Yet it soon became apparent that only I knew that. Edward had no idea what I meant and demanded that I explain. I knew full well the folly of attempting that, so I just smiled and let my robe fall to the floor and pool round my ankles in a silken caress. Edward did not press me for an explanation; he pressed me onto the mattress instead.

Later, as we lolled back against the pillows, it was decided that Meg, being so young and accustomed to country living as she was, should depart forthwith for my castle of Wallingford, the traditional seat of the Earl of Cornwall, and take up her duties there as chatelaine, while I remained with Edward as he had greater need of me.

I was half asleep when he said: "Piers, it occurs to me that you might send Agnes to Wallingford to look after Meg. She is young and still of an age to have a nurse."

"Then she may choose someone of her own liking, and you may pay her wages since you feel so strongly about it," I replied, "but Agnes stays with me."

"You are too familiar with her, Piers!" he accused.

"And you are aloof and kingly in your bearing when you consort with ditch-diggers, thatchers, and bargemen?" I countered.

"That is neither here nor there; when men labor together beneath the hot sun they should be on friendly terms! But you are three-and-twenty and in excellent health, so what need have you of a nurse? You are too affectionate with her, Piers, it is not seemly!"

"Really, Edward!" I sighed and rolled my eyes. "Agnes is almost seventy and is a second mother to me, so it is absurd for you to be talking about her as if she were a love-rival! After my mother died she took care of me, and I assure you she was under no obligation to do so, and received no remuneration for it either!"

"Then give her a gift of money and send her to Wallingford to look after your wife!"

"*Never!*"

"But what if she *wanted* to go?"

"*You would not dare!*"

"I am the King of England, Piers, so do not presume to tell me what I will and will not dare!"

"Very well then," I shrugged, "if the King of England dares to persuade Agnes that she would be happier elsewhere then Perrot will leave Nedikins and go elsewhere too!"

"Oh Perrot!" Edward gasped, clutching his heart as if it ached. "No! *Please!* You would not leave me! Would you?"

"For those I love, I would dare *anything!* Just because you are my lover, Edward, does not mean you rule my heart! Love comes in many guises; lust is not the only robe it wears; methinks you have forgotten that! I love you, Edward, and I have forsaken dignity and peace of mind to be with you! This very day I have committed a grievous wrong against an innocent young girl to satisfy a whim of yours, so do not presume to dictate who deserves a place in my heart! Forsooth, you would have me love none but you! You even object to my dog coming into bed with us when it storms, and you know Blanche is terrified of thunder!"

"When you turn away from me to hold her and give the impression of having forgotten all about me, then yes, I most certainly do object! Last time there was a storm you fell asleep with your back to me and that animal in your arms! How do you think that made me feel?"

"And how do *you* think that made *me* feel?" I retorted, taking him completely by surprise. "You know I like nothing better than to fall asleep lying on my side with your body curled around mine, and your arms about me; it reminds me of our first night together. Now I ask you, Edward, how do you think I felt? I lay there with my back to you, expecting, wanting, waiting, to feel the warmth of your skin as you nestled against me, and to feel you put your arms about me, and you never did! And there was no reason for you not to; you know Blanche doesn't bite! I assure you I passed a most miserable night! And thinking of it now, I am made miserable all over again!"

"Oh Perrot!" he cried, instantly contrite. "Can you *ever* forgive me?"

"I always do," I shrugged with a sigh worthy of a martyr, "so why should this time be different from any other?"

"My darling, you are as tender-hearted and generous as you are beautiful!" he declared and would have taken me in his arms again but I held back and pressed my palm against his chest.

"There will be no more talk of sending Agnes away?"

"Not a word, my love! I want my Perrot to be happy; he is too beautiful to be anything else! And Blanche shall have a new jeweled collar! And what shall my beautiful Perrot have for himself? Name it and it is yours!"

"*Your love!*" I answered fervently, lying back and reaching up to draw him down to me. But just before his lips met mine I pressed my palm against his chest again and turned my face away. "But *first*, I would have you send to Agnes; I would like her to brew me a posset of rosemary to settle my nerves; this has been a trying night and they are most sorely jangled."

Edward looked at me as if he would gladly murder me, but I held his gaze, and in the end he did as I desired, though not without murmuring that the Devil could take my nerves and that I would be the death of him. Methinks Time will prove it to be the other way around.

THE REGENCY

Of the many titles and endowments Edward has given me throughout the years I only requested two—the first being to be appointed Regent when he crossed the Channel to wed the French Princess Isabelle. I asked not out of a desire to lord it over all and sundry, but in the hope that if my enemies saw that I would do nothing to take advantage of the power such a position entails then, perhaps, in their eyes I would be redeemed. And if I performed my duties well and displayed good and sound judgment, maybe Edward would realize that there is more to me than what his eyes see.

Of course, Edward readily acquiesced. But all my good intentions came to naught. My Regency only fanned the flames of hate that already surrounded me. Otherwise, it passed uneventfully. It lasted exactly two weeks.

Perhaps "uneventfully" is the wrong choice of word, as something important of a personal rather than a political nature did occur. It was at this time that I began what was, until recently, a longstanding affair with the Earl of Richmond.

I had known the Earl since my early days in the old King's army. He was a highly valued friend and trusted advisor of the King. He was also a friend of my father, but to me he was merely an acquaintance.

Then, two years after I joined Edward's household and became his "beloved Perrot," I was summoned to Winchester to attend my father's funeral. The Earl of Richmond was there and, after offering his condolences, invited me to dine with him. I eagerly accepted. Richmond was a renowned conversationalist and I looked forward to a pleasant evening with him. It is a sad truth to tell, but with

Edward I often felt the lack of stimulating conversation so keenly that it was like wandering in a desert, lost and longing for a taste of cool, sweet water.

John de Bretagne, Earl of Richmond, was a man of intelligence and learning, a seasoned soldier, courtier, and diplomat, famous for his affable charm and ability to get along with everyone. He was the kind of man whose enemies—if he had enemies—liked him. He was exactly the sort of man I always longed to be. He was also very handsome, with a full head of unruly brown hair kissed with golden lights and jolly blue eyes. He was, at the time of my father's death, five years past thirty.

I spent that afternoon with Edward clinging to me like a drowning man, weeping on my shoulder, and marveling at how stoical I was being in the face of my great loss. In truth, I had hardly known my father. He had been so often away and, even when we served in the army together, we were more like strangers than father and son, though our relations were always cordial. But Edward took my words as further proof of my bravery and declared me "stalwart in the face of grief."

"Now my Perrot is really and truly an orphan!" he sobbed. "I promise I will always take care of you! Here is my shoulder, do not hold back, drench it with your tears even if they be vast as an ocean and flood this palace and drown everyone in it!"

In the end, I was forced to feign a headache and steal away to lie on my bed and enjoy the blessed peace that ensued as Edward tiptoed around shushing any noisy servants and courtiers nearby lest they disturb "poor Perrot who is prostrate with grief."

Much to my surprise, Edward did not object to my dining with the Earl of Richmond. On the contrary, he insisted that it would do me good; the Earl had been my father's friend and Edward was certain it would prove comforting for me to talk to someone who had known him. He even selected my garb to spare my grief-stricken mind the torment of such trifles. Thus, I sallied forth to meet the Earl of Richmond in a tunic of bright purple velvet with long silky fringe that jiggled teasingly about my thighs when I walked and black silk hose embroidered with purple roses along the sides. Agnes deemed it a most provocative ensemble—the tunic was cut daringly short—and professed serious doubts about its suitability for such an occasion. I was inclined to agree, after all, I was supposed to be in mourning. But Edward insisted I was as beautiful as an angel.

"Mayhap he means a *fallen* angel?" I whispered to Agnes as Edward knelt to smooth the silken fringe over my thighs.

Clearly he had no qualms about the Earl of Richmond seeing me so alluringly arrayed. But since the trail of brokenhearted ladies Richmond left languishing in his wake wherever he went provided fodder for so much gossip, I daresay it never occurred to him that he should be concerned.

We dined in his private apartments, seated at opposite ends of a long table. The Earl dismissed the servers, summoning them by bell only when we had need of them.

Alas, the conversation failed to meet my expectations! Richmond seemed troubled and preoccupied, as if weighty issues preyed upon his mind. Then the conversation changed. His questions were delicately phrased and politely probing as he tried to discern in what direction my desires lay. He had heard rumors, but one seemed to contradict the other. My father used to laugh about my exploits with lusty widows, while my brothers sanctimoniously declared that such antics were all too typical of "mother's witch-child." And someone else claimed they had heard me complaining to Agnes that I had gotten a bad bruise on my middle bending over a table with the weight of a certain captain on my back. I was disconcertingly sophisticated for one so young, and I had more clothes than anyone had ever seen without seeming to have the means to afford them. I rode blood horses instead of the usual army nags, and traveled with my own bathtub, two eccentric servants, and was rumored to be a witch. Yet, in spite of all this, I was not effete, and anyone who assumed I was, was quickly disabused of this notion by my sword or fists. And none could say for certain whether it was lads or lasses that I fancied.

His interest surprised me. Richmond was a man renowned for his prowess with the ladies; from serving wenches to countesses they all capitulated to his charms. He was proud of his conquests, and not above carrying on more than one love affair at the same time.

"*Damnation!*" In frustration Richmond banged his fist upon the table. "This is so unlike me! My mind is all a muddle and I do not know …"

"*I do,*" I interrupted softly with a look of invitation in my eyes as I raised my goblet and took a sip of wine. "You are trying to seduce me."

Richmond blinked in surprise and blushed to the roots of his hair.

"Do not be discouraged, you are doing splendidly! Here, allow me to help you; I shall meet you halfway."

I left my chair and walked half the length of the long table then paused and stood expectantly, waiting for him. He came to me and, in a surge of passion, seized hold of me and kissed me hard and long.

Verily, I was overwhelmed by the intensity of it, and by my own emotions; I found myself truly stirred, and to feign desire there was no need.

It occurred to me that I should feel guilty because of Edward, but since he did not know ... And did he really *need* to know? After all, it would only upset him! And Edward is *so* emotional! Besides, this really had *nothing* to do with him!

The Earl stepped back and stared at me, startled and amazed.

"Have you no respect for yourself?" he demanded.

Then it was my turn to be startled and amazed; this is *not* how my lovers usually respond to our first kiss.

"You're only seventeen, yet you behave like a practiced tart!"

Before I could respond, he grabbed my wrist, dragged me to his chair, sat down, put me over his knees, and *spanked me. Hard!* And this was no amorous love-play; I would have the bruises to show for it!

When he was done he took me by my collar, dragged me out the door and all the way back to my room. To my immense relief, Edward was not waiting for me, only Agnes.

"This child is up far past his bedtime, Madame," he curtly informed her, "see that he retires at once! He is not yet ready to sit at table with his elders!" And with that he left us, slamming the door behind him.

"I'm not a child!" I shouted after him. "I'm almost eighteen!"

"Child, what ails the Earl of Richmond?" Agnes asked in wide-eyed amazement.

"He made advances to me, and when I responded he became angry and ... spanked me!"

"Spanked you?" Agnes asked incredulously. "Do you mean a proper spanking?"

"I thought it most *im*proper, but yes, it was what would be called a proper spanking. It was certainly not done in play! How dare he? I've never been spanked in my life!"

"Well of course not!" Agnes exclaimed. "Your lady-mother would never have sanctioned it even if it had ever occurred to me!"

"And to tell you to put me to bed as if I were a child of five!" I fumed.

"Naturally, you may stay up as late as you like, my sweet," Agnes said soothingly. "Come sit by the fire now and try to calm yourself."

"I can't sit down!" I responded petulantly.

"Oh the brute! The savage monster!" Agnes cried, taking me in her arms and hugging me tight. "To raise his hand against my darling!"

It would be years before either of us forgave the Earl of Richmond for that spanking, or the attending difficulties it caused. I had to explain the bruises to

Edward, and believe me, it was no easy task! I told him that in my grief for my late father my tear-blinded eyes had caused me to misjudge my distance to a chair and I had missed the seat and fallen onto the floor. When Edward replied that I must have fallen very hard indeed to account for such bruises, I told him that if he really loved me he would never have brought me to a place with such hard floors in my grief-stricken condition and retreated behind my locked door. Edward spent the rest of the day lamenting his thoughtlessness and insensitivity while I played cards with Agnes and Dragon until I decided to forgive him.

Therefore, it was a great surprise when, six years later, the Earl of Richmond sought me out the very day Edward departed for France and asked me to dine with him.

"Are you going to spank me again?" I asked.

"You are no longer a child, so do not be childish and hold a grudge! Say that you forgive me and that you will dine with me tonight. His Majesty says you are as generous as you are beautiful!" Confusion flitted across his features when, at these words, I began to laugh.

When he left my bedchamber that morning Edward's opinion of my generosity had not been very great. But it was not my fault! He had kept me up far past midnight, and then to shake me awake at dawn just to tell me that he had lost his shoe when I was sleeping so soundly … it was most unkind! Edward is the King of England and if he cannot find one misplaced shoe which he knows is somewhere in a single locked room then no wonder his subjects have no confidence in him! I burrowed deeper into the warm bed, but Edward would not let me be. He shook my shoulder again. "Piers, Blanche has taken my shoe and run under the bed with it!"

It was a cold morning and I was not inclined to stir, so I yawned and said: "Surely you have others!" and went back to sleep.

"I do not know why you are laughing, but it is music to my ears!" Richmond ardently declared. "*Please*, say you will have dinner with me!"

"And what of you, My Lord?" I asked. "Have you forgiven yourself? Methinks you were angry that night, and not only with 'the practiced tart of seventeen.'"

"I was angry because I desired you," he admitted. "All my life I have been a devout admirer of the fairer sex, and then to suddenly discover that I desired you … Can you even imagine my horror, my shame? Yet try as I might—and I have spent these six years trying—my desire for you lives on. Now *please*, punish me no more, Piers, and say you will have dinner with me! Or must I beg you on my knees?"

"Very well, My Lord," I sighed with a wave of my hand both magnanimous and grand. "If you insist, then yes, I will have dinner with you tonight."

This time our dinner was a much more convivial affair. Our conversation was lively and free, and he bade me call him by his given name—John. And afterwards, this time it was he who stood and walked half the table's length, paused, held out his hand to me, and asked: "Will you meet me halfway?"

And I did. The kiss that followed was even better than our first. And then, instead of dragging me over to his chair and spanking me, he took me by surprise in an altogether different fashion. He stooped and, before I knew what was happening, had slung me over his shoulder like a sack of grain. He carried me into his bedchamber, dumped me on the bed, and kicked the door shut with his heel. It was one of the most interesting nights of my life!

Maybe I should have felt guilty about going into another's bed when Edward had scarcely quit the country, but it would be a lie if I said I did. I have been untrue with many while he was in England or even under the same roof, so why should I regret dallying in his absence? Richmond offered me something Edward could not give me, so I took it; people generally do take what they are offered.

As my Regency neared its end, and Edward's return was imminent, we decided that we did not want our affair to end, so it didn't. Of course, I explained everything to Edward, how in my eagerness to do well as Regent I had sought the advice of the Earl of Richmond whom I had always respected and admired. With a knowing smile, Edward said he had known all along that the Earl would be as a second father to me. This remark gave birth to a private jest; henceforth in our letters John and I would always address one another as "Father" and "Son."

Incredibly, there has never been a whisper of gossip about me and the Earl of Richmond. In the eyes of the world we are exactly what we seem: two friends, one considerably older than the other, who are like father and son. John and I have deceived everyone; while Edward and I fool no one, for no one is fool enough to believe our love is brotherly.

Though our times together were few and brief—diplomatic missions often took him away—I found a certain contentment with John, for a time at least. Unlike Edward, he is confident and strong, a man of the world neither gullible or naïve, and he could be so gentle and caring, though now I must force myself to remember that.

Edward and John were two very different men, and I loved them both in different ways, but if I had to choose ... as hard as it may be to believe or understand, it is Edward I always come back to, and not because he is a king. I close my eyes and see the endearing smile and tousled golden hair of the boy I loved at

Langley and my heart swells with love for him! Judge me not too harshly; remember instead that Love has made fools of far wiser men than me!

THE KING AND
QUEEN RETURN

In January of the year 1308 Edward married Isabelle, the daughter of King Philip IV of France, in a lavish ceremony at Notre Dame. It was accounted a splendid match by all, both being young, blonde, and beautiful. And hope ran rampant that "Isabelle the Fair" would cure Edward of his ridiculous obsession with me.

"Isabelle the Fair," that was what they called her, though I always thought the name I gave her, "The Ice Queen," much more apt. Hers was not a vibrant golden beauty like Edward's, but the very opposite, a frosty white-blonde pallor. She was like an untouchable virgin goddess with a latent voluptuousness lurking just beneath the ice; ice which she hoped Edward would be the one to melt. I knew the first time I saw her that she was in love with him; it was there in her eyes when she looked at him, until humiliation and pride taught her to hide it.

When they returned to England the court assembled to meet their ship at Dover. I shivered in the salty breeze and felt at the same time giddy and nervous as I stood there at the fore of a large and splendid retinue, waiting to meet the woman Edward had married.

My brothers were with me, and I was nearly rendered deaf with Arnaud on my right and Raimond on my left, clamoring to be heard, both of them insisting that their wives be appointed ladies-in-waiting to the new Queen. And Guillaume swaying before me, staggering drunk even at this early hour, imploring me to find him a wife, "a blonde with pretty paps and plump thighs," so that she too might serve the Queen. I tried very hard to ignore them and sought to divert myself by watching the other courtiers instead.

Once again Edward's arrogant cousin Tom of Lancaster had proven himself worthy of the name "Buffoon" in his diamond-patterned tunic and hose of blue, red, and yellow satin, with a mountain of silk roses and ostrich plumes dyed to match piled upon his hat, and his emerald velvet mantle dripped with row upon row of multicolored silk fringe. He adopted a haughty pose and held his chin high and stroked his little gold beard as if it were a cat. His wife Alice stood nearby and I whispered to her: "Do you think he bleaches it with the juice of lemons to keep it so golden?" causing her to shriek with laughter and draw many disapproving eyes in our direction.

Pembroke stood beside Lancaster, somber but elegant in black velvet, pointedly ignoring my attempts to flirt with him. Burstbelly stood nearby, his stomach straining and bulging against his white and silver tunic. And Warwick glowered darkly at me and caressed the hilt of his sword while the wind vainly endeavored to comb the tangles from his long black beard.

As for myself, I was dressed to dazzle and all eyes and mouths were agape at my magnificence. I wore a turquoise brocade tunic embossed with a pattern of emerald and gold vines and blood red roses, the same shade as my red silk hose and the long flowing liripipe attached to my hat. A bevy of peacock feathers swayed gracefully atop my diamond-spangled hat and a matching fan dangled from my bejeweled belt. I wore rubies, emeralds, and diamonds on all my fingers, about my neck, wrists, and waist, and on my shoes, and my mother's crescent moon brooch sparkled on my shoulder.

As soon as the ship docked and the gangplank was in place Edward was racing towards me, deserting his bride in a flurry of sky blue brocade and ermine, heedless of the wind taking his fine feathered hat and carrying it out to sea. His face was all aglow and he laughed joyously in that way he has—like a donkey braying, only much more melodious.

"Perrot! *Darling* Perrot! *Beloved* Perrot! *Beautiful* Perrot!" he cried and threw himself upon me with such force that he nearly knocked me off my feet. Never had he hugged me with such tight urgency or kissed me so hungrily.

I glanced past him at the new Queen, standing amidst her ladies-in-waiting and other members of the royal entourage, which included several of her relations who had come to attend Edward's coronation on King Philip's behalf. As she watched us, I saw her confusion and amazement rapidly turn to anger. It was obvious that she knew nothing about me; no one had thought to inform her that Edward's heart belonged to another, and that other was a man.

I could well understand what a shock such a discovery could be. Remember, I've plied my trade for a long time; I've seen wives discover that their husbands are prey to unnatural desires. Some weep and rage, others accept meekly, some blame themselves, others withdraw from the world entirely and take refuge in a convent, some are sophisticated women of the world who accept and think nothing more about it, and others harbor unnatural lusts themselves and are quite content with the situation. It was something I now often had cause to contemplate in regards to my own marriage. A day was sure to come when Meg would learn the truth. I knew it would wound her to the quick, but there was nothing I could do to spare her. The wisest thing would have been never to have married her, but the past was a knot I could not untie. And the knowledge that I would one day cause her pain was always there like a thorn in my heart. But it was plain to see that Edward did not cherish similar sentiments about his own bride.

"So easily forgotten," I mused as we strolled back to the ship with my retinue trailing after.

"What?" Edward stared back at me blankly.

"I am speaking of your wife. She vanished from your thoughts entirely the moment you saw me. It makes me wonder if as soon as I was beyond your sight did you also forget about me?"

"*Perrot!*" Edward gave a wounded cry. "How can you even *think* such a thing? I thought of *nothing* but *you* the whole time I was away! And I have brought you many fine gifts from France!"

"None of which could ever please me more than having you back does," I answered. And I meant it. I felt such a twinge of impatience to be alone with him, it was altogether maddening! No matter how vexed I am with Edward when we say goodbye, after a few days apart I am pining for him desperately. "I missed you," I said softly.

"Oh Perrot! Did you *really*?" Words do not exist that can do justice to the glory of his smile.

"Did you think I would not?" I teased.

"Well ..." he hesitated, blushing sheepishly and studying his shoes. "You are *so* beautiful I feared that someone might make advances and that you, in your loneliness, might accept them."

"Just because I am beautiful does not mean that the concept of loyalty eludes me."

"Then you *were* faithful to me?" he asked hopefully.

"In my fashion," I answered with a little shrug and a smile to further tantalize. "But, Nedikins, should you not look to your wife now? New circumstances and a new land; anyone would be made anxious by that."

"*What? Who?* Oh, yes, *my wife!* Verily, it shall take me some time to grow accustomed to this married state! Come and meet her, Piers, I *know* she will love you just as much as I do!"

"Oh Edward," I hung back in dismay, "it would be the death of me if anyone else were to love me even half as much as you do!"

Edward just laughed. "My Perrot is *so* witty! No one can make a jest like he can!"

I let Edward lead me up the gangplank and introduce me to his bride. Edward really had no thought of sparing her, the way he continued to gaze upon me, devouring and undressing me with his eyes ... anyone could see he was in love, and not with his wife!

Isabelle looked me up and down with regal disdain.

"Does Your Majesty not find it demeaning that this person should appear here in the garb of an oriental potentate with the intention, I think, of outshining you?"

"How could I possibly mind?" Edward breathed without taking his eyes off me.

"And what exactly does this person do?" she asked.

There was a sharp intake of breath all around. Burstbelly nervously gnawed his nails. Warwick's grip tightened round the hilt of his sword, and Lancaster glared daggers at me. Pembroke sought my eyes and shook his head vigorously, *begging* me not to tell. They were afraid I would be blunt and tell her *exactly* what my duties consisted of! I confess I was sorely tempted to, but instead I said sweetly with an insinuating smile: "I am His Majesty's Principal Provider of Entertainment." Anyone with a soupçon of sophistication could figure it out and my eyes flashed a challenge.

"Ah," she nodded, "I should have guessed from your attire; you are His Majesty's clown and not some vulgar popinjay after all!"

I was so outraged I could not even speak. *A clown? Me?*

"No, no, Isabelle!" Edward interjected hastily above the courtiers' laughter. "Piers is my dearest friend in all the world! He is styled the Earl of Cornwall and in my absence has acted as Regent."

Isabelle turned incredulously to Edward. "Surely you jest, My Lord? Such a position belongs to a man of more mature years and an even more mature mind!"

There were murmurs of agreement and laughter all around. Edward saw that I was in serious danger of losing my temper and began hustling me towards the gangplank.

"Now, now, my dear, Piers is a man of many talents! But I know you are weary from the journey, so let us away to the palace now where we can all take our ease! You can make friends with Piers later. I know that when you are better acquainted you will be the very best of friends!"

"*I would not count on it if I were you!*" I murmured through tightly clenched teeth, and I could tell from her expression that Isabelle felt *exactly* the same.

"I object to being referred to as 'this person,' Edward!" I fumed, shaking free of his hand and stalking towards the row of horses, litters, and carriages. "She insulted me, repeatedly, and all but called me a fool! And did you hear what she said about my clothes?"

"Oh Perrot, let it be!" Edward implored. "You won't be wearing them long, so ..."

"*That,*" I said pointedly, swinging round to face him, "is a matter open for debate! Do not be so presumptuous, Edward!"

At the royal coach Isabelle paused and regarded me uncertainly. "Is this person to ride with us, Edward?"

"Yes, Edward," I turned to him and asked sweetly: "Is this person to ride with us?"

Edward knew he would have to make a choice then and there.

"My dear, this coach is beastly uncomfortable! Yes, it is luxurious, to be sure, but I would not subject you to this torture! You take the next one!" He put his hand on her back and pushed her firmly towards Lancaster's coach, which stood next in line. "Piers and I will make do as best we can in this one; you ride with Cousin Tom and Alice! No, no, I insist!" And, ignoring her protests, he shoved her inside and slammed the door, catching her purple velvet and ermine train in it. Then he was at my side again. "Get in, Piers, get in!" he urged, shoving me just as he had Isabelle. And before I was even seated his hands were upon me.

"Can you not wait until we reach the palace?" I demanded, hastily reaching out to draw shut the heavy velvet curtains as his hands found their way beneath my tunic and began peeling down my hose.

"No!" he answered, his voice husky with desire. "If you asked me to wait even another moment it would be a torture more than I could bear! Drive on!" he shouted to the coachman. In response there was the crack of a whip and the coach lurched forward as the wheels began to turn, bearing us the short distance to the cliff-top castle.

As we climbed out of the coach, Isabelle and those who had accompanied her from France looked startled and askance at our flushed faces, ruffled hair, and rumpled clothing.

"That coach is fit only to be broken up for firewood!" Edward said to Isabelle. "You see what a rough journey we have had, my dear!"

"It was very thoughtful of Your Majesty to spare her the ordeal," I simpered.

Then Edward took my arm and whisked me into the palace, abandoning Isabelle once again.

JEWELS FROM FRANCE

The gifts Edward brought me took my breath away. Buckles, brooches, chains, collars, clasps, cameos, and rings. Diamonds, rubies, sapphires, emeralds, amethysts, garnets, and pearls in settings of silver and gold and a plethora of loose stones that I might have set according to my fancy. They dazzled my eyes and made my heart sing! I spent hours sitting cross-legged upon my bed with them all spread out before me while Edward sat in a chair nearby watching me.

"I love the way jewels make your eyes sparkle!" he sighed.

"And the way I express my gratitude?" I teased, crooking a finger and beckoning for him to come join me. We made love on my gem-strewn bed. And to please him, that night when we dined alone together in the privacy of my bedchamber, I wore nothing but pearls, great long strands of priceless white Orient pearls girded round my loins.

The following day found me lounging on a velvet-cushioned chaise and looking languid and alluring—the way Edward likes me to look—in crimson velvet, while Edward sat on a low stool beside me, cradling his lute.

He was serenading me with a song of his own composition and I was pretending to listen. It really was a *dreadful* thing, something about love being like honey and not being able to be bought with money.

In an imperious swirl of ice blue velvet Isabelle swept in. She stopped short and gasped at the sight of us, nearly causing the lady-in-waiting following her to collide with her back.

"My Lord, I am sorry to disturb you, but I wish to show you something …"

She motioned for her attendant to come forward and I saw that she was carrying a large ornately carved wooden box. Isabelle opened it and displayed its empty red velvet-lined interior.

"*Oh!*" Edward breathed. "What a *beautiful* box! Isn't it a beautiful box, Piers? Wouldn't you like to have one just like it?"

"He might as well take this one since he already has its contents!" Isabelle exclaimed.

Her eyes raked over me, burning with fury as they fastened upon each of the ruby and diamond ornaments I wore.

Now I understood and turned expectantly towards Edward. Like Isabelle, I was eager to hear his explanation.

"*Edward!*" Isabelle stamped her foot and struggled to hold back the angry tears she was too proud to let flow. "Edward, you insult me! You have made me a laughingstock, and worse, an object of pity, before the eyes of the entire court! Nay, *two* courts, for they will have much to say of this at my father's court in France! You deck your simpering catamite with *my* gems; jewels my father gave *me* to celebrate our marriage!"

"But my dear!" Edward exclaimed. "Look at him! Rubies are Perrot's favorite! And they look so much nicer on him than they do on you; do you not think so?"

I had to clamp a hand over my mouth to stifle my laughter. Oh Edward, I thought, how fortunate you are that I am not in Isabelle's shoes! If I were, you would have a fearsome headache, for I would not hesitate to smash that beautiful box over your dear idiotic, thoughtless, tactless, insensitive head!

"No, Edward, I do not!" Isabelle said emphatically. "And you miss the point entirely! Those are *my* gems, bridal gifts from my father, and you take them, *steal* them ..."

"Have you forgotten, Madame, that I am the King of England?" Edward demanded. "I can do as I like, and whether one is speaking of the lowest or the highest in the land, the Law says that a wife's property becomes her husband's on their marriage day, therefore, they are *my* jewels and I can do with them as I see fit! Now leave us; Perrot is impatient to hear the rest of the song I have written for him and it is most unkind of you to deprive him of that pleasure!" And he turned his back on her and took up his lute again.

But I was in no mood for songs. I was *furious!*

"Edward ..."

"Yes, my love?" he asked anxiously. "Is anything the matter? Do you not like the song?"

"Yes, of course I do!" I lied. I could not quote a verse of it now to save my life. It was one of those songs that is better forgotten or better yet never written at all. "Edward, how could you do this?"

"Oh I slaved over it for *hours*, I wanted every word, and every note, to be *perfect*, and a fitting tribute to you!"

"*The jewelry, Edward!* How could you do such a thing? Do you not see how this makes me look? And you? Here ..." I started to remove the heavy ruby and diamond encrusted chain, "you must give them back!"

"*No!*" Edward howled. "Oh no, Piers, *I cannot!* Giving them back would make me look like a fool!"

"Edward, you have already made yourself look like a fool, so it is too late to worry about that! Come now, be reasonable; let us try to set things right before ..."

"*No!* I am the King, Isabelle is my wife and as such her property belongs to me, and if I go back upon my word it will undermine my authority! She will think me of a changeable and pliant mind! The jewels are yours, Piers, I have given them to you, and with you they shall stay! Now lie back and take your ease, and I shall continue my song; there are still eleven more verses you haven't heard."

Oh Edward, I thought, you maddening, vexatious, sweet, darling fool! How little you understand yourself and the people around you! You *are* of a changeable and pliant mind and nary a soul does not know it!

But Edward merely smiled, strummed his lute, and sang on about the similarities of love and honey.

CORONATION

Edward's coronation brings back such bitter memories I can hardly bear to write them down. All the arrangements were left entirely to me. I felt that the greatest gift I could ever give Edward was to see that his coronation ran smoothly and was such a splendid affair that it would be talked about for centuries.

Even now I am not sure exactly what went wrong. I cannot prove it, but I feel certain that money changed hands. Warwick and Lancaster were too serene and smiling while Edward was in France, and there were times when I would catch them trading smiles and knowing glances. Be that as it may, on the 25th day of February 1308 my dreams of a glorious coronation collapsed like a house of cards, and what had been so perfect on paper was, in true life, a travesty.

There was a shortage of seats, and many important guests were left standing. They took this as a personal insult and never forgave me since it was I who must dash about and decide who should have the much-coveted seats. The crowd was so dense that their jostling caused a wall to collapse and several people were injured and a knight was killed. And the ceremony itself exceeded the planned length by a full three hours.

And, of course, they took umbrage at my role in the ceremony. But Edward would have me walk before him carrying his crown on a velvet cushion. And rather than appear in cloth-of-gold like all the other earls, I wore royal purple velvet encrusted with pearls instead; "one for each lover I've had!" I boasted, inadvertently causing Edward to burst into tears.

When he saw me just before the ceremony began, Warwick snarled at my audacity and threatened to tear my presumptuous garments off my back.

I stood my ground and smiled back at him. "And I thought you weren't interested!"

He lunged at me then and it was all Edward, Pembroke, and Richmond could do to keep The Black Dog from murdering me right there in Westminster Abbey. Then the fanfare sounded and we frantically rushed to find our places.

As I began to lead the long stately procession down the aisle, Edward reached out a leg from beneath his weighty velvet and ermine robes and playfully kicked my backside.

"That is for daring to flirt with The Black Dog!" he whispered.

"Forsooth, My Lord, do not scold me for that; you know I am very fond of dogs!"

Pembroke cleared his throat reprovingly, but Edward ignored him, and I glanced back at him and winked.

"It is heaven to watch you walk! Verily, you do not walk, you glide like an angel!" Edward whispered ardently.

"Aye, a *fallen* angel!" I quipped.

Afterwards, in the banquet hall, fresh horrors awaited us. The old rushes had not been swept out and new sweet-smelling ones strewn in their place. Verily, I loathe rushes and they cannot be changed often enough to suit me; in my private rooms I always have carpets upon the floors. Men and dogs alike relieve their bodily needs, and food falls, by accident or intent, into the rushes, causing vile odors and attracting all manner of vermin. I nearly fainted when I beheld the state of the rushes in the banquet hall. They raised such a noxious stink that I felt my stomach turn as if it were an acrobat.

And though we sat expectantly round the long trestle table there was no food for us to eat even though we were more than three hours late. When, at last, the food was carried in, it was cold as death and either overcooked until it was black and hard as stone or underdone to the point of being bloody and raw. The elaborate marzipan subtleties had collapsed so none could discern their intended shape. And the roast swan, re-dressed in its snowy feathers, lay limp as if its neck had just been wrung rather than sitting regal and proud upon its silver platter. And there were hardly any servers to wait on us. Those who were there moved as if they had lead weights in their heels and were clumsy as buffoons, stumbling and spilling food and wine upon the guests and knocking the ladies' tall headdresses awry or entangling the serving spoons and carving knives in their veils.

I sat beside Edward, smoldering with anger and struggling to hold back my tears. All around me people were whispering that I had scrimped on the arrangements for my own enrichment. It pained me deeply for nothing could be further from the truth. A coronation comes only once in the life of a king, and I would not have robbed Edward of that glory. I wanted it to be as special and flawless as the most perfect pearl, and I wanted him to be proud of me for arranging it all so splendidly! I lifted an eel from the platter before me and found it so raw I would not have been surprised to see it thrashing on my fork. With a sigh I let it fall and sat back feeling sick.

Edward noticed my silence, it was so unlike me; usually at table I am all smiles and merry wit, and he would not let me be until he knew the cause.

"But my darling," he exclaimed when I had at last unburdened myself, "whatever do you mean? Everything *is* perfect! *You* are here! And as for the food," he glanced down at the untouched mutton oozing blood on his golden plate, "it was so clever of you to arrange to have us served a cold supper! You must forgive me if I abstain, but all the excitement of this glorious day has robbed me of my appetite! And to have buffoons masquerade as servers! That was not clever—it was *brilliant!* Ha! Ha! Look! See how that one has dropped the gilded calf's head in Lancaster's lap!"

He lied so sweetly, and with such love and sincerity, that tears filled my eyes.

"Oh Piers, *please* be happy!" he pleaded as tears rolled down my face.

And then he took me in his arms, and even though we were surrounded by courtiers, foreign dignitaries, servants, and our own wives, he kissed me long, deep, and passionately.

It meant so much to me, his declaration that all was perfect, the way his lies transformed a disaster into a delight, that all my pretense at discretion crumpled and I melted in his arms and returned his kiss wholeheartedly.

We were both oblivious to the appalled gasps that echoed round the table. Even the musicians stopped and stared at us.

By the time the banquet ended we were *very* drunk, on wine and each other. Our progress down the passageway to Edward's bedchamber was marked by hungry kisses and fumbling hands clawing impatiently at our clothes, tearing them in our haste to be rid of them. Pearls fell like hail onto the flagstones as Edward tore at my purple velvet tunic, even resorting to his teeth and jewel-studded dagger to free my flesh. We left our clothes where they fell, heedless of what those who saw the trail of tattered garments might think. At last, we reached his chamber, slammed the door behind us, and fell as one onto the bed, casting the last remnants of our clothes—or more aptly rags—onto the floor.

That night was … to describe it as amazing does not begin to do it justice! A revelation perhaps? Never before had I been so much in love with Edward, and to this day nothing has ever surpassed, or even matched, it. Before I had always been the passive participant in our passion; I let Edward make love to me. But this night was different; I was *wild* to make love to him. My desire knew no bounds; it was like a cauldron boiling over.

Edward was astonished at my ardor.

"My love, I do not know what has wrought this change in you, but if it has anything to do with the banquet ... henceforth I want you to plan every one!"

I took his face between my hands and kissed him. "It is not the banquet, Edward, it's *you!*"

Later, when we were resting between bouts of frenzied lovemaking, we heard footsteps and voices in the corridor. I recognized Warwick's voice just before a heavy object thudded hard onto the floor. He had slipped upon my pearls.

"*Curse Piers Gaveston!*" he roared, prompting Edward to bolt up in bed and shout: "*You mean the Earl of Cornwall!*" He had decreed that everyone was to call me such and he expected to be obeyed.

I laughed and pulled him back down into the bed, silencing him with my kisses.

I awoke later to find Isabelle standing over me in her elegant night-robes of icy blue and white silk with her white-blonde hair unbound. The light of her candle cast a golden halo about her face, ghostly pale and wet with tears, as she watched me sleeping in her husband's arms.

Before my eyes, I saw her harden; I watched the heart of a young and eager girl who had fallen in love with her husband at first glance grow hard as stone. All the warmth within her withered and died; like frost forming on a beautiful white rose. And I knew I had made an enemy. Our eyes met. It was a declaration of war, a duel to the death, and Edward, slumbering peacefully and obliviously with his arms about me, was its cause.

In the gray light of dawn I slipped softly from Edward's room and encountered the Earl of Warwick in the passageway. Had The Black Dog been lying in wait for me?

"So," he looked me up and down, "now that the coronation is over you see fit to robe yourself in gold."

He was referring to the breach of etiquette I had committed by disdaining the requisite cloth-of-gold in favor of the royal purple, and also to the opulent fur-trimmed gold brocade dressing gown I was at that moment warmly enveloped in.

"His Majesty was kind enough to lend me this robe as I seem to have lost my clothes."

"Yes," Warwick nodded, "and we all know how you lost them. Here at court we are all too accustomed to such disgusting displays, but the Queen's relatives were appalled."

"Indeed? Verily, My Lord, I am surprised! The French are accounted such a sensual and worldly race!"

"And what of your wife, Piers Gaveston?" he continued, pointedly ignoring Edward's edict. "How will you explain your absence last night to her, I wonder?"

I smoothed my rumpled hair as I considered this. "I shall simply say that I was unavoidably detained. Now if you will excuse me, My Lord, my feet are cold," I indicated my bare feet. "And," I yawned, "I am rather tired; I hardly got any sleep last night!" And I continued on down the corridor, now cleared of our clothes, to my chamber where I fell exhausted into bed.

I was awakened a few hours later by the tentative touch of Meg's hand. And it was with great trepidation that I rolled over and sat up to face her.

She could not even look at me. Instead she sat with her eyes downcast, repeatedly clasping and unclasping her hands as they lay in her lap and her tears dripped down on them.

"Is it true? Is it true what they say ... about you ... and Uncle Edward?"

There was really nothing to be gained by lying, so I told the truth.

"Yes, my sweet Meg, it is. I am sorry. It was never my intention to hurt you."

She shook her head uncomprehendingly and there was such pain in her eyes.

"Look at me, sweetheart," I reached out and gently tilted up her chin. "There is something I would have you understand—the love I feel for Edward takes nothing from the love I feel for you."

"Then you *do* love me?" I saw her hope bloom anew and it pained me to my very depths.

"Yes," I answered as I caressed her face. "Who told you, my sweet? About Edward and I?"

"The Queen. I was sitting with her and her ladies. We were sewing and Her Majesty said that though she commended my fortitude she personally found the situation intolerable and would not be able to follow my example. I did not understand, and she ... explained. I ... I had seen you kiss last night at table, but I ... I did not understand! And all the French ladies laughed and called me 'the dear innocent,' though I do not think I am dear to them at all!"

"Well you are *very* dear to me!" I assured her. "And you must not heed what they say; your innocence is far more beautiful than their worldliness can ever be! *Never* lose it, Meg! *Never* envy the French ladies, or anyone else, their sophistication. It is bought at the expense of the goodness we are all born with and chips away at it little by little until there is nothing left. Be innocent and good, Meg, do not end up like them—or me."

"But I think you are *wonderful!*" she cried, flinging her arms around me.

"See?" I nodded. "It is because you have such a good heart! Truly I do not deserve you, and you deserve a husband far better than I!"

"*No!*" Meg insisted, clinging to me. "I would not have anyone else for the world!"

"My darling, you cannot mean that, but I thank you for it just the same." I kissed her tenderly. "Now that you know the truth, can you truly abide with it?"

Meg sat for a moment deep in thought then nodded and began to speak slowly, choosing her words with care. "I know little about these things, Piers, and I cannot pretend to like it or even to understand, but, if you love me, I am content. I come but little to court, my life is in the country, the solitude suits me, and there none would ever speak of this to me. It is only at court that people are so unkind. And now that I know the truth I would rather not dwell upon it. I know I cannot forget it, but I would rather not think about it either."

"I understand," I said gently, taking her hand in mine, "but, my darling, we cannot always govern our thoughts, often they come unbidden to our mind and are like to lodge there despite all our attempts to banish them. And if, in time, you find that you cannot suffer this and would rather seek an end to our marriage I shall do everything I can to assist you."

Meg shook her head. "It shall not come to that. And now, my husband, I shall leave you to your rest." And, shyly, she kissed my cheek and left me.

After she had gone I lay there feeling wretched and melancholy and despising myself. And I was angry with Isabelle. Regardless of how she felt about me, and I knew she hated me right down to my fingernails, it was needlessly cruel of her to hurt Meg. Not for a moment did I believe it was done unintentionally. She knew that Meg was innocent and sought to disillusion and hurt her—just as she had been herself—as a means of striking back at me; I was the one she blamed for depriving her of Edward's love, and we always hate the one who has stolen the life we longed for. I've seen it so many times, that look, that pain, the envy and hate, in the eyes of a man or a woman as they watch the one they love walk away with another. I daresay she thought that if she must suffer then Meg should too; misery does love a companion. But that did not change anything; it was still a cruel and malicious thing to do!

And Meg—she accepted it so easily! She is a little like Edward, I think, she would rather run away from the truth than confront it boldly, or else mask its unpleasant face the way spices are used to disguise the flavor of rotting meat. The country will be her refuge from the truth and the scandalmongers' tongues, and what she does not know will not hurt her.

TROUBLE BREWING

Contrary to what Edward wished to think, the subject of the jewels was not closed. Isabelle wrote angry letters to her father, describing herself as "the most wretched of wives," and complaining of Edward's treatment and neglect; her husband, she said, was a stranger to her bed. And the relatives who had attended the coronation confirmed everything she said and more, stating plainly that Edward preferred my bed to hers.

The Black Dog and his pack rallied round her. They said I was an arrogant foreign upstart who had used sorcery and forbidden sex to enslave the King, and that with my extravagance I had depleted the treasury and put the country into pawn with foreign moneylenders.

Yet it was not until Edward and I ventured incognito into London that I realized just how hated I had become.

We went not as the King and his Favorite but as two gentlemen of means out for an evening's pleasure. Dragon and two of Edward's strongest guards accompanied us at a discreet distance and in ordinary clothes instead of their liveries.

We roamed freely about London, navigating the maze of winding streets and narrow alleys, and merging with the crowd in the marketplace; arm-in-arm, clutching gold pomander balls to our noses, drinking from a silver flask we passed between us, and trying to avoid soiling our fine boots in the muck and dung that covered the streets, and laughing all the time.

A scarlet-haired strumpet ran up to Edward and showed him her breasts as an enticement. And a peddler tried to sell us the hair of a boiled weasel as a tonic against the ague, we had but to drink a single hair in our breakfast ale every morning and never again would we suffer a fever or a shivering fit. And, in a discreetly lowered voice, he offered us an ointment made from the fat of a hanged man to slather our cocks with; it would protect us from the pox so that we might enjoy the whores of London without peril.

Clinging close as laughter shook us, we said nay and went merrily on our way to find a wine shop where we might refill our flask.

Everywhere we went we heard ribald jests, indignant exclamations, and wild tales about the King and his Gascon Favorite. They spoke of my satanic powers and the Devil's Mark I bore upon my hands, and Edward and I nearly fell to brawling because I was not wearing gloves. They said I performed dark rites to render Edward blind to the Queen's beauty and impotent in her bed, and that I used curses and poisons against my enemies.

When last he came to London, the Earl of Lancaster had fallen off his horse after leaving a tavern. While he floundered in the mud the whore he had been with snatched his purse and fled. Was that not clear proof that The Gascon had bewitched him? And was it not peculiar that the Earl of Lincoln, that fine old gentleman whom I had insolently dubbed "Burstbelly," often suffered a bellyache after sitting at table with me? Poison; it *had* to be! And what about the rheumatism that nowadays afflicted the Earl of Pembroke's knees? Gaveston, they nodded knowingly, no doubt he fashioned a wax poppet in the guise of Pembroke and stabbed a pin into its knees!

No one would send their sons and daughters to serve at court without first providing them with a charm to protect against the evil eye and witchery lest it be their misfortune to wait upon me. Indeed, there stood an old woman upon the corner selling charms. "Charms for love, for luck at cards, to guard against witches and the evil eye!" she bellowed, holding up a handful of amulets for all to see. She beckoned to us, and though Edward frowned fastidiously, I insisted that we go and speak with her.

"Greetings, young Sirs!" she smiled, shaking back her stringy gray hair and displaying a mouth full of blackened stumps. "And do you fine gentlemen go often to court? Well then, you shall need a charm, a *very powerful* charm, to protect you from Gaveston! Nay, young Sir, do not scoff!" she chided Edward. "Never has England been blighted by a more powerful witch!"

"And have you a charm to protect *me* from Gaveston?" I asked.

"None more powerful than mine!" she declared and reached into her basket and drew out a little bulging brown pouch with three talismans dangling from it—a crudely carved frog stained with woad, a bit of horn, and a wooden cross bound with dirty twine.

My curiosity aroused, I inquired what was inside the pouch.

"Herbs, powerful and secret, and the things that witches fear—salt and a holy wafer from the Church!"

Utter Nonsense! We often use salt in our rituals, and, like everyone else, to season our food. Nor do we fear holy wafers either, it is but bread with a blessing upon it, and without belief it has no power.

"Long ago when I was a young maid," she confided, "our village priest discovered a witch. And though she swore herself innocent, he had her bound in a chair and they poured a sack of salt down her throat and she could not swallow it. Aye, it saved our village the trouble of burning her it did! And I heard tell of another witch who choked to death on a holy wafer. Had she been innocent she would have been able to chew and swallow it! Will you have the charm, fine Sir? It is only a penny and it will keep you safe from Gaveston, I guarantee it will!"

I *despised* her tales; they *sickened* me! But, to be done with her, I accepted the charm and took a penny from my purse. It was then that she noticed my hands. There was fear, stark and strong, in her eyes as they darted up to scrutinize my face then dipped back down to regard my hands again. Her eyes went wide with terror and, dropping her basket, she raised her hand in the sign against witches and fled, pale and trembling, stumbling and speechless, down the filth-strewn alley.

"*Now* will you put on your gloves?" Edward asked peevishly.

A herder was at that moment passing with his pigs, no doubt seeing them safely on their way to slaughter, and in answer I took my pearl embellished gloves of purple velvet from my belt where I had tucked them and flung them down before the swine.

"*Piers!*" Edward groaned and rolled his eyes. He snatched the charm from my hand and flung it after my gloves into the muck. "Now come along! Our moods are darkening, so let us find a tavern and try to lighten them!"

It was at the Mermaid Tavern, a squalid little place deep in the stews of London, that Edward found his temper could brook no more.

The sun had long since set and we were drinking wine and playing dice with a bargeman, a great big bull-necked, blunt-nosed fellow named Harry, who had no idea who we were. Our coins were nigh gone; Edward habitually suffers high losses, and luck was not with me that night.

Beneath the table I nudged Edward's thigh as I mischievously addressed the bargeman: "I've no coin left but I am not ready to quit the game; will you have me instead?"

Edward choked on his wine and I had to pound his back.

"Aye, I will!" Harry the bargeman nodded, smiling broadly.

Verily, I was surprised! I had not thought myself to his taste; I had meant only to amuse and startle Edward, but … I had made the offer … and, before Edward could stop me, I rolled again—and lost.

"Shall we go upstairs?" Harry asked, jerking his head towards the rickety staircase leading up to the inn's private rooms. "I've won coin enough off you and your friend to afford a room, and I want you to be comfortable."

I was distracted by the sound of ripping cloth. In his haste to remove a gold brooch to settle my debt, Edward had torn a goodly sized piece from the front of his tunic.

"Would you offer yourself in my stead?" I laughed, seeing his bare chest exposed through the gaping hole.

"Nay!" Harry shook his head adamantly. "Do not get me wrong now," he turned to Edward, "you're a comely enough fellow, but the dainty, dark-haired one is more to my taste." Then, turning back to me, he asked: "So, where do you hail from? What's that accent of yours?"

"I was born in Gascony," I answered.

"Were you now?" His coarse, thick brows shot up in surprise. "The same as the evil male sorcerer that has bewitched our dim-witted King?"

Poor fellow, he really did not know that the "comely enough fellow" sitting across from him was actually that "dim-witted King" or that I was that bewitching "evil male sorcerer!"

"Yes," I affirmed, "*exactly* like Gaveston!"

"Well now, if the evil Gaveston is anything like you I can well understand why the King is so smitten with him! Aye, it is a pretty piece you are!" He leaned forward then, with a lascivious grin, and asked eagerly: "And have you whorish talents like Gaveston?"

"That you will have to discover for yourself! But it is true I do bear a marked resemblance to him. Is that not so, Ned?" I nudged Edward's thigh again, and smiled cajolingly, urging him to play along. Then, turning back to Harry, I explained: "Ned's business takes him often to court and he has seen Gaveston numerous times."

But Edward was in no mood for games and I *really* should have known better. He stood up abruptly and jerked me to my feet. And in that moment I knew I had gone *too* far.

"We are leaving! Here!" He flung the gold swirl-patterned brooch, and the piece of red cloth that was still attached to it, into Harry's lap. "This should cover my friend's debt!"

Undaunted, I flashed Harry my most enchanting smile. "Another time perhaps?"

"*Out!*" Edward shoved me towards the door.

"Aye, I hope so!" Harry called after me. And I looked back to see him smile and nudge the fellow at the next table and say: "Fancy that, I almost had me a Gaveston of my own!"

Edward's mood grew darker as we passed a rowdy bunch seated round the hearth swilling ale and singing a bawdy tune about a certain lack-brained King Neddy and his passion for Gavy, and pity the poor fair young Queen with her broken heart and empty bed, so evilly trespassed against by this shameless pair. "Send not your daughters to court," another verse said, "if you aspire to royal favor send your sons instead, for if the boy be comely he could rise to an earl as Gaveston did!" Actually, I thought it quite clever, but Edward was *furious.*

"*How dare they?*" he fumed. "How *dare* they speak so about their King?"

"They are not speaking, Ned, they are singing."

"I *know* they are singing, and the tune they are singing is *treason!*" he flared back at me.

"Oh surely it has a better title than that!" I quipped.

Edward just glared at me and tightened his grip.

"Edward, you are hurting me!" I cried, pulling away from him and rubbing my arm.

"Let that be a lesson to you then, to comport yourself with more dignity!" And he turned on his heel and left me.

I tossed my head defiantly, signaled to Dragon, and hastily whispered my instructions. Harry the bargeman, this tavern, tomorrow at two o'clock. "And under no circumstances are you to tell him who I am! Do not mention my name or give any hints, even if he offers you money!"

I had almost reached the door when Edward stormed back in, knocking aside a serving wench with a tray of pewter tankards, and seized hold of my arm and hustled me out into the night.

He was in a vile temper, and hidden behind the blue velvet curtains of the barge he gave free rein to the beast in him. Fury made him stronger still and he easily overpowered me, strong though I am, and struggle though I did. I would not give him the satisfaction of hearing me cry out, so I bit the velvet cushion my face lay upon and concentrated on the sound of the oars slapping, the water lapping against the sides of the barge, and the sickening stench of the Thames, though it angered me that it made my eyes water for I would not have Edward think he had made me cry.

Outside the curtains the guards heard Edward's groans, grunts, and curses. "Hark unto that! His Majesty is putting The Gascon in his place!" And there was much laughter as the joke was repeated amongst the oarsmen.

And in those brutal moments I was nine years old again and back in the best room of my uncle's inn with the lecherous lodger. It all happened so quickly, even now my memory of it is a series of blurs and violent flashes. My uncle told me to take him his dinner. There was a boisterous crowd downstairs in the Common Room celebrating a wedding so no one heard my screams when he grabbed me. I remember the clatter of the pewter tankard and the dull thud of the wooden trencher that held the greasy mutton hitting the floor. He rammed his knee hard into my back, pinning me facedown upon the bed, pressing my face into the pillow to stifle my screams. I could not breathe! His nails raked my skin, leaving long red scratches, as he tore my clothes away. And then the pain, like an iron rod being hammered up inside me. Then his lust was spent and he was panting and sagging over me. He pressed a sickening, slobbery wet kiss onto the nape of my neck. And it was over. He flopped back on the bed, smiling and exhausted, sighing: "There's nothing like a virgin!" I pulled on my torn clothes and hobbled away with a burning pain inside me and his seed dripping out of me.

As soon as the barge docked I leapt out and ran up the damp, slime-coated steps, slipping perilously, forcing myself to ignore the burning, throbbing pain, and hugging my cloak tight about me to hide my tattered clothes.

I did not stop running until I reached my bedchamber. But I could not outrun the mocking laughter of the guards and oarsmen.

I sagged against the locked door, but at the sound of Edward's footsteps I backed away and sank down onto my bed. I yelped at the pain and leapt back up again as tears sprang to my eyes. The footsteps stopped and Edward began his infernal pounding, pleading for forgiveness and entreating entry. I ignored both the King of England and the repentant Nedikins and gingerly lowered myself onto the bed and stretched out on my stomach. Never again would I believe that my body was precious to Edward, henceforth such declarations would be only hollow words; empty flattery.

Edward was discovered at dawn lying just outside my locked door, sleeping, curled up like a faithful puppy, upon the cold stone floor.

In spite of my bruises, aches, and pains, I kept my rendezvous with Harry the bargeman the next day. It was my way of striking back at Edward.

In a surprising contrast to his rough appearance Harry treated me royally; his calloused hands were surprisingly gentle, and his caresses almost reverent. He kissed my bruises and called Ned a brute and swore that if he ever saw him again he would crack his skull open like an egg.

For a moment I feared my scarred hands would give me away. "It was a play upon words when I told you I bore a marked resemblance to Gaveston," I explained. "He is not the only Gascon in England with burned hands."

"Aye," Harry said as he took my hands and covered them with kisses, "and I'll warrant yours weren't caused by hellhounds licking!"

"My mother died in a fire," I explained. "I tried to save her."

"But I must call you something!" he insisted when I refused to tell him my name.

"Since I remind you of Gaveston you may call me Perrot; that is what Lack-wit King Neddy calls his male whore!"

Harry laughed and asked no more. It was the perfect revenge on Edward even if he did not know!

When I returned to the palace Edward demanded to know where I had been, so I told him.

"I've been betraying you with a bargeman!"

Edward erupted in gales of laughter. He thought it was a joke. I laughed with him and let him think what he liked.

THE BOGS AND
MISTS OF IRELAND

Clad in full armor and led by Warwick and Lancaster, the peers of the realm clanked and rattled their way into the council chamber and presented Edward with an ultimatum—either Gaveston goes or civil war will rage throughout the land.

I sat back in my chair, irreverently propping my legs up on the council table, nibbling a pear, and pretending not to care while I watched Edward make a fool of himself, his voice growing increasingly desperate and shrill as he insisted that he could not live without me.

These grim unsmiling men have never understood me, but I understand them all too well. What they really want is what they think I want—power. They have already adjudged Edward incompetent and would have him be their puppet king, or like a figure on the prow of a ship, while the *real* power resides with them. The fact that I do not want power is incomprehensible to them because it is all they have ever wanted. Only Pembroke is devoid of personal ambition; yet he stands with them because Edward's obsession with me does neither king nor kingdom credit.

"*Oh leave off, Nedikins!*" I snapped petulantly.

The earls gaped, gasped, and exchanged incredulous glances. Had they heard right? Had I actually dared to call the King of England "Nedikins" in the council chamber before the assembled peers of the realm? Was there no end to my audacity?

Edward blushed to the roots of his golden hair.

"*What?*" I affected innocence. "You *did* ask me to call you that!"

"Yes," he hissed, "but only when we are alone!"

"Well," I shrugged, "if these gentlemen insist on making affairs of the bed-chamber into affairs of state then you must pardon me if from time to time my tongue slips. It may well be that tonight I shall cry out 'Your Majesty!' in the heat of passion!"

"Have you *no* shame?" Pembroke demanded of me.

"When the day came when I must decide between shoes and shame, My Lord, I chose shoes and would again!" I answered saucily.

"Oh, you are a silly thing!" Pembroke threw up his hands. "For the life of me, I do not know what His Majesty sees in you!"

"I would be most happy to show you!" I offered and leaned back in my chair, caressed my silk clad thigh, and licked my lips, my eyes on Pembroke all the while.

"*You will not!*" Edward cried hotly. "My Lord of Pembroke, I will thank you not to encourage him!"

"Your Majesty, I assure you, I *never* … I …" anger and embarrassment mottled Pembroke's face. "He needs no encouragement!"

"*None!*" I assured him ardently.

"*Enough of this!*" Warwick roared. "Take heed, Gaveston, when you cross us you play with fire!"

"I think he rather likes it," Lancaster sneered. "To play with fire; observe his hands, I think long ago he discovered fire to be the most diverting of playthings!"

"*Tom!* Take care!" Burstbelly cautioned. "Do not speak of the Devil's Mark; you cannot know what he might do!" And he crossed himself as he saw the fury upon my face and my hands clench tightly round the arms of my chair.

"Aye, you'd best not!" I warned. "Else I cast a spell and turn you into a frog and only the Lady Alice's kiss shall restore your manhood!"

The mention of his wife plunged The Buffoon into a mad red rage. He drew his sword and sprang at me. I drew mine and, blades clashing, we circled round the council table while Edward stood by wringing his hands, uttering shrill pleas that we desist, and shouting for the guards.

The guards came rushing in and Edward ordered them to restrain Lancaster while he swept me up into his arms and carried me, kicking and struggling, indignant and protesting, from the council chamber and set me down outside the door. Hastily, he kissed my cheek then rushed back inside and slammed the door.

I was so outraged at such treatment that I seized a tray from a passing servant and flung it full force against the door. The earthenware bowls and pewter tankards crashed against it and porridge and ale dripped down onto the floor. And with a satisfied nod, I turned and strolled leisurely back to my apartments.

An hour later Edward came to me, his face bathed in tears, and informed me that I was banished and could no longer call myself Earl of Cornwall. I must quit the country by June 25th otherwise Holy Mother Church would excommunicate me.

To show how much I cared for that I would purposefully delay my departure by three days, leaving Edward to bombard the Pope with letters beseeching him to lift the ban, and also causing great distress to my devoutly religious bride.

While Edward had continued to whine, grovel, and rage before the council I had been turning my mind to more practical matters.

Edward was forever telling me that anything that was in his power to give me was mine, so, for only the second time, I asked for something.

I asked him to appoint me Lieutenant-Governor of Ireland. It was a calculated choice. From my conversations with the Earl of Richmond and much frustrated and tedious discourse in the council chamber, I knew ruling Ireland was a burdensome, bothersome task and all the men the Crown dispatched there seemed loath to do their duty and were wont to laze and fritter their time away instead, pining for a return to civilized society. But in their complaints of this wild, heathenish land and its uncouth denizens I saw the gleam of promise and a chance to prove myself.

"I do not want to leave you, Edward," I said, kneeling before him with tears spangling my lashes and my hand upon his thigh. "But since I must, do not let them send me away in disgrace, but send me yourself in honorable estate."

"It is done, my love," he bowed his head solemnly and kissed my hand.

Of course, my appointment was heatedly protested. But, in the end, my enemies decided to make the best of things and hope that I would wander into a bog and drown.

While Edward remained in England behaving like a petulant child deprived of his favorite toy, I ruled Ireland in his stead.

Unlike the men who had held my post before me, I was not content to sit idle. I took immediate action and rode out with my troops to quell the rebellious wild Irish chieftains, and in so doing, I won their admiration and respect. We routed the rebels from the Wicklow Mountains, and the outlaws William Macbalator, Dermott O'Dempsey, and the O'Byrne clan were captured, condemned, and hung to great public acclaim.

Each time I returned to Dublin at the head of my army, with the outlaws chained and snarling surly in a cart, the people lined the streets to cheer and throw flowers at me. Maidens came to braid ribbons in my horse's tail and mane and tuck posies in his bridle. And the crowd, old and young alike, surged forth to touch me, their fingers lightly, reverently, brushing my legs and seeking my hands. Mothers even held their babes up to catch a glimpse of me as I was proclaimed a hero.

Once I saw Meg standing with her maids in the crowd and I beckoned to her. Ever shy, she hung back, but her companions urged her forward. I lifted her into the saddle before me and rode onward with my arms about her as she leaned back against my chest. The crowd roared with approval and tossed their caps in the air, so pleased were they to see their governor's affection for his lady.

The next day a celebratory mass was held in the church of Castle Kevin. And I played my part so well I was accounted quite devout and given many jeweled crucifixes in consequence, but I didn't mind; I could always have the stones pried out and reset in more pleasing settings.

When I was not with the army, I busied myself with matters of justice and administration. The roads were in a deplorable state and I ordered them repaired and also dispatched masons to repair the crumbling castle fortresses. And, most important of all, I strove to maintain peace between the Irish chieftains. I even accomplished what was deemed impossible and persuaded these wild, stubbornly independent men to sit down and discuss their grievances with compromise and resolution in mind.

For most of my life I had believed that I was worth only what someone was willing to pay for me, but that year I spent in Ireland showed me that I was wrong, and that I could be so much more than just a whore. For the first time in my life I had accomplishments of which I could truly be proud of. I had proven myself an excellent and able military commander and governor, and no one, not even Warwick and Lancaster, could fault me. Pembroke even acknowledged that I had been "conscientious and dedicated" in my undertakings as governor.

And the Irish liked me! They praised my valor, charm, integrity, and earnest enthusiasm. And my court set a tone of elegance the likes of which they had never seen. It still amuses me to remember their awed whispers that the new governor owned four silver forks wrought especially for the eating of pears and his white greyhound wore jewels about her neck and had her meals prepared in the kitchen and served in a silver bowl instead of having to make do with bones and table-scraps.

After England, where all but a few despised me, it was wonderful beyond words to be so highly esteemed, and to have no one hovering over me telling me I was too beautiful to be encumbered by such burdensome things as thoughts.

Edward, or "Lovelorn Ned" as he once again signed himself, wrote that he pictured me as a priceless diamond dropped in the mud and he longed to pick me up and bring me home, and everyday he strove to convince the council to allow him to do just that.

Poor Edward, it will pain him much to know that I did not mind the separation. Please do not misunderstand me, for I love him dearly, but his is such a jealous and possessive passion that at times I think it will surely squeeze all the life out of me. His love can be so cloying, so sickeningly sweet, that I feel as if I have gorged all day upon sugary sweets, cream tarts, and marzipan.

Apart from my official duties, I gave much of my time to Meg. In that year we spent together we came to know each other better, we went walking and riding, and for picnics under the trees when the weather was fine. And I tried to coax her out of her shyness, for her new and more prominent role as governor's lady terrified her. But I never truly succeeded in breaching that wall; though upon her modesty I made several playful assaults. One fine day I attempted to teach her to swim as I had taught Edward. Her shift grew heavy with the weight of water and impeded her limbs, so I lifted it over her head and cast it onto the grass. And oh how she blushed and tried to shield her pert little paps from my eyes when I remarked that her nipples were like rose-clad sentries standing at attention!

Every night when my duties did not compel my absence, I went to her chamber before she retired and brushed and braided her hair. I felt such a great tenderness for her that it saddened me that I could not fall in love with her. But together we lack that special alchemy that makes a couple go together like thunder and lightning instead of chalk and cheese. And though we talked much, there were many things I never told her. As my hands deftly plaited the silky red-gold strands we never spoke of Edward or my past. And of my many other lovers she never knew; she thought Edward was her only rival. It was not that I desired to enshroud myself in mystery or to pretend to be something other than I was, but her innocence is precious to me, and I would, if I could, protect her from how ugly and unkind the world and the people in it can be. Who knows better than a whore what a treasure innocence truly is? Once lost it is gone forever; there is no going back.

And then an unexpected joy came into my life when Meg shyly announced that she was with child. It was something I never expected, to feel joy at such a pronouncement. But I was happy, truly happy! I knew that I would never be one of those cold and distant parents, the sort of rigid, intimidating figure that children respect but fear, to whom love is given only as a duty. Instead, I would be warm and loving. And mayhap in fatherhood I would find the true and lasting love that had eluded me all these years.

I must take steps to set my life aright; I would not have my child be ashamed of me and taunted to tears because I had earned everything I possessed in the King's bed.

And then the summons came. And I obeyed it. I returned to a land that despised me and Edward's eager arms. *What a fool I was!*

THE FOLLY OF
GOOD INTENTIONS

When I set foot on English soil for the first time after my yearlong Irish exile I had such hopes. Foolishly, I thought everything would be different now that I had proven myself. The earldom of Cornwall and all the honors I had lost were restored to me, and Edward's pestering of the Pope had returned me to the Church's good graces. I was brimming over with good intentions. I promised myself I would strive to be on agreeable terms with everyone and to curb my wicked tongue. Ah, how miserably I failed!

And to delight Edward, I who am accused of taking all and giving nothing, brought back musicians and storytellers, beautifully crafted ornaments and musical instruments, finely bred wolfhounds, and the best Irish horseflesh, as gifts for him. But the moment he saw me, dressed in emerald velvet and surrounded by a bevy of Irish attendants, all of them chosen for their wild, uncouth appearance, the better to accentuate my slight build and the elegance of my clothes and bearing, the only flesh Edward was interested in was my own, everything else could wait. He seized my hand and rushed me straight to his bed, intent only upon his own pleasure, ignoring the startled, angry, and appalled faces of the Queen and court as they stepped aside to hastily make way for us. Aye, things were off to a rollicking, but not a very promising, start! I had not even been back at court an hour and everyone was already damning and reviling me for consuming the King's attention and leading him into degeneracy.

Shortly afterwards we celebrated my return with a magnificent tournament at my castle of Wallingford.

Edward had given me a suit of red-gold armor studded with emeralds. I was so proud of it that I would have nothing shield its magnificence and left off my silk surcoat; I would have only the green and yellow ostrich plumes swaying atop my helmet to represent my colors. Truly it was the most beautiful armor, when the sun struck it glowed fiery as a sunset!

To receive my favors, I rode up to the royal box where Edward and Isabelle sat comfortably ensconced in cushioned chairs with servants to fan them and serve wine, sweet cakes, and meat pies.

There had been a slight disagreement about whose favor I should wear. Thus it was both my young wife and royal lover who leaned down to present their tokens to me while Isabelle sat stiff-backed and icy-eyed in her chair looking every bit the Ice Queen in white satin.

Ignoring Edward's scowl, I went first to Meg.

Smiling softly, she took the diaphanous pink veil from her headdress and bound it carefully round my upper arm, making sure the knot was secure and that it would not hamper my movements. When she began to draw away I reached up and lightly caressed her cheek and, rising in the gilded saddle of my great black charger, I kissed her gently.

At Edward's wounded cry I smiled and went to him. His blue eyes stormy with jealousy, he leaned down and hung round my neck a blue ribbon embroidered with silver lilies from which a gold leopard with black enameled spots dangled; royal emblems—the lilies and leopards of England. And then he cupped my face in his hands and kissed me hard upon the mouth, leaning so far over the edge that he nearly tumbled out of the box.

My horse snorted and pawed to signal his displeasure as I grasped Edward to keep him from falling even as I struggled to stay in the saddle. Edward's attendants hastened to pull him back into the box while my squire retrieved his hat from the ground where my horse had trampled it. I took it and, with a pert little half-bow, returned it to His Majesty.

With an embarrassed frown, Edward set the battered bonnet back on his head and tossed the tattered, dirt-streaked gauzy blue liripipe over his shoulder.

"Well, if no one else desires to kiss me ..." I paused playfully, "then I shall away to the tiltyard and try for the gold ring!"

The prize that day was to be a circlet of gold, to be presented to the winner by the Queen, which he was then, in best courtly tradition, supposed to give to his lady-love.

"Go then, My Lord," Isabelle said coldly, "no one else here desires to kiss you, though you might ride round to the other boxes and inquire there!"

"Nay, it would only weaken me," I sighed, "and I need all my strength for the joust!" And I turned my horse and rode off to arm myself for the first contest.

One by one I rode against them, Lancaster, Lincoln, Warwick, and Pembroke, all great jousters in their day.

My lance caught Lancaster's side and he toppled backwards from the saddle in a flip.

As the crowd cheered me, I gave my lance to my squire and spun my horse round and called to Lancaster: "What a *splendid* back-flip, My Lord! You are not only a buffoon but an acrobat as well! Shall you entertain us tonight while we are at table? Oh *do* say you will!"

Lancaster tore off his helmet and flung it aside. "You impertinent strutting cockerel, may the Devil take you!"

With a wink and a wave to him I went to prepare myself for the next contest.

I rode against Lincoln next. And it took *all* my skill! Just as my lance was about to strike, the leather straps upon his armor snapped, strained to breaking by his great belly, and the breastplate fell away. It would have been a fatal blow to an unarmored chest. My horse was going at full charge and it was only at the last instant that I managed to veer aside.

With a great sigh, the crowd, tense and white-faced, sat back, relieved that tragedy had been so narrowly averted.

Burstbelly dealt the offending breastplate a savage kick and vowed he would never ride against me again. It was my witchcraft, he insisted, that broke the straps and only the infinite mercy of the Lord in Heaven had saved him from certain death.

"Blame your great belly, My Lord, and not me!" I retorted as I turned away, incensed and saddened.

It took two passes before my lance splintered against Warwick's shield and down he went. Indeed, the blow struck so hard I was nearly unhorsed myself.

He lay flat in the dirt, struggling beneath the weight of his armor to sit up. When his squire came rushing to assist him, Warwick kicked the boy and sent him sprawling. And then he looked at me with such black hatred in his eyes as I sat triumphantly astride my horse, preening the plumes upon my helm and smiling.

"May God have mercy on you, Gaveston, for if you ever fall into my hands you shall *not* have it from me! Call me The Black Dog if you like, you insufferable devil-damned popinjay, but, mark my words; you *will* feel my bite someday!

As God is my witness, I shall send you back to Hell where you belong if it is the *last* thing I do!" he roared then stormed off the field. When another of his squires came running with a goblet of wine he cuffed him soundly on the ear, downed the wine in a single gulp, and dashed the goblet onto the ground.

"I see that losing graciously is a lost art!" I said as my eyes followed him to the bench where he sat down alongside The Buffoon and Burstbelly, all of them glowering murderously at me. How it maddened them, to be bruised, defeated, and begrimed, while I remained in the saddle unscathed, preening my plumes and flaunting my prowess.

I see now that I was blind that day. I did not realize how much I hurt their pride. I never thought how they must feel, these proud, war-hardened men, not a one of whom, save Lancaster, was under forty, to be unhorsed with such ease by the foppish, arrogant, young, willow-slim peacock who adorned the King's bed. Had I let them unhorse me things might have gone better for us all, such a gesture might have salved their injured pride and given them a small measure of satisfaction at my expense, which my own pride could so easily afford.

The Earl of Pembroke was the last to challenge me. We missed each other on the first pass.

"One moment, My Lord!" I called, circling round to face him before we returned to our marks. I rode up to him and grasped the blunt end of his lance. "Did I never tell you how much I *long* to feel your lance?" I asked as I suggestively caressed the tip.

Angrily, he snatched it away. "Can you not leave off flirting and jesting long enough to joust?"

On the second try his lance glanced lightly off my shield in a blow that I would term "caressing."

"There, Gaveston, now you have felt my lance!" he cried.

"My Lord of Pembroke, are you flirting with me?" I teased.

"Certainly not!" He slammed his visor down with a sharp clang and rode back to his mark.

"This time you shall feel mine!" I called. "Though be forewarned, my caresses are bolder!"

On the third try the tip of my lance bounced off his shield and struck his chest.

There was a great cry of alarm as he fell with a fearsome crash and lay silent and still. I quickly dismounted and ran to him.

With a groan he sat up and removed his helmet.

The crowd sank back, sighing with relief.

"Do not look down upon me, Gaveston!" he said as he glared up at me and disdained the offer of my hand. "Remember instead that the day *will* come when you also shall be forty and some insolent young puppy will unhorse then stand gloating over you!"

"Nay, My Lord, you mistake my intent!" I cried. "My mother told me never to look down upon someone unless I meant to help them up."

I offered him my hand again and this time he grudgingly accepted it.

"Sound advice," he nodded, grimacing as he rose. "It is a pity your mother did not also tell you not to get into the King's bed, mock your betters, or let money flow through your fingers like water!"

"I was but seven when she died, My Lord, and there were many subjects we never touched upon."

"I am sorry to hear that as it is plain you lacked proper guidance. You may relinquish my hand now."

"Must I?" I pouted as he snatched it away.

"Yes, now go and claim your prize!"

"That is what I am trying to do, My Lord, but you rebuff me at every turn! My friend the Earl of Richmond accuses me of fancying you," I confided. "Naturally, I denied it, but only because it's true!"

"Aye, you are trying!" Pembroke asserted. "Trying my patience!"

"Confess it, My Lord; I rattle you like the glass in a casement when it thunders!"

"Nay, Gaveston, I will not! Methinks you would deem it flattery if I were to tell you what a damnable nuisance you are!"

"Well ... if it were done in the right spirit ..."

"Oh, go away! Go fetch your gold ring and leave me be! I daresay the King has begun to wonder why you tarry!"

I shrugged. "If he asks I shall tell him."

"I daresay you would!" Pembroke snapped and stalked off to join the other earls I had defeated.

"Verily, My Lord, I shall have to don mourning for your dead sense of humor again!" I called after him.

As a fanfare of trumpets announced my triumph, I approached the royal box where Isabelle angrily thrust the gold ring onto the end of my lance then resumed her chair.

My horse shook his mane and stamped his hooves impatiently as everyone waited to see what I would do.

At one such tournament, years ago before I married, I had given the gold ring to Agnes, causing Edward to weep for nearly a week. It would be the height of chivalry to present it to the Queen. Or I might provoke Lancaster to the point of murder by giving it to his wife. Or … I darted a mischievous glance at Pembroke whose expression told me not to even consider it. Meg would be the most proper recipient. And, of course, there was Nedikins toying anxiously with the frayed ends of his liripipe and gazing at me hopefully. So many choices and everyone waiting for me to make up my mind!

I nudged my mount and approached the royal box.

Dipping my lance, I deposited the gold ring gently on the lap of Meg's pink silk gown.

"For our daughter, Madame," I said with a bow, and it was thus that I announced that we were expecting a child.

Meg laid a hand tenderly upon her belly though it had barely begun to swell.

"A daughter, My Lord? You sound so certain!"

"I *am* certain! A daughter it shall be! Agnes is never mistaken about these things!"

Then, seeing the furious scowl with which Edward was regarding me while his fingers shredded the ends of his liripipe, I thought it best to bow and retreat, leaving all to exclaim in wonderment that The Gascon had actually made a child.

Naturally Edward followed me. He found me in the tiring pavilion amidst the clutter of knights and squires, barber-surgeons, weaponry and armor. I had already doffed my armor, and, stripped to the waist, my chest glistening with sweat and my hair thoroughly damp with it, I sat on a bench drinking wine, which Dragon urged me to sip slowly lest I become ill from imbibing the cold liquid too quickly.

"*Out!*" Edward ordered. "*All* of you!" he added, his gaze lingering meaningfully upon Dragon. Edward dislikes Dragon only a little less than he does Agnes. He loathes his scaly skin and ravaged face and cannot bear to see him touch me.

There was laughter in my eyes as I shrugged and got wearily to my feet, jerking my head for Dragon to follow me, as I joined the weary and confused throng heading back out into the hot sun.

"*Not you!*" Edward glowered.

"But Your Majesty did say you desired everyone to depart!" I exclaimed innocently.

"You know perfectly well that you are the exception to every rule! All others may go! *Now!*"

The scene that followed was not a pretty one. I was weary to my bones and in no mood to smile and beguile. So I told the truth without bothering to coat it in sugar.

Edward was aghast. How could I possibly want a child? It was bad enough that I doted excessively upon my greyhound! He stormed and raged and declared himself betrayed, calling me a Brutus and a Judas and likening himself to both Julius Caesar and Jesus Christ.

"There are *three* people in this marriage, Edward!" I reminded him. "You are not the only one whose feelings count! What of Meg? She came innocent to this marriage while we both knew it was all your scheme to quiet the tongues that raged against your endowing me with Cornwall! If you did not mean for me to be a husband to her then you should not have married me to her, or else laid the truth before her and let her decide if it was something to which she would willingly be a party!"

"Now really, Piers! Would you have me negotiate with a girl of thirteen?"

"By the Law, she became a woman at twelve," I reminded him. "And laws be damned, Edward, woman or child, she has feelings to consider! I have tried to do right by her and as long as our marriage endures I shall continue to do so!"

"Do not speak to me of rights and wrongs, feelings and laws, you did this because you desired it, because you desired *her!*" he charged as tears poured down his face.

"No, Edward," I flared back at him. "I did it because it is what the role of husband requires; indeed, that is something you would do well to remember yourself! Have you forgotten that all England is waiting for you to produce an heir?"

Edward sank down upon the nearest bench and buried his face in his hands and wept. Violent sobs shook his shoulders and tugged at my heart until I could not help myself and knelt before him uttering soothing words. That was a mistake. The sailors have a saying: "If you do not like the weather at sea bide awhile and it will change." The same is true of Edward's temper; even lightning cannot flash as fast as his emotions veer. He sprang on me like a serpent striking and I found myself flat on my back with my wrists held fast as he straddled me.

"Have your precious child if you will, but *never* forget that you belong to *me!*"

He flipped me over onto my stomach and struggled to wrest the hose from my sweat-slick body.

"*Edward! No!* This is not the proper place! Others will be coming soon to doff their armor! We have delayed them too long; we will be seen!"

"I don't care!" he breathed, his hands roughly brushing aside my hair so he could nuzzle my neck.

"But I do!" I cried as I tried to wriggle out from beneath him. "I care very much!"

"You do not!" Edward scoffed, nuzzling my neck again.

But I *did* care. Yet I ceased to fight, I accepted defeat and let my body go limp. And, closing my eyes and pillowing my cheek against the warm green grass, I let him do as he would. It was the easiest way, and I wanted it over and done with even though I despised myself for surrendering.

Outside the tent I heard voices and the rattle of armor.

"But what nonsense is this?" Warwick's voice boomed. "We cannot stand about out here in our armor being baked by the sun; we shall be burnt to a cinder!"

I heard the rustle of heavy silk as the entrance flap was brushed roughly aside, then the startled and outraged oaths and gasps before it was quickly whisked back into place again.

I never turned my head or opened my eyes. I didn't want to see them seeing me, seeing us, like that.

Edward was too intent on his purpose to notice them, but such was ever the case with Edward.

Loss

It was at Wallingford that Meg caught the toe of her shoe in the hem of her gown and fell down the steps descending into the rose garden. Our child was lost.

I was at court with Edward when it happened. I journeyed swiftly to Wallingford, ignoring Edward's clinging and frantic pleas that I was in no fit state to travel, and the royal physician's complaint that I must pay for the jar of leeches I had hurled at the wall when he would apply them to my temples to "soothe my nerves back into serenity."

Meg lay in her bed, sobbing her heart out. When she saw me she wept all the more. Poor child, she feared I would be angry and blame her.

I bade her attendants and sister leave us and lay down upon the bed beside her and took her in my arms.

"I was so afraid you would be angry!" she cried, her frail little body wracked by sobs as she clung to me.

"Nay, love," I assured her, "of course I am not angry! It was an accident and you are not to blame! Our daughter has merely decided to delay her entry into the world, but I think we shall see her soon; we must only be patient and wait a little while. But now we must think of you and of getting you well! Come now, sweeting, no more tears!"

"It is not true what Eleanor said?" she ventured timidly. "That you would account it no great loss. You truly do want us to have a child?"

"Verily, my sweet," I said lightly, hoping to make her smile, "I never listen to my brothers, so why should you heed your sister, especially when she says such false and foolish things? Indeed, it shall be my great pleasure to have as many children as you care to give me!"

There was a knock upon the door and Agnes came in with a strengthening tea brewed from raspberry leaves. I sat with Meg while she drank it then left her to rest and went to walk in the garden.

I breathed deeply of the roses and felt the breeze from the river ruffle my hair. Suddenly a fanfare of trumpets shattered the silence and I nearly jumped out of my skin. Servants started running about hither and thither, like chickens in a barnyard frightened by a fox, shouting "The King! The King!" Verily, there are times when I think Edward cannot go to the privy without blaring trumpets, silk banners, and pageboys shouting "Make way for the King!" I wanted to *scream* and tear the walls down; it was either that or murder Edward, I was *so* angry!

"*Not now!*" I clenched my teeth and seethed. "*Oh please, not now!*" *Why* couldn't he leave me be? *Why* must he always come running after me, following me like a kitten's tail?

Then I turned around and there was Edward, standing regal in his royal purple riding vestments at the top of the stone steps, his hands upon his hips and his golden hair glistening in the sun. He thrust his feathered cap, gloves, and riding crop into the hands of his squire then brusquely waved him away.

"Leave us!" he commanded as he descended the steps. "The Earl of Cornwall and I have much to discuss!" And the boy bowed and scurried away.

"I bid Your Majesty welcome," I said, sweeping into a low court bow.

"Do you indeed, Piers?" he asked, arching his brows dubiously.

"Why have you come, Edward?" I asked wearily.

I turned away from him and went to stand gazing out upon the river.

He came to stand behind me. "I am glad that Meg shall recover. I am fond of her, you know."

"Are you? Indeed, My Lord, I did *not* know."

"Piers, upon my soul, she is my favorite niece, and I like her well! But I cannot help it; I resent any who would take you from me, even if it be for only an hour!"

"Edward, there is more to life than me, than us!" I turned round to face him. "Do you *really* not want more than what we have?"

He reached for my waist. "Only more of you!" he said ardently, gripping me tight. And he would have kissed me if I had let him.

Gently, I drew away from him and turned my eyes back to the rippling waters, so cool, blue, and inviting. How I *longed* to strip off my clothes and plunge in!

"It is where we differ then, for I would have more. Mayhap I am greedy, Edward, but I find my life lacking."

Edward grabbed me roughly and spun me round to face him. "Do you mean that *I* am not enough? That what I have given you is not enough?"

"I am not speaking of *possessions*, Edward! Do you remember those happy days at Langley when I first came to you? When we would swim together in the River Gade—it was I who taught you how to swim!—and how we would laugh and splash! And then we would lie upon the grassy bank and let the sun dry us. Or else we might spend an afternoon fishing, but you would always have me bait and afterwards take the fish from the hook for you! Sometimes we would go boating. How you loved to row! You never seemed to tire! And you would never let me help, you would have me sing to you and play upon my lute instead. And when we grew hungry we would knock upon the cottage doors and buy bread and fresh churned butter, a round of cheese, and the makings of a stew from the farmers' wives. And then we would sit and talk by our fire while our stew simmered. Verily, that stew was more pleasing to my tongue than the finest court banquet! And all the festivals and fairs we attended in common clothes! Do you remember dancing round the Maypole on the village green and the bonfire and bobbing for apples on All Hallow's Eve? And we would ride, racing our horses over the countryside, and fence with wooden swords so your father could not accuse you of neglecting your training. And the day you made your first horseshoe at the smithy, how proud of it you were, you went around showing it to everyone for days afterwards! And the plays we devised and acted in! I can still see the costumes, so bright and gaudy; I can even hear the music! And in winter we would frolic in the snow and pelt each other with snowballs, and then we would fall to wrestling, and *always* we would end in laughter! And in the evenings we would sit by the fire and tell each other stories and riddles. And the jests we played upon others! Do you remember the special pie we made to welcome Burstbelly? When he broke the crust dozens of little green frogs came hopping out! How we scurried about trying to catch them all! And the next morning he complained that he had hardly slept for the frogs croaking and had even wakened during the night to find some perched upon his great belly! And we would play at archery, and bowls, and bandy-ball, and fly our hawks. And once you wagered me that I could not learn to juggle, and I did and won a purse of silver off you! And your pet camel that was kept in the stables! Oh, Edward, do you remember how the people would stop and stare as we rode past upon it? Their eyes were fit to pop and their mouths would gape until I feared their chins would touch the ground! They didn't know what to make of such a curious beast! Oh Edward, we were *so* happy then!"

"Aye," Edward nodded, smiling, "it was before I had all the cares that come with a Crown, and it was also before you became mine." He reached for me again. "But when I became a man, I put away childish things ..."

"For now we see through a glass, darkly; but then face to face," I continued the quotation. "Only *we do not*, Edward, *we do not*! Forsooth, Edward, I was more yours then than I have ever been!" I cried desperately, wishing with the whole of my heart that I could make him understand.

Abruptly, his hands released my waist. "Do you think I do not know that? You were mine alone then and now you are untrue!" His voice broke upon the last word and tears filled his eyes and I knew it cost him much to say it. "Cousin Tom and the others trip over each other and nearly break their necks in their haste to be the first to tell me that you have been seen with someone or entering or leaving another's room; they think to kill my love for you, but it will *never* die!"

"Edward," I sighed, "Edward, I am not the person you think I am!"

"You are Piers Gaveston and I love you!" he declared, pulling me close to him. "And, by my soul, I wish you loved *only* me! *Why*, Piers, *Why*? *Why* am *I* not enough? I am the King of England, so what need have you of any other? What is it they give you that I cannot? Titles, lands, revenues, wardships, and manors I have given you! All the gold in my treasury is yours to command! I have raised you until you are like a second king, and for no luxury do you lack! No one in the world wears jewels or garments finer, guards protect your precious person, I would even give the Great Seal of England into your hands so that you might honor and condemn as you please! And greater even than these gifts, I have given you my heart! *Why*, Piers, *why* isn't it *enough*?"

How could I explain to him what I scarcely understood myself? Now all these honors, and even the beautiful gems, left me cold. For me power held no allure. As King's Favorite and the Earl of Cornwall I no longer needed to play the harlot, yet I went on the same as always. Only now it was not the need and greed for gold that drove me. It was something else ... something even more elusive that I sought in all those beds and hasty fumblings in alcoves, darkened corridors, and moonlit gardens. I needed to find someone who could see past the flamboyant and flippant façade of the King's Favorite, the persona of Piers Gaveston, my beauty and the sensual delights my body promised, and love *me* for myself alone, whoever, whatever, I am. I want what I thought I had found with Edward, a companion, a friend, and lover combined in one wonderful, loving person. Someone I can laugh and play with, talk and take walks with, someone who can touch my hand without dragging me to the floor or taking me to bed. I *know* I shouldn't be so free and easy with my favors, all these casual encounters that actually mean nothing are surely *not* the *right* way to go about it, but it's what I *know*, it's become a habit, and a way of acting out, of spiting Edward for being so clinging, possessive, and jealous, and for failing to understand *me*, and for giving me everything but the *one* thing I *truly* need. I want to be something more than beautiful, because I know I will not always be beautiful, I want to be secure in the knowledge that old age, wrinkles, and gray hair or a bald pate will not oust me from my beloved's heart. If I am loved *only* for my beauty's sake, when that withers and fades, what else is there, and is what remains worthy of love? *I do not know!* And that *scares* me! I've been playing games and pretending for *so long* that the lines have become blurred, the boundaries confused, black and white have melded into murky gray, facts have become distorted, and I have lost myself. I was born Piers Gaveston, but I also *created* Piers Gaveston, and others have had a hand in that creation as well. Life and experience mold and shape us. But along the way I became something I never wanted, never intended, to be—infamous; notorious. The legends and rumors and lies have taken on a life of their own, and I want to shed this Piers Gaveston like a snake sheds its skin and start again, reborn fresh and new! If only I had the courage and knew how! I feel like I've been spinning round and round, fast, out of control, and wild, for a *very* long time; I'm dizzy and tired, and *I want to stop!*

I had thought, mayhap naively, that my success in Ireland would herald a new beginning for me. I had proven myself, so why not give me something, some useful work, to do? But no, once a whore always a whore, just a pretty plaything, both an objet d'art and an object of contempt, to be dismissed, insulted, ridiculed, despised, and used as those about me see fit. Edward loves me, Edward wants me, Edward needs me to be always at his beck and call and to never stray too far from his side, and what Edward wants is all that matters. Everyone laughs at me, both behind my back and to my face, but what they don't realize is that *I* laugh *first* and loudest at Piers Gaveston. But only I apparently hear the bitterness in my laughter. I know full well what I have become, but I also know what I could have been!

"I am lost, Edward," I said softly, as tears filled my eyes. "I am lost and I would be found!"

Edward gripped me tighter still. "Perrot, you are here in my arms, so you are *not* lost! You are *found*, Piers, *you are found!*"

"Nay, Edward," I said, pulling away from him, "*I am lost!*"

I turned and ran up the stone steps.

"Piers!" he called after me. "I love you more than life itself!"

I halted and looked back at him. "I would not mind if you loved me less if you understood me more."

That evening Edward sat alone at the great trestle table, waited upon by servants, with musicians playing in the gallery overhead, and a jester capering before him, while I kept to my chamber, "sulking behind my locked door," to quote Edward.

"I wish Edward would go away," I said petulantly to Agnes. "I want to visit my daughter!"

It was a well-kept secret, but I was the father of a little girl. She had been born while I was in Ireland and I did not learn of her existence until after I returned.

Before we left England, I escorted Agnes to visit her friend Grunella, an ancient midwife who lived in a cottage in the forest near Wallingford. It was then that I met Sarah, Grunella's granddaughter. I saw her for the first time making an offering to the Lady in a forest glade. She had apple green eyes and hair the color of spiced red wine served warm. She was wonderful; warm, caring, and wise, and utterly devoid of jealousy, ambition, pretense, and spite. I did not know her long or well, but I regret her loss deeply to this day. When she looked at me there was no contempt in her eyes or the cunning avarice of favor-seekers. She died giving birth to my child. Grunella tried but could not stop the bleeding.

I named my daughter Amy after my little sister who was lost so long ago. I remember how happy and proud I felt the first time Grunella laid her in my arms. My heart swelled nigh to bursting and I wanted to take her home with me, but Agnes prevailed upon me to be sensible: "Anyone can tell she's yours, Child, she looks just like you!"

And, credulous though they are, it would truly be asking *too* much of Edward and Meg to believe that I had just happened to find a baby girl with my hair and eyes lying abandoned on a tree stump in the forest or that my tender heart had compelled me to buy her from a band of gypsies.

So we thought of a plan. I would persuade my perpetually drunken brother Guillaume to claim her as his baseborn daughter. Given his feckless and volatile nature, no one would look askance if I were to take her into my household and raise her alongside any children Meg and I might have. And such was his behavior when he was in his cups, making amorous advances to statues and dancing wild jigs to the accompaniment of fiddles played by giant frogs that no one else could hear or see, that even if he revealed the truth doubt would always cling to it. But now, for kindness' sake, I must delay a little while, it would be cruel to bring a child into the household when Meg's grief was so fresh and keen. But in time …

"I know you do, Child," Agnes said gently, "and if you are not averse to rising early, before the King does, we might arrange it."

"I shall be up with the sun if need be!"

"Nay, love, not quite so early!" she chuckled. "You must have some rest!"

Early the next morning I crept out of the castle and, with Agnes and Dragon, hastened to Grunella's cottage.

Amy recognized me and reached out her plump little arms to me. Even now I bask in the memory of the love and trust I saw in her dark eyes as she nestled against me and reached up a soft baby fist to grasp a handful of my hair. When I raised my hand to gently pry it free her fingers closed around mine. She gurgled and cooed happily when I kissed and tickled her. And when she grew weary she slept with her head upon my shoulder, her black curls soft against my cheek.

In those fleeting hours true contentment and complete acceptance were mine; they were my daughter's precious gift to me.

My dearest Amy, I never expect your eyes shall gaze upon these words. And no illusions act as a comforting balm to my mind. I know if you ever know anything about me it will be only stories and slander, you shall never hear a single laudatory word spoken about me, for upon the scales of decency I weigh feather-light. But by the grace of the Lady, may the memory of my love for you remain in your mind, even if it be dim as a dying rush-light. In those all too brief hours I spent with you, you restored to me what I thought was lost forever. You loved me for myself alone. With your innocent mind unfettered by what others say and think of me, you saw and loved the *real* me. And with all my heart I thank you for it!

LORD OF MISRULE

It was I who found the bean in the custard, so I must take the Lord of Misrule's gaudy motley-colored crown and preside over the Christmas festivities and lead the court in their games and revelry.

As I stood at the head of the great trestle table, in Edward's accustomed place, and raised my cup of wassail in the traditional toast of "Drink and be well!" the Earl of Warwick grumbled: "Now Gaveston has been given his proper title, for he is Lord of Misrule indeed, and not just at Christmas but the whole year round!"

"Indeed!" seconded Lancaster.

"Indeed!" chorused Lincoln.

"Indeed!" agreed Pembroke.

"Forsooth, My Lords," I laughed, "all these 'Indeeds!' Why not an 'Aye!' or a 'To be sure!'? The parrot His Majesty gave me has a greater diversity of phrases than have you three!"

Laughter rang loud and long around the table. The earls frowned and had the disapproval in their eyes been daggers I would most surely have been struck dead.

"Well you can be sure that I would not care to hear any of the phrases your parrot has acquired!" Lancaster pompously informed me, still smarting no doubt because of the gaudy colored ribbons I had tied in his beard when I found him sprawled senseless by the hearth that morning after a night spent carousing. He did not notice them before the entire court had seen and I tweaked them and danced round him as if he were a Maypole asking if he had mistaken Christmas for May Day.

"Verily, My Lord," I said with an impish shake of my bell-trimmed cap, "you have put me in my place indeed! And, I must confess, my parrot says naught but 'Pretty Piers' as Edward taught him until I am like to scream or dine on roast parrot!"

"Oh husband!" Meg exclaimed. "You would not *really* harm the poor bird? He is so pretty and clever!"

"Nay, sweeting," I smiled down at her, "I spoke only in jest. I shall not have the parrot roasted, nor baked or boiled either; instead, I shall send him home to Wallingford with you."

"Oh Piers!" she cried, her face wreathed in smiles. "I would love that! But will you not miss him? Uncle Edward gave him to you!"

I leaned over and kissed her cheek. "Only as I would miss a splinter that had been plucked from my finger. Be of good cheer, my sweet, it is your parrot now and he will be far happier with such a pretty mistress as you. Perhaps you can even teach him some phrases of which My Lord of Lancaster will approve!"

"Oh Piers, you are so good to me!"

"Thank you, my dear Meg, I have always tried to be; I am glad I have not failed." I raised her hand and pressed it to my lips.

Over the elaborate marzipan subtleties and wobbling jellies I saw Edward glowering at me from the other end of the table. With a saucy smile I raised my cup to him.

The Lord of Misrule had decreed that the King and Queen should sit together at the foot of the table, in the seats of honor, to be sure, but surrounded by the dullest members of the court, so that they must either sit in silence or turn to each other unless they would be bored to tears or slumber. An ancient and decrepit countess sat beside Edward, recounting her numerous ailments in vivid detail. And beside Isabelle was a crusty old general who lived and breathed for precise military maneuvers and the glory of his past campaigns.

Edward glared back at me and stabbed his fork into a roast capon as if it were his mortal enemy.

Now I was ever mindful of the need for a royal heir, and the persistent charge that I kept Edward from Isabelle's bed. I bade Agnes learn the pattern of the Queen's courses and made Edward go to her when her womb was ripe for planting. Quarrels, chicanery, potions, I shamelessly made use of them all, *anything* to send him from my bed to hers. Indeed, I did everything but follow him into her chamber and sit by the bed and give instructions! I would have done that too, but I daresay Isabelle would have disapproved.

I always did love to keep Christmas at Langley and see the Great Hall arrayed with boughs of holly and evergreens. I can see it now, lit with candles all around, and the rushes heady with the scent of spices. I can even taste the little Yule Men crafted of gingerbread and the warm, sweet wassail. There were brightly clad minstrels, acrobats, jugglers, and mummers, masques and pantomimes, merry country dances, full of leaps and turns and kicks, and games galore. Edward's favorite was Hoodman Blind and he could play at it for hours, as carefree as a child.

I danced, drank, and whirled about; jesting, laughing, and teasing, until my head grew light, then I let Edward lead me to a window-seat. I beckoned a servant to bring me one of the mincemeat pies, baked oblong to represent the Christ Child's cradle and seasoned with cinnamon, nutmeg, and cloves for the gifts of the Three Magi. I broke it in two and gave half to Edward then sent him off for another game of Hoodman Blind, promising that I would join him soon, then I settled back to watch the merry company.

Oh how I laughed to see Lancaster in his gaudy green and blinding yellow stripes clumsily demonstrating dance steps to a group of ladies. He stroked his little gold beard and sidled close to one to whisper in her ear and ended by tangling his jeweled collar in the veil dangling from her tall brocade headdress. His eyes often sought his wife, and every time they found her, surrounded by a bevy of admirers, his attentions to the ladies grew more ardent as if to say "I care as little for you as you care for me!" though everyone knows he would leap to death and woe to win her. Yet there is not a man in the world that Alice despises more than Tom of Lancaster. When they were betrothed she declared that she would rather starve to death than wed him, but hunger pangs proved mightier than her convictions. After all, she *is* Burstbelly's daughter, and she has inherited his appetite, but fortunately not his rotund figure. To be avenged on Tom, Alice plays the wanton and keeps from giving him his much desired heir by taking the herbs Agnes gives her. But I know that her heart truly belongs to Ebulo L'Estrange, a humble squire in her husband's service. I chanced upon them once, coupling in the royal stables while The Buffoon's horse looked on, no doubt neighing his approval. That was how Alice and I became friends; we like to trade confidences and saucy banter, and I have sometimes connived to help her spend an hour alone with Ebulo. And yes, we have bedded together a few times, just because we could, laughing at the thought of what it would do to Lancaster if he ever found out.

The Black Dog sat apart, nursing his ale, glowering by the fire with a pack of wolfhounds resting round his feet and nosing for scraps in the rushes. I really do not understand why he hates me so! But upon one another we have this strange effect. Whenever I come into his presence he is like a bull seeing red and snorts and seethes as if he would charge at me. While I at the same time feel I must provoke him just because he is there glaring at me and the veins in his temples are throbbing as if they would burst free from beneath his skin and slither away like snakes. It *excites* me, like risking everything on a single throw of the dice. I cannot help myself, I know what I am doing, and I know that I should not, but for the life of me, I just cannot behave whenever Warwick is near!

The Earl of Lincoln sat watching the dancers and calling out greetings to his friends, a Yule Man in one hand and a mincemeat pie in the other, his ample belly straining against his yellow silk tunic. He really is a jolly man with his white curls and apple cheeks. Burstbelly is an apt name for him; he strokes his paunch and gazes down upon it fondly like a mother-to-be, so I cannot imagine why he took such grievous offense when I dubbed him such. Yea, I do admit, one night when I was far into my cups and acting wild I jabbed him with a pin to see if it would burst and go flat, but on the morrow I did apologize and offer a soothing rose salve. But he would not accept my apology and said the Devil could take me and my salve.

The Earl of Pembroke stood amongst those watching Edward play Hoodman Blind, a slight smile upon his lips and a cup of wassail in his hand. Mayhap as Lord of Misrule I should go and command a kiss? But, nay, I would rather it was given freely! Of all my enemies, Pembroke is my favorite. He is like a candle burning steady at the heart of a storm and I am drawn to him like a moth to a flame. Perhaps someday I shall succeed and make him shake with laughter. would puncture his pomposity the way I tried to burst Lincoln's belly!

The elder and the younger Hugh Despenser were also of this crowd stern-faced amongst all the smiling ones. Can they not leave off talking of state craft even at Christmas? Forsooth, they do sore vex me, and I shall not write another word about either of them until it becomes necessary! Hugh Despenser can write a chronicle of his own life when he is facing death and justify himself he can!

Isabelle was amongst the players. She was a vision of beauty and grace in her cloth-of-silver and purple velvet gown with amethysts round her neck and on the coif that contained her fair hair.

Meg sat nearby, watching, too shy to join in the game, but she seemed content and was smiling and applauding the players' crafty dodges. The pretty little spaniel I had given her lay upon her lap. "Methinks your arms and your heart long for a warm little body to hold," I said when I placed the silky-haired brown and white puppy in her arms, "and I thought this little girl might please you."

And young ginger-haired Hugh Audley stood nearby, watching Meg with his warm brown eyes. Whenever I see this sweet, shy lad gazing wistfully at my wife I feel sick with self-loathing. Here, given time, might have been a true love match. But Meg never notices him; I stand in the way and past me she cannot see. It is true, life touches life, and one person *can* be like a pebble dropped into a pond creating ripples that spread far and wide. Poor child, she thinks she loves me!

As I sat upon the window-seat, content to watch the others and eat my pie, I spied my three brothers coming towards me. In that instant my appetite fled and I called Blanche and fed her the rest of the mincemeat pie. It was pointless to run away; I could tell by the determined set of their faces that they would track me down like a pack of hunting hounds.

"Piers," Arnaud, the eldest and our father's namesake, began, "we would speak with you."

"But I would not speak with you, it is Christmas and I would enjoy myself, *now go away!*" I snapped peevishly.

"And so you may!" Raimond said indulgently. "We would only have a *little* speech with you! Surely that is not *too* much to ask of one's brother at Christmas? Remember, Piers, it *is* the season for charity!"

"Very well," I sighed, "say on then; to the point, please, and quickly!"

"I want to be a governor!" Arnaud announced.

"And I also want to be a governor!" said Raimond.

"And what would you be governor *of?*" I asked.

Neither had anywhere particular in mind, it was only the honor, the title, the stipend, they coveted.

"And what of you, Guillaume?" I asked the youngest of this avaricious trio. "Do you want to be a governor too?"

Arnaud and Raimond chortled. "His head's too muddled by drink to be a governor!"

"Nay, Piers," Guillaume answered, his voice slurred and a silly grin spreading across his face, "it is the wine merchant again! Not another drop will he vouchsafe me until I settle with him! Come along, Piers," he draped an arm about my shoulders, "do your duty towards your brother as you know you should! I shall tell Edward you bedded the wine merchant if you do not help me!"

"Mayhap I did," I shrugged, freeing myself from his unwelcome embrace, "many merchants have had me."

"*Catamite! Whore!*" Arnaud hissed. "You are a *disgrace* to the name of Gaveston! You will lie with anyone! And we will tell Edward so if we are not created governors!"

"Anyone who is not poxed and has money enough to pay me," I corrected, "I am not entirely without standards. And if I am such a disgrace to you then by all means disown me, go back to soldiering," I glanced at their middles once fit and firm now grown paunchy and soft with easy living, "and trouble me no more!"

"Now Piers," Arnaud interjected quickly, "perhaps I spoke hastily ..."

"Aye," Raimond nodded vigorously, "Arnaud you *did* speak hastily! It is Christmas as Piers said and we should not be troubling him when he wants only to enjoy himself! Now, Piers, if you will just give us your word that you will speak to Edward about our governorships ..."

"What about the wine merchant?" Guillaume interjected.

"*Oh a pox on the wine merchant and you, you drunken sot!*" Arnaud cried, elbowing Guillaume sharply aside.

And then, as was bound to happen sooner or later, my first and third brothers were rolling upon the floor, grappling amongst the rushes, and making free with their fists, teeth, and kicks, screaming insults and curses above the lively Christmas music, and attracting a small crowd, some of whom even placed wagers upon who the victor would be and cheered them on accordingly.

"Piers! They are killing each other! Will you not do something?" Raimond cried as he flung himself down, struggling to separate them, and promptly had his nose bloodied by Guillaume's fist for his pains.

"Nay," I sighed, standing and stepping carefully around them, "let them; it will be two less worries with which I must contend."

Verily, those three have knocked enough teeth out of each other's heads to string a necklace!

Ignoring their cries of "Piers, you care nothing for your family!" I went to join the game of Hoodman Blind and positioned myself behind Isabelle.

"You must let him catch you!"

Isabelle stared coldly back at me. "Why must you forever mock me? You *know* it is not *me* he wants to catch!"

"Then you must *make* him want to!" I said and shoved her straight into Edward's arms.

Those standing round applauded to see the Queen in the King's arms and I withdrew quickly, before Edward could take off the hood and notice me, and stepped out into the courtyard to let the clean, crisp winter air refresh me.

The snow lay like an ermine blanket upon the flagstones. Some of the palace servants and guards were having a celebration of their own around a small bonfire. They sang and passed around a flagon of ale while a serving wench handed out meat pasties and honey cakes. I heard a woman's shrill, happy giggle and saw movement in the shadows against the castle wall. I smiled as I drew my motley-colored mantle close about me and shook back the colored streamers on my cap, causing the little golden bells to jingle.

"Piers!" I turned at Edward's voice calling my name.

"*Oh Edward!*" I wailed. "Isabelle was in your arms! What happened?"

"It was her turn to be Hoodman, so I put the hood over her head and came to find you!" I saw lust dancing in his eyes. "Perrot," he softly crooned, "I have something for you!"

"*Please* tell me it is not another parrot," I said warily.

"No!" He giggled and showed me a sprig of holly. He held it above my head and leaned in swiftly to kiss me. "There now, is that not a pleasing trick?"

"Indeed it is," I said, "though it should rightly be mistletoe."

"Nay, love," Edward shook his head adamantly, "do not speak of mistletoe! The Church will not have it, it is an evil, idolatrous plant; the Druids favored it and used it in their rituals. Far better to have the holly, its sharpened leaves and red berries will ever remind us of the crown of thorns placed upon Christ's head and the blood He shed for us."

"To my own beliefs I shall cling true, Edward, and you to yours. And, now, let us forget it; it is not a night for Christian and Pagan to parry! Indeed, it is a most pleasing trick and you must show it to your Queen! Come!" I took his arm and guided him back to the doorway.

"Nay, Perrot," Edward hung back, "I would rather into the shadows with you!"

"But you shall not! I am Lord of Misrule and tonight you are mine to command!"

"I have *always* been yours to command!" Edward protested, trying to get his arms around me again.

"Then you must into the light with your holly sprig and show this charming trick to your Queen! The passion you would give me, give to her tonight," I urged, giving him a little push. "I both desire it and command it!"

"Forsooth, Piers, it is a bitter medicine you would have me take!" Edward whined, staring sullenly at Isabelle. "And at Christmas too! It is most unkind of you!"

"And after the bitterness comes the honey," I reminded him. "Come to me tomorrow and I shall chase *all* the bitterness away! But remember, be passionate! If you are cold to her, I shall be cold to you!"

"Then I shall be hot as the fires of Hell!" he vowed and ran back inside.

He seized hold of Isabelle and ripped the hood from her head. With it came her amethyst spangled coif. Her white-blonde hair tumbled down her back and Edward twined his fingers in it as he drew her close to him. He showed her the holly sprig then held it aloft and kissed her heartily.

Isabelle was delighted, all the coldness and anger melted from her, and I saw the love and desire clear upon her face as she returned his kiss wholeheartedly.

Edward swept her up into his arms and spun around wildly, his head thrown back, laughing all the while, until I feared he would fall down dizzy or drop Isabelle, and then he carried her from the hall and up the stairs to resounding applause. The court was ecstatic! This Christmas it seemed the Queen had triumphed over The Gascon!

Watching from the doorway, I smiled and, with a nod of approval, lifted the Lord of Misrule's crown from my head. And, swinging it by its colorful streamers, I went alone to my bed.

SCOTLAND

The lofty peers of England finally lost what little of their patience was left and, led by Warwick, Lancaster, Lincoln, and Pembroke, they swore a solemn oath to right the many wrongs afflicting the land and rid it of my evil and lascivious presence. Banded together, twenty-one strong, they dubbed themselves the Lords Ordainers and presented Edward with a list of grievances and the Ordinances by which they proposed to correct them.

Verily, they want everything but to sit upon the throne and call themselves "King!" If Edward accedes to their demands, all the power will be in their hands and he will count for nothing. He will be a puppet and they the masters who pull the strings and make him dance to their tune. If they have their way, they will control the royal household. Edward will not be able to appoint or dismiss servants, courtiers, or officials, depart the realm, declare war, or give gifts, not even trifles, without their consent. Nor will he be able to issue pardons or orders of protection. And any doubtful points of Law will be left entirely to their interpretation.

As for the "evil male sorcerer who has enslaved the poor besotted King," I must be deprived of all the honors Edward has "wantonly and recklessly" lavished upon me and be banished perpetually from the realm.

Edward promised to accept without quarrel, comment, or question all Ordinances concerning himself and his kingdom as long as I be allowed to remain, my position unaffected, at his side, but to this they would not agree.

As Pembroke rightly said: I "engross His Majesty's attention to the exclusion of all else."

"But nothing else is of interest to me!" Edward exclaimed, hoping to rouse Pembroke's sympathy.

"Does Your Majesty think that those who reign after you, England's future kings, will take pleasure in knowing that they have lost the power that should rightfully have been theirs because of your passion for that wanton, wicked Gaveston?" Pembroke asked, stalwart and unmoved.

It was at that point that Edward decided we should face our problems by running away from them, it having suddenly occurred to him that he had neglected affairs in Scotland far too long.

A victory, he hoped, would put a stop to all this talk of Ordinances.

But I saw something more, one last chance, one final hope for me to grasp at. If I could succeed in Scotland as I had in Ireland perhaps a new door would open for me. But it was not meant to be, and I should have known that from the start.

Heedless of the fact that all of them possessed lands in Scotland that required protection lest they be taken by the Bruce, Warwick, Lancaster, Lincoln, and Pembroke all refused to marshal their forces and march with us, and many other noblemen followed their example. All of them were willing to defy a royal command and risk their lands rather than fight alongside me. Their decision stands testament to how greatly I was despised and how little Edward was respected.

While Edward made his headquarters at Berwick, I rode out with an army two hundred strong, harrying the countryside as far as Perth and the Grampian Mountains, and even leading a foray into the Ettrick Forest. But the wily Scots refused to engage, fleeing afore us and hiding in the marshes and mountains. Edward tried vainly to negotiate with Robert the Bruce, but he would not consent to a meeting lest he be taken captive. And while we endeavored to lure the Scots into battle the Bruce dispatched a party of raiders into northern England to rape and pillage. Thus I returned to Berwick weary, frustrated, and heart-sore, knowing no one would appreciate my efforts.

I found Edward slumped and yawning over his map and parchment covered desk.

"My Lord," I said from the doorway, "your general has come to make his report."

Edward looked past me, a quizzical frown furrowing his brow when he saw no one standing behind me.

"*I* have come to give my report," I clarified.

Before I went to him I had gone first to my quarters. Fastidious creature that am, I wanted a hot bath and a change of clothes. That was a mistake. If I had gone to him sweat-stained and stinking instead of immaculate and fresh in dan ask the reddish-purple of a plum with pendant pearls dripping like tears from my silver belt he might have received me differently.

Grinning broadly, Edward pushed back his chair.

"And I am eager to hear it! Come sit on my lap!"

When I hesitated, Edward reached out and drew me round the desk and onto his lap.

"There now; isn't this nice? Couldn't you sit like this all day?"

"I daresay I could," I shrugged, "provided Your Majesty does not stand up, of course."

Edward laughed so hard he nearly shook me off his lap.

"Well now, did you face the Scots in battle?" he asked.

"No," I shook my head and sighed. "We tried, but they would not engage. My spies report that they fear my witchcraft and believe I have the power to summon storms."

"Most interesting!" Edward nodded, his hand steadily advancing up my thigh to steal beneath my tunic's hem.

"Edward," I shifted my position in an attempt to dislodge his hand, "wouldn't you like to hear about our foray into the Ettrick Forest?"

"Nay, love, I find it tiresome!"

He stood up and set me on the desk. And then he was upon me, all eager hands and questing lips.

"*Edward!*" I twisted my face aside and struggled to sit up; an inkwell was pressing painfully into my back. "What of the Grampian Mountains then?" I persisted.

"*Well what of them?*" Edward snapped. "I find mountains even more tiresome than forests! Hush now, my sweet Perrot, your mouth is far too beautiful to talk of these dreary matters! Don't you know God fashioned it solely for the pleasures of love and the passion of kisses?"

Never in my life have I felt more like a whore, not even when I sought custom in the taverns and bathhouses and held out my hand for the coins before I lowered my hose. I felt so worthless lying there with the inkwell pressing into my back and Edward pressing into me that I would gladly have welcomed death if it would set me free.

Afterwards, when Edward sat back in his chair, grinning like a fool, his eyes glassy with lust sated, I sat up, rubbing my back, and began to put right my clothes. It was then that I saw his seed pooled and glimmering upon the maps and dispatches and I felt *sick* to my very heart. How could *this*, what he had just done to me, mean everything and his crown and kingdom nothing? And in that moment I fell out of love. Once and for all, I said goodbye to the boy I had loved and admitted that into this man he had been completely submerged like a poor drowned soul lost at sea. Any glimmer of his shade I might glimpse was but an illusion, a ghost from the past come to tempt and torment me with tender memories of what had been but could never be again. The Edward I loved was gone.

I rose unsteadily and, without a word or a backward glance, I left him.

As I walked down the corridor, lined with soldiers and messengers waiting to see the King, I felt sick with shame when I saw the way they looked at me. Their animosity and contempt was so palpable it seemed to squeeze all the air from my lungs. They knew what had just happened and that they had been made to wait while Edward had his way with me. Some whistled and puckered their lips in mocking kisses and called me "Pretty Piers." I forced myself to hold my head up high as I walked past them. Let them call me arrogant and peacock proud! But once I was beyond their gaze I had to hug the wall for support until I reached my chamber and staggered inside. I fell to my knees beside the bed and groped beneath it for the night-pot and vomited.

I wanted so much to remain in Scotland as Edward's lieutenant, to take charge of the campaign and match my wits against the Bruce. Had I been allowed to, my story might have had a different end. But the men's reception of me killed what little hope I had left. Even if by some miracle I had persuaded Edward, the moment he left me alone with them ... I trembled at the thought of what might befall me. Would they kill me outright or pass me amongst them like a common whore to put me in my place? And if I fell into Scottish hands I would be burned as a witch unless the lure of the ransom Edward would pay proved more powerful than their rampant superstitions.

When Edward came to me I was lying curled up on my bed. Agnes had covered me with a fur blanket and sat beside me stroking my hair and holding a goblet of mulled wine that I, from time to time, sat up shakily to sip.

Slowly I stood up to face him.

"Your favor has destroyed me! I have tried to make a life for myself, but you will not let me! I realize now that I shall *never* know peace of mind or respect as long as I stay with you, therefore, I must seek it elsewhere! I am weary of being your *Principal Provider of Entertainment*, Edward, your *Lord of Misrule!* When we return to England I shall set my affairs in order and then into exile I shall go! I must learn from my mistakes and make a new life for myself! I need to rebuild the walls and lock up my heart again; the only way I can survive is to teach myself to feel *nothing* again!"

We quarreled violently. I said such awful, ugly, bitter things to him, yet every one of them was true. We screamed, shouted insults, abuse, and curses, wept tears enough to rival a rainstorm, and threw things until the room looked as if a storm had swept through it. At last Edward ran weeping from the room to have his physician apply leeches to his temples.

That night as I lay wakeful and restless in my moonlight-flooded chamber Edward came to me. He stood gazing down at me then tentatively bent and placed a kiss upon my bare shoulder. When I did not protest he lay down beside me.

"Why do we say such terrible things to one another?" he asked softly.

"The truth is often ugly and unkind, Edward, yet it must be faced. No one can run away from it forever, not even a king."

"What is to become of us?" he wondered.

And in all honesty I answered: "I do not know."

It was the only night we ever lay together sleepless and in chastity.

Into Exile Again

His whole body anxiously aquiver, Edward clutched my hand tightly as we sat side by side in the cold and cavernous council chamber awaiting the arrival of the Lords Ordainers. My own hands were steady and I felt no fear. I *knew* exactly what was about to happen and I was tired of playing this game, but, for Edward's sake, I forced myself to smile and squeeze his hand reassuringly.

"Tell me the nicknames again, Perrot," Edward pleaded, his voice tremulous and childlike, "you know it always amuses me. Tell me why you call Warwick The Black Dog and Lancaster The Buffoon."

And though I had long since come to regret them, I leaned back in my chair, propped my silk-clad legs up on the table, and complied.

"Why should I *not* call Warwick The Black Dog? Is his voice not like the growl of a mad mongrel? And when angered he foams at the mouth like one. And his long black beard is as unkempt as the coat of a wild dog; it is rare indeed that one does not see burrs or bits of food caught in it. He has told me on more than one occasion that he means to bite me one day!"

Edward giggled and clapped his hands. "Now tell me why Cousin Tom is The Buffoon!"

"Well, I shall tell you plainly, Tom of Lancaster is just as much of a strutting peacock as I am. We are both gaudy in our plumage and proud. Yet there is a difference; I have that which Thomas lacks—*Style!* Every chance he gets he struts and preens before the ladies, seeking to impress them in clothes so fussy, gaudy, and bright and weighed down with tinsel and trimmings, hoping to lure them into his bed. I remember him on my wedding day preening in his pink and orange striped taffeta with a whole garden of roses blooming on his hat! I told you then that you should send him to the Tower for his crimes against fashion. All his attire lacks is the cap and bells of a jester—a buffoon! What a shame he lacks the wit to actually *be* one!"

"Yes, yes," Edward applauded, "that is my cousin Tom! And Pembroke is Joseph the Jew because ..." he prompted.

"Ah, My Lord, it is because he hoards his smiles and laughter like a Jewish miser does his coins and is sore reluctant to part with them! Forsooth, I meant no insult when I named him such, only to tease!"

"Methinks you tease Pembroke overmuch!" Edward said petulantly. "It is comforting to know that nothing shall ever come of it!"

"Verily, My Lord, I am not yet ready to admit defeat!" I smiled.

Grim-faced and wearing armor, to show the seriousness of their intent, and that civil war was not an idle threat, the Lords Ordainers marched in and ranged themselves before us, with Warwick, Lancaster, and Pembroke at the fore. Burst-belly was absent, having recently died of gluttonous excess; though many persisted in the belief that I had poisoned him.

They declined to be seated which I could well understand; the chairs in the council chamber are beastly uncomfortable. They frowned and stared pointedly at my legs propped up upon that most highly esteemed of tables but I just smiled and nodded graciously back at them.

"By your leave," began Lancaster, "I shall read the charges."

"As you like, My Lord," I smiled amiably. "I shall sit here and strive to appear languid and alluring while I pretend to listen; but do not worry, if you stumble upon a word you do not know I shall be most happy to assist you."

Edward smiled dotingly and laid a hand upon my arm. "Dearest Perrot, even in times of adversity your kindness and generosity never desert you!"

"Your air of levity ill becomes the gravity of this situation," the Earl of Pembroke reproved me.

"Oh woe that I should ever be ill-becoming in *your* eyes!" I cried.

Edward tapped my thigh sharply and shook his head to signal his disapproval. And then the charges were read against me.

According to them, I had dabbled in the black arts to gain ascendancy over Edward, and enticed him to do my bidding in various nefarious and deceitful ways—namely by dangling the promise of forbidden sex, or sodomy, before him like a carrot on a string held just beyond a donkey's nose. I had squandered the country's wealth, thus emptying the treasury and putting the nation into pawn with foreign moneylenders, the worst by far being the Florentine banker,

Amerigo dei Frescobaldi, my personal banker and sometime lover. I had used my influence to feather the nests of my kin, shiftless, good-for-nothing Gascons all, to the detriment of good and able Englishmen. My arrogance knew no bounds, and to no one, not even the Church or my lover the King did I show proper respect. They declared me an enemy to King and country alike.

And, found guilty of treason, I was once again stripped of my earldom, and all other honors, properties, and revenues, to be banished in perpetuity from England, Scotland, Ireland, Wales, and all English dominions across the sea, including my native Gascony. I was ordered to be quit of the country by fortnight's end or else, for the second time, I would be excommunicated. Why they thought this would strike fear in the heart of a man they accused of worshipping the Devil I do not know. It merely meant Edward would worry himself to a shadow, wear pens out by the bushel, and annoy the Pope until he lifted the ban.

"Well, Piers Gaveston, have you anything to say?" Warwick asked as Lancaster clumsily rolled up the condemnatory parchment.

After indulging in an exaggerated yawn, I shook my head, clucked my tongue, and said: "For shame, My Lord of Lancaster, this story has scandal, intrigue, danger, and romance, high comedy and drama, and it just *drips* with sex, yet you tell it *so* dully! I daresay you could make Robin Hood sound as dreary as a banker's clerk!"

Lancaster said I should consider myself fortunate that they did not sentence me to burn as my mother had and doubtlessly continued to do in the dominion of Lucifer, the master she had served so well. And I was doubly deserving of such a fate, sodomy and witchcraft both being burning offenses.

"*Damn you!*" I leapt to my feet. "You know *nothing* of my mother or me!"

"None save one bewitched," he stared pointedly at Edward, "would want to know Satan's minions!"

"Away with you, pretty little Gascon catamite," The Black Dog growled with a swatting motion as if I were nothing more than a bothersome fly, "before I see you ablaze myself!"

At these words Edward burst into tears and flung himself upon me, entreating them not to hurt his beloved Perrot whom he loved more than life itself.

"For shame, Your Majesty!" Pembroke reproved him sharply. "Regard yourself! See how besotted you are! Clearly you are bewitched; he has cast the glamour over you! Were he to cut off one of your limbs you would smile and say: It is nothing; I still have one left!"

"With all due respect, My Lord," I said saucily, "it would depend on which limb it was, they do not *all* come in pairs." I glanced boldly down at Pembroke loins and licked my lips. "A certain one springs to mind that has no twin and if lost would be sorely lamented, especially in bed!"

Edward's tears instantly turned to laughter. He collapsed into his chair, clutching his sides as laughter convulsed him and his face turned red.

"Oh Perrot! Your wit is like rubies, sparkling and beyond price!"

"My Lords," I stood to address them, "since you have raised the subject, a subject it is plain you know *nothing* about, pray give me leave to answer you. Look at me, vain, foppish peacock that I am, and know that *never* have I required more than what you see here, this face and body, to attain anything I desired. I have never had recourse to poppets and pins, evil incantations, or to traffic with the dead, and the only potions I have any acquaintance with are medicinal. And your Church, which you rightly say I do not respect, murdered my mother, chained her to a stake and set her on fire, then confiscated all that she possessed, leaving me an orphan without a mother, means, or a home! Verily, it gives a whole new meaning to the words Christian charity!" With that I turned my back and left them. As I went, I heard Edward's heartrending wail as he fell forward, weeping and pounding his fists upon the table.

"Your Majesty must sign the decree," Pembroke insisted, laying it before him.

"You would have me sign it with my heart's blood!" Edward sobbed.

"No, Your Majesty," Pembroke assured him, dipping a quill into the inkwell and handing it to him, "ink shall suffice."

"I cannot wear my crown upon my heart!" Edward wept as he shakily scrawled his signature.

But I was *glad* to have it over and done! Certainly I would go; I *wanted* to go! I would not stay and see Edward made into a laughingstock before the entire world by plunging his kingdom into civil war just to keep me in his bed!

A few days later an attempt was made on my life. I had gone into London, quietly and unobtrusively, with only Dragon and one other guard. We were returning to our barge when two men, wielding daggers, burst from the bustling dockside crowd and made straight for me. It happened so quickly. We struggled to disarm them, but mindless rage swelled their strength. I had no choice, it was either kill or be killed.

Miraculously, I escaped without a scratch, and, covered in my would-be assassins' blood, they hustled me to the barge with such speed that my feet scarcely touched the ground. They threw me in and ordered the oarsmen to make haste; there would be extra coins for them if they got me back to the palace soon and safe.

When word reached Edward he sped breathlessly to my side, no doubt expecting to find me languishing in bed with my life's blood pouring out of me. Poor Nedikins, how surprised he was to see me sitting by the fire, freshly bathed and dressed, sipping wine and conferring with Agnes while my servants sorted through my clothes and carried in sturdy wooden traveling chests.

"I shall travel lightly since my destination is at present unknown, so have them pack only the most simple, serviceable things that are easy to care for and launder ..."

"*Piers!*" Edward exclaimed. "*What are you doing?* You *cannot* mean to leave me!"

"Has Your Majesty forgotten that I am banished?" I asked, calmly taking another sip of wine.

"But, my love, you must not abandon hope!" Edward rushed to kneel before me. He took the goblet from me and thrust it at Agnes then clasped both my hands. "By my very soul, I swear, I shall find a way to keep you!"

I pulled my hands away and stood up. "Did it never occur to you that I no longer *want* to be kept by you?"

"You cannot mean that!"

"Oh, but *I do!*"

"You have grown cold, Piers!" he accused. "And I do not know what has wrought this dreadful change in you!"

"*Life* has changed me; *you* have changed me, Edward! No longer shall my lovesome mouth lie to you! I shall no longer play the pastry chef who rolls the truth in sugar before it is served to you! But if the truth pains you, then you may take comfort in knowing that it is a dagger embedded deep in my heart as well."

Edward seized hold of me, clutching me tight against his body. "Then let me pull that hateful, hurtful dagger free and make you warm again with my love!"

"Nay, Edward," I said coolly as I pulled away. "The fire within me is doused and never again shall it kindle for you. I have experienced fire all too well," I displayed my scarred hands, "methinks I prefer the cold."

"Do you mean you no longer love me?"

"That is precisely what I mean," I said and turned away from him. "Agnes, I have been remiss; I have forgotten entirely the matter of shoes ..."

"*How can you sit there talking of shoes?*" Edward wailed. "*I love you more than life itself!*"

"Then you must have very little regard for life," I shrugged.

"No; you cannot mean this!" Edward persisted. "The shock of the assault has robbed you of your senses!"

"No, Edward, it has opened my eyes and I see the world and my place in it with an all new clarity! Verily, I feel as a blind man who has suddenly, miraculously, regained his sight must feel! But what happened today really has nothing to do with my decision. I went into London today to consult my lawyers; I have signed documents empowering them to act upon my behalf and in Meg's best interests for the next five years …"

"*Five years!*" Edward shrieked, his face deathly pale. "You mean to leave me for *five years, five long years?*"

"No, Edward," I shook my head and said placidly: "I mean to leave you *forever*. The Lords Ordainers have banished me and I mean to make my exile a permanent one. By my actions I mean only to be practical. Though I have been restored to the state in which I came to you, a foreigner possessing neither title, lands, or inheritance, the Lords Ordainers have graciously consented to allow Meg to retain Wallingford, sans the title of Countess of Cornwall, until such time as she remarries or perishes. Beyond her housewifely duties she is inexperienced in the management of such a large estate and someone must look after her interests. I have also charged them to find a suitable tutor to educate her in such things; knowledge is power and blind faith is rarely rewarded. After five years I shall see how matters stand, but it shall all be done by correspondence; onto English soil I shall never again set foot."

"But she is my niece!" Edward protested. "Do you think that I will not look after her?"

"The same as you have looked after me?" I arched my brows. "Verily, Edward, I pity anyone to whom you decide to give your protection or love; to the brink of destruction it will bear them!"

"Then I am *glad* you are leaving!" Edward cried, blinded by tears and rage. "Never have I known such heartless ingratitude! *Everything* I have ever done has been for you; my every thought has been of you! And *this* is how you repay me, by tearing out my heart and stomping on it?"

His hand flew out and slapped me hard across the face and a trickle of blood snaked slowly from my nose. And with that he left me, slamming the door behind him.

I sank down onto the settle again, rubbing my cheek, which bore a stinging red print of Edward's hand, while Agnes brought a cloth to staunch the blood-flow.

"It will be better if he hates me."

"Aye, Child," she agreed, "you may even leave him a wiser man."

"I hope so, Agnes, *I hope so!*"

Again I delayed my departure for three days and was promptly excommunicated. When presented with the document I thanked the messenger heartily, saying that his arrival was timely as I was just on my way to the privy and would take
it with me and put it to good use.

This time when I left only Agnes, Dragon, and Blanche would accompany
me. My plans were uncertain and since Meg was once again with child it was
ill-advised for her to travel. No, she would remain in England, and, in time, I
hoped, forget and maybe even forgive me.

She wept copious tears and clung to me until I feared for her and the child. I
had never seen her so upset. She begged me to stay at least until the child was
born even though she knew I could not; the Lords Ordainers would not allow it.
Agnes hastened to brew a soothing posset and, to quiet her fears, I promised I
would return, in secret, to be with her when our child was born.

"I am not a child, Piers, even though you think I am! I am seventeen!" she
sobbed. "So do not make me promises that you do not intend to keep!"

"I promise faithfully," I said solemnly, "and by my word I am bound." Only
then would she consent to drink the posset and lie back quietly and rest.

Edward could not look at me without tears flooding his eyes. And neither of
us could speak except to say "yea" or "nay" to innocuous questions like "Are you
cold? Shall I put another log on the fire?" or "More wine?" otherwise tearful
lumps filled our throats and we were always trying to swallow them down.

My last night, I sat alone beside the fire in the Great Hall. Everyone made a
great show of avoiding me, but I didn't care. I sipped my wine and watched as
they rallied round Edward. Isabelle was at his side, radiant in red velvet and
cloth-of-gold, rubies glittering like drops of blood around her fair neck, a propri-
etary hand upon Edward's arm and a smile of triumph upon her lips. It annoyed
her immensely I am sure that I did nothing but smile and lift my goblet to her
whenever she looked my way with gloating eyes.

The Black Dog, The Buffoon, and Joseph the Jew showered Edward with
praise as if he were a puppy newly learned to obey his master's voice. There was
dancing and a new troupe of Welsh minstrels to divert him, and a few ambitious
young men even dared to smile invitingly.

Edward glanced often at me then quickly looked away, his bottom lip atremble. He tried to lose himself in the revelry and wine, and he danced every dance
with Isabelle.

The younger Sir Hugh Despenser came to join me. He stretched out his
ink-stained hands to the fire's warmth then drew up a chair beside me.

"Ah, Sir Hugh, I hear you have lost your place on the council because you spoke out against my banishment. I hope you have not come expecting my thanks."

He stared back at me unsmiling. Never have I know him to smile except in condescension or mockery. Though he is of an age with me he seems far older. His stern face is seriousness itself and his muddy gray eyes are like trampled snow. He cares nothing for any of life's pleasures, though he attends all the court ceremonies and revels like a carrion bird circling over a carcass. And he dresses without style or cheer, and only in colors dark and earthy.

"Nay, do not flatter yourself, Gaveston, I know how you render your thanks and it appeals to me not at all."

"Nay, Sir Hugh," I retorted, "do not flatter *yourself!* I know you take me for a fool, but I also know that you care nothing for me or my cause. Favorites and councilors come and go, but as long as his life endures, unless he abdicates or is overthrown, Edward shall be King." He looked startled but sought to hide it by signaling a servant to refill his cup. "You aspire to rise higher than the stars, Sir Hugh. And Edward *never* forgets a friend, and to side against me is to also side against him."

"He has told me as much, yes," he affirmed. "When I left the council chamber he clasped my hand and said: I never forget a friend. You surprise me, Gaveston; your perceptions are not only apt but unexpected. Whoever have you been talking to?"

"My perceptions are my own. Do you think I could not have thought of them myself? Unlike Edward, I see you for what you are, and I *know* what game you play."

"Because you have played it yourself and lost! But I shall not go *your* way, Gaveston; *I shall win!* Poor, foolish catamite, you had *all* the power in the land, but you did *nothing* with it! You frivoled and frittered your time away and now all you have to show for it are your fripperies and baubles! Someday when I, as King's Favorite, reign ..."

My wild burst of laughter interrupted him. "Verily, Sir Hugh, you cannot mean you seek to wear *my* shoes? Do not take it amiss, but I do not think you are to Edward's taste; you are far too serious and unsmiling!"

"Nay, Gaveston, *I shall not take the King to my bed!*" he said scornfully. "I shall win Edward's favor, but others shall slake his lust. London is full of creatures like you, pretty hell-bound men with whorish talents who lust after their own sex, so when the need arises Edward shall be sated. But they shall dance to *my* tune, I shall choose them with care, and none shall he see twice, so none can win his favor. I mean to be Edward's rock, a shoulder of granite that shall always support him, he will come to depend on me for *everything*, and he will make no decision lest it be my own! Those who say there are two kings in England—Edward who reigns and Gaveston who rules—are mistaken. For you do not rule, Gaveston, and never have, you are but a pretty whore for whom Edward has paid too dear a price! But when my day comes—and it *will*—there will indeed be two kings and Hugh Despenser will be the one who rules!"

"Verily, you are a confident, boastful fellow! And do you not fear the people will revile you as they do me?"

"*I do not fear the people!*" he sneered. "But I shall bide my time. Not now, while your memory still burns bright, but once it dims, and it will … *My day will come!*"

"And have you no fear that I will tell Edward of your ambitions?" I asked.

"Do you honestly think he would believe you?" he taunted. "Has Edward *ever* believed evil of one he considers a friend? And you are in no position to even try! It is known all about that you have quarreled and no longer speak or share a bed. So much for witchcraft, Gaveston, your spell is broken! *You have no power!*"

"*Indeed?*" I asked softly. "When one plants a seed, Sir Hugh, one knows not whether it will wither or flourish, one can but hope. And as for power …" I smiled as I stood up, the diamond brilliants on my black velvet sleeves flashing in the firelight as I smoothed down my tunic which was cut daringly short to expose my black-silk-sheathed thighs. "There is power, Sir Hugh, and there is *power*. Be not so dismissive of witchcraft; I am my mother's child."

Edward's eyes turned my way again as the musicians finished their tune and the air betwixt us seemed to crackle and hum. I smiled and began wending my way slowly across the crowded hall. As I passed all fell silent and stepped away, clearing a path for me. Hostility hung heavy as a hanged man upon the air. On the threshold I lingered and looked back over my shoulder. My eyes met Edward's and, giving him only the briefest of nods and a small, beguiling smile, I moved onwards towards the shadow-shrouded stairs.

Edward's chest heaved mightily and sweat beaded his upper lip like a moustache of seed pearls and shimmered upon his brow while a crimson flush suffused his face. His hand trembled as he grasped the golden goblet and wine sloshed out over his fingers. My foot had scarcely touched the first step when I heard his anguished cry and the startled, angry gasps of Queen and courtiers alike as he dashed the goblet to the floor, the wine spattering Isabelle's gown, and ran after me, shouting my name. And with a satisfied smile I continued upstairs, the flickering pitch-tipped torches lighting my way.

"Once again the glamour has been cast!" Pembroke bemoaned.

"Devil damn that popinjay!" The Black Dog bellowed.

"How does he do it?" Lancaster wondered aloud.

Edward caught up with me in the torch-lit corridor. And then my back was against the wall and his body and mouth were pressed hungrily to mine and we were moving as one to his bedchamber.

"Silly thing!" Edward chided me afterwards when we lay in a tangle of naked limbs and rumpled sheets. "Will you admit now that you truly love me?"

"It was why I called you back to me tonight. I would have gone away and left things as they were. Indeed, it would be far better for you if you did hate me. Yet I could not, knowing what I know, turn my back and walk away. I would ever regret it if I did not warn you."

"Nay, love, I could *never* hate you!" Edward cried, throwing his arms about me and covering my face and neck with kisses. "You and I, we are passionate people, in our anger and our love! Now what would you warn me of?"

"Deal carefully with the young Hugh Despenser; his sympathy is false and he has an insatiable lust for power."

Edward began to laugh and flung himself back onto the bed, wallowing like a pig joyous in the muck; and I knew then that it had all been in vain. Yet I had spoken the truth and appeased my conscience, so it need never reproach me.

"Nay, my love, be not jealous!" Edward exclaimed. "It is men like Hugh and his father I need about me to govern, not The Black Dog and his ilk! The elder Despenser was held in high esteem by my father and he raised his son on statecraft as if it were mother's milk. And, by my soul, I like them well! I trust them! Whenever I must make a decision they do not lecture me like Pembroke, nor ramble on until I am bored to tears, no, they tell me plainly what I should do, and the decision is made, and I am on to more amusing things! Oh Piers, *please* do not sulk! Saint's above, I like it not!" He sat up and put his arms around me, but I sat rigid and would not be drawn into his embrace. "If I must decide whether to wear the liripipe on my hat draped round my neck in cunning fashion or to leave it flowing free, no opinion save yours would I more readily seek! Just be beautiful and witty, Piers, and leave governing and politics to men like the Despensers!"

He kissed my brow and would have kissed my lips but I turned away.

"If you choose not to heed my warning then be it on your own head."

Undaunted, Edward pressed a kiss onto my shoulder. "My sweet Perrot, you must trust me to know a friend when I see one!"

I left the bed then and began gathering my clothes up from the floor.

"Verily, I can see it now!" I cried as I pulled on my black silk hose. "I need no crystal ball to scry the future! He shall play you like a fiddle! How glad I am that I shall not be here to see it! I would save you if I could, and by going away I shall save you from myself, I shall *not* be the instrument of your destruction, neither you nor anyone else shall use me as such, but I *cannot* save you from *yourself*, nor apparently from Hugh Despenser either!" And I snatched up my black velvet tunic and turned my back on him.

"Speak not of partings, my love! You know I shall have you back in my arms again before much time has passed! Have I not always found a way to bring you back to me?"

"No, Edward, not *this* time!" I stood before him now, fully dressed. My eyes filled with tenderness and regret and I leaned down and kissed his brow. "I shall always remember you with affection, Edward, but I shall not warm your bed again. *We are done!*"

I was gone before he could summon wits enough to speak. There was a stab of pain in my heart when the anguished, keening sobs began, so like a wounded animal, but I kept walking, I would not turn back.

I waited in the courtyard while my coach was brought round from the stables. In spite of my furred cloak I shivered in the biting November wind as I paced back and forth in the new-fallen snow with Blanche trotting alongside me. And I remembered how, almost a year ago, Edward and I had stood in this same courtyard and he had held a sprig of holly over my head and kissed me.

I started and turned at the sound of someone clearing their throat and beheld the cloaked figure of Hugh Despenser.

"I have come to see you off, fair catamite, and bid you farewell. Methinks victory is mine. Did not the seed you planted in the King's mind fail to prosper?"

"Only time will tell, Sir Hugh. But I have one more seed left to plant; you may consider it my gift to you."

"What, *more witchcraft*, Gaveston?" he sneered.

"Call it what you like, Sir Hugh," I said mysteriously, smiling as my fingers caressed the diamond-paved crescent moon pinned upon my cloak. "You are *wrong*; the people of England will *not* forget me! *You* shall remind them! The memory of Piers Gaveston the man may fade into the mists of time, but the legend shall burn as bright as a bonfire blazing in the night! My shade shall haunt thy every step, and thy every deed with mine they shall compare!"

"Forsooth, Gaveston, have you not had enough of games? *You would curse me now?*" he chuckled and it was the closest I ever knew him to come to genuine mirth.

"Nay, Sir Hugh, I curse you not, my memory shall do it for me, so I need not speak the words that bind! And now, farewell," I smiled, drawing up my hood, "my coach awaits!"

But he had more to say and called after me: "You are like a child, Gaveston, playing at sorcery the way children do at battle, knights, and ladies-fair! Only a *fool* would fear *you!* Vainglorious peacock, you think too highly of yourself! I say the people *will* forget, even as I shall forget; indeed, I have forgotten you already!"

As I climbed into the coach I lingered for a moment and looked back, up at the frost-rimmed window behind which Edward stood weeping. I raised a velvet-gloved hand to my lips and gently blew him a kiss, then I ducked inside and drew the heavy velvet curtains shut. I settled back against the cushions beside Agnes. Dragon knocked on the roof to signal the coachman that we were ready to depart. The whip cracked and the heavy wheels began to turn, churning and crunching over the snow.

I journeyed first to France, but the enmity of Isabelle's father made that country an inhospitable clime for me and I soon fled, narrowly evading arrest, amidst a flurry of rumors that King Philip would have me burned on charges of heresy, sorcery, and sodomy. I traveled next to Flanders where Edward had assured me that his sister Margaret, the Duchess of Brabant, would make me welcome. To her credit, she did try, but her forced and fragile smile betrayed the truth, that my presence was an embarrassment, and I soon took my leave.

Every place I ventured made fresh the fear that there was no place in the world for me. Wherever I go I am an object of embarrassment, curiosity, and scorn. My infamy has spread far and wide, it follows me wherever I go, I cannot escape it, and I know now that I shall never be free. People's expectations are like a set of heavy chains weighing me down. I am the villain in "the poor besotted king's tale," a warlock dabbling in the black arts, and my sex is my magic wand. It is common knowledge that I have cast a spell over Edward and they expect me to do the same to them, whether they are willing or not, they expect it just the same. I am a figure of dark fascination; they are at once frightened and intrigued. Even as I live, I have become a legend. And I have grown so weary of the world that I think I shall not be sad to leave it.

When I returned to England a few months later I tarried for a time in Cornwall. I did not go to Wallingford, I knew I would be recognized there and my presence betrayed, besides there was no need; we had arranged that Meg would go to York for her confinement. Instead I sought refuge in Grunella's cottage in the forest nearby.

I spent nearly a month in that tiny cottage. And it was a joy immeasurable to have this precious time with my daughter. To hold Amy in my arms, play with her, sing to her, and to have her near me every hour of every day. To watch her toddle across the earthen floor and pick her up and kiss away her tears when she toppled, to feed her porridge every morning, and lay her tenderly in her cot at nightfall. I treasure these memories, only, selfish creature that I am, I wish there were more of them!

As the time drew nigh for us to begin the journey to York so that I might keep my promise to Meg, a day came when my confidence and hope seemed to bloom anew. Grunella was away, birthing a babe, and I was sitting by the fire with Agnes, glorying in my new-cropped hair. I had bade her take the shears to it, and now it covered my head like a glossy black cap, baring my neck to the breeze. My head felt pleasingly light and Agnes and the little square mirror I held told me that it suited me and made me appear younger than my years.

"After the child is born," I said, as, with mounting excitement, I began to devise a new life, "you shall give me a henna rinse, Agnes, to lend it a reddish cast, and we shall away to Rome. I shall take a new name, as must we all. And you must bandage my hands as if they were newly burned, so that none shall link me with Gaveston. We shall invent a tragedy to explain it all and say that we have come to Rome on my physician's advice. I shall dress in celestial blue and be carried about the city on a litter; like any merchant I must show the goods I have for sale. And you shall be my grandmother, and Grunella shall come with us as nurse to my daughter. We shall take a fine house and bide our time while we wait for my hands to heal. Then I shall send for the finest glovemaker in the city and pick his mind; before I open shop I want to know who the best customers are, who to expect, who to avoid, and who to entice. And we shall see what fortunes the Holy City may hold for us. Rome is a fine city for courtesans, and I have heard there are many who fancy my kind there, and as a witch no one will expect me to go there; we will hide in plain sight! And I am still young and comely enough to make us another fortune! I am only seven years past twenty! But I must look to the future! I have worked *hard* to preserve my looks—all the baths, massages, creams and lotions, and the ivory picks, polishing cloths, herbal and vinegar mouthwashes, and spice comfits to keep my teeth clean and white and my breath sweet, the weekly enemas, daily exercise, and restraint at the banquet table to maintain my slender figure. I've always looked younger than my years, and I think, with the Lady's blessing, and if my luck holds, I have another ten years left before my value starts to fall. I'll make us rich again, Agnes, and this time I'll make it last; there will be no Lords Ordainers to take it away! And if we find that

Rome is not for us, then there is always Spain, and from there, if we like, we can take ship to some faraway exotic land, somewhere warm where the scent of cinnamon hangs in the air!" I clasped her hands. "There *must* be a place in the world for me; we have but to find it!"

"Aye, Child, and we *will!* But how are we to pay for this now that all your wealth has been taken from you?"

I smiled and held up my left hand. "*With this ring!*" The ruby cherry on its band of gold flashed in the firelight. "La Cerise! It is worth £1,000!"

"And you would part with it, my love?"

"It is like a ballast stone weighing me down and holding me steady to a course I would veer from, and I would be *free*, Agnes," I said adamantly, "*I would be free!*"

THE BEGINNING OF THE END

It was after midnight when Agnes and I forged our way across the snow-covered courtyard, the wind whipping at our cloaks, and our boots sinking ankle-deep into the snow. We made our way up the backstairs, Agnes preceding me to make certain the corridors were clear of those whom it would be in my best interest to avoid. But fortune was with us, the hour was late, and the night cold, so none who did not have to be were abroad.

I heard Meg's anguished cries and my heart froze.

"Come, Child," Agnes said gently, "like as not it sounds worse than it is. Sit you down by the fire now and I'll go in and see." And taking her old brown leather satchel, she hurried into the birthing chamber. A little while later she came to the door and beckoned me inside.

My poor Meg, she lay writhing upon the bed, clutching her stomach, her knees making twin tents beneath her shift which, despite the cold, was soaked with sweat.

The ladies attending her greeted my appearance with glowering eyes and deep frowns. The birthing chamber is a woman's domain and they resented my intrusion. And being all too familiar with my history, my presence was even more unwelcome. Just by being in England I was risking my life, like a common outlaw, there was a price on my head. "I daresay he trusts the Devil to protect His own!" I heard one of them whisper loudly as they made a great show of busying themselves around the hearth with the boiling water and stacks of clean linens.

"Piers!" Meg gasped and stretched out her hand to me.

I sat on the bed stroking her sweat-matted hair, kissing her tears away, murmuring soothing words, and holding her hand.

"I *knew* you would come!" she said, smiling through her pain. "I *knew* you would!"

I stayed with her until Agnes signaled that I must depart.

I do not know whether it was hours or moments I passed sitting, lost in thought, by the fire before the door opened and I heard an infant's weak, quavering, shrill cry. I came instantly alert and leapt to my feet.

"Another girl, my sweet," Agnes whispered as she placed the baby in my arms, "but we knew that all along!"

I could only nod; I was too overcome to speak. Indeed, I could do nothing but smile as I gazed down at my newborn daughter's red and crinkled face.

"She does not appear very lively," I said worriedly, tracing my fingers lightly over the sparse growth of carroty hair that covered her scalp.

"The birthing was long and arduous," Agnes reminded me.

"*Meg!*" I realized with a sudden pang of guilty alarm; I had not asked about Meg! "How fares she?"

"She's fine, Child, sleeping like a babe herself," Agnes assured me. "She's really not built for bearing and the strain wore her out."

"She *will* be all right?" I asked anxiously.

"Aye, though she may be some time in regaining her strength. Cease your worrying now, love," she slipped an arm about my waist, "and take joy in your beautiful new daughter!"

Lost in admiration, we did not hear the door open behind us and started at the familiar voice. My heart seemed to stop and sink like a stone and my blood ran cold as ice water.

"You do that very well," Edward remarked as he strode into the room in his purple velvet slippers and dressing gown. "To look at you one would think you had vast experience of holding babies!"

"Is Your Majesty implying something?" I asked, striving to appear nonchalant though my heart was beating like a drum. "Come look at my *beautiful* new daughter, Edward. She is to be called Joan after Meg's mother, your favorite sister."

"She looks like a very tiny bald and toothless crone!" Edward pronounced decisively with a grimace of distaste.

"*There! Now* see what you've done!" I fumed as Joan began to scream, her little red face scrunched up in rage and her tiny fists weakly pummeling the air. "And she is *not* bald; when she is older she will have a fine head of red-gold hair just like Meg!"

"Here, give her to me," Agnes directed, reaching out her arms to take the linen and lace swathed bundle.

"Yes, *do!*" Edward urged, fastidiously shooing Agnes and the mewling babe away. "And now, Piers," he turned back to me, "kindly explain what you have done to your hair!"

"Do you not like it?" I ran a hand over my glossy black crop. "I felt like a change so I bade Agnes cut it."

As soon as the door closed behind Agnes, Edward smiled and said confidently: "I *knew* you would come back to me."

"But you are mistaken, Edward. I have *not* come back to you. I came only for Meg, to keep my promise to her. I shall be leaving soon and you will see me no more. I have taken back my heart and mean to put the past behind me and start a new life."

With a sudden lunge Edward pinned me against the wall. The stone was cold against my back and I shivered. His hand caressed my face, from my brow to my neck where it came to rest, curling lightly round my throat.

In spite of myself, I felt the familiar stirring. I was aroused and Edward knew it and a smile of triumph spread across his face. I squirmed uncomfortably against the wall, *furious* with myself, trying to suppress the surge of desire I felt. I wanted to twist round and bash my head as hard as I could against the wall, but I was trapped, Edward held me fast.

"Look at me!" he ordered. "Tell me you do not love me and I will let you go!"

His grip tightened, reminding me just how easily the delicate bones in my throat might snap.

"I think that if I do you will strangle me."

"I think you are right," he nodded, his voice eerily calm as he subtly increased the pressure on my throat. "Tell me that you do not love me and you are free to go, to the Devil or anywhere else it may please you to go!"

"Will you believe me if I do?"

"No!"

"Then there is no point, it has long been my practice to only tell you lies that you are likely to believe."

"So you *do* love me then?"

"I suppose I do," I shrugged as his grip slackened, then before I could extricate myself from my uncomfortable position against the wall, his lips were pressed to mine, hard and bruising.

"Come to my bed, you have been absent from it far too long!" It was not an invitation, it was a command. He grasped the front of my tunic tightly in both hands and began backing towards the door, pulling me along with him, never noticing my expression of weary resignation or my leaden steps.

When I awoke I was in Edward's bed. It was morning and the pale winter sunlight was streaming into the room. I was alone except for a diamond brooch that was like an exploding star pinned on the pillow beside me.

Heedless of the cold against my naked skin, I went to the window and stood staring out at the feeble golden light, like a delicate coating of butter upon the snow. The door opened behind me, but I did not bother to turn round, if it were an assassin come to plunge a dagger into my back then so be it. If it were Edward better that I should act cold and aloof because I felt the distinct desire to murder him. I heard the clatter of breakfast dishes being set down, then the heavy fur coverlet was being whisked off the bed and draped around my shoulders.

"Child, whatever are you thinking of? You'll catch your death!" Agnes chided.

"I think we both know I already have. Death thy other name is Edward!"

There was a scroll lying upon my breakfast tray and I picked it up, expecting my usual reward of a castle or market dues. All the color drained from my face and my hands began to shake. I dropped the scroll as if it were searing hot and sank down onto the bed, hugging the fur coverlet close about me.

"Child, what is it? You've gone white as a ghost!" Agnes picked up the scroll and stood squinting down at the small, tightly formed black script as if sheer concentration could give her the power to read.

"My death warrant," I answered, and, taking it from her, I read aloud: "I Edward the Second, King of England by the Grace of God, hereby proclaim Piers Gaveston to be a good and loyal subject, and hereby restore to him the earldom of Cornwall and with it all the lands and titles previously held by him. Formerly exiled contrary to the laws and customs of the land, he has returned and stands ready to justify himself before his King."

I let the scroll fall from my hands. This time neither of us bothered to retrieve it. We sat silently upon the bed staring down at it as if it were a snake poised to strike us.

After that it all happened very quickly. Warwick and Lancaster began marshaling an army to march against us, using tournaments to hide their true intent and justify such large gatherings of armed men.

In desperation, I turned to the Earl of Richmond. For the first time, he failed to welcome me warmly and there was a rigid coldness about him that I had never seen before. And though esteemed as the perfect host, he offered me neither a chair nor a goblet of wine. Instead, we stood face to face alongside the table where our affair had begun, and I wondered if he was also remembering those two most interesting dinners and the "practiced tart of seventeen" he had spanked and the King's Favorite he had carted off to bed over his shoulder like a sack of grain. How time changes us! I marveled.

I took a deep breath and began: "I've come to ask your help. I want you to plead my case before the Lords Ordainers and explain that I came back only for Meg, because I promised her I would be with her when our child was born. It was never my intention to stay or to see Edward again! I planned to steal away as quietly as I came! Then Edward issued that accursed proclamation! By the Lady, I swear, I knew nothing about it before I saw it on my breakfast tray! And now I dare not set foot outside the King's protection! I would be hunted down and killed! I would willingly tell them myself but the very sight of me sends their anger soaring! But they will listen to you ..."

"I am sorry, Piers," he said abruptly. "I cannot help you."

"Cannot or will not?" I asked pointedly.

"Both. They would never believe that you came back for the wife you so shamelessly neglect. I'll wager I could count the number of times you've bedded her on one hand. Many jest that the conception of your daughter was immaculate; another virgin birth." I started to protest but he held up his hand. "I know you have had a fair number of women, Piers, including Lancaster's wife, but in the end it means nothing; it does not amount to evidence you can present to prove your husbandly devotion, far from it in fact. Nor would they ever believe that one so cynical and self-centered as you is likely to be sentimental about a child, especially a daughter. Granted, you display great affection for your greyhound, but that is neither here nor there. You are a luxury that has grown too expensive for this realm; find another protector, Piers, neither Edward nor I can afford you."

"It is a bitter blow to find you so cold and distant, My Lord," I said quietly. "I thought you loved me."

"Then you are rightly deserving of your reputation as a fool. We all make mistakes, Piers, and mine was ever to have become smitten with you. Since I do not believe in witchcraft, I can only ascribe it to a brief madness of which fortunately I am now cured, had it endured it might have cost me dearly. I will not be dragged down by or with you, Piers. Edward may do as he pleases but thankfully I have better sense. Goodbye, Piers, if you will excuse me, I have guests and I have neglected them far too long." And he returned to his bedchamber. As the door opened and closed I caught a glimpse of two young women, naked and giggling, in his great four-poster bed.

I stood there for a long time beside that table, feeling like the oak shattered after the lightning. Against my enemies I stood defenseless and alone. None with any influence would bestir themselves to help me. I knew better than to believe Edward that he would save me. Verily, I would not risk a penny bet on his succeeding!

NEWCASTLE

Pursued by Lancaster's army, we fled north, to Newcastle, taking the reluctant, and newly pregnant, Isabelle, and as much treasure as we could carry, with us. Edward was certain we would find supporters there aplenty, ready to rally to our cause, but he could not have been more mistaken.

It was at Newcastle that Isabelle and I reached an understanding. One afternoon when we sat playing chess by the tall arched windows overlooking the sea, she captured my king. She arched her brows and regarded me expectantly, no doubt expecting some insolent or witty rejoinder from me. But I merely smiled.

"I wish you well with him. Time has taught me that often the prize isn't worth winning."

Isabelle stared back at me, and I knew then that she understood. And with a nod and a knowing smile she answered: "It is the victory that matters most I think."

"Then the victory is yours, Madame."

"Methinks I find it cold," she said softly, gazing down at the ebony chessman in her hand.

"Allow me, Madame," I stood and, taking her velvet cloak from where it lay upon the hearth-side settle, draped it round her shoulders. Isabelle looked up at me, our eyes met, and we both knew it was the victory that she found cold; without Edward's love it meant *nothing* to her.

In spite of all our difficulties, Edward's spirits remained buoyant; truly he is endowed with the confidence and hope that is unique only to innocents, fools, and saints. While he plotted strategy, ate heartily, slumbered deep and peacefully, and urged me to be of good cheer—"Love conquers all, and victory shall be ours!"—I was consumed by weariness, anger, and despair. I could neither eat nor sleep. I felt desperate and caged and paced the floor for hours, gnawing my nails. Finally I could stand it no more and lashed out at Edward.

"You would kill me to keep me!" I railed. "*Why* did you issue that proclamation, Edward? *Why?* You *knew* I meant to go away again! Now I am trapped! They would kill me to make certain I could never come back! And it is *you*, Edward, who has signed my death warrant!"

"It was not a death warrant, my darling, it was a pardon!" Edward explained with an indulgent smile. "It was the *only* way I could keep you! I love you too much to ever let you go! I am hopeless without you, Piers!"

"Do not lay *that* charge upon me, Edward!" I rounded on him furiously. "You were hopeless *long* before you met me! Shall you cherish my corpse as much as you cherish this living body, I wonder? I shall soon be one; it is folly to think otherwise!" With that I turned and headed for the stairs.

"Do not say that!" He called after me. "You *know* I will not let anyone harm you!"

"Little King, as if *you* could prevent it!" I said contemptuously from the top of the stairs. "Oh Edward, face the truth for *once* in your life! If you said 'Boo!' to a goose it would not run; it would stand its ground and stare you in the face or else fly up and bite you on the nose!" I didn't linger to hear his reply, instead I returned to my chamber and slammed the door behind me and flopped wearily onto my bed.

By nightfall I was delirious, writhing and tossing upon my bed, on fire with a raging fever. Over and over again I dreamt of an hourglass, a most peculiar hourglass, as the sands were red. Then suddenly a broadsword would swing out of nowhere, out of the darkness, severing it in half, and at that moment the sands would turn to blood, spurting and spilling out, like a gurgling red fountain. Again and again I saw it. As I writhed upon my sweat-soaked sheets I kept sobbing: "*Please* make it stop! Make it go away!" In my delirium I babbled prayers to the Lady, called for my mother and Agnes, and screamed that I was burning. I kept seeing Warwick and Lancaster standing menacingly at the foot of my bed with devilish smiles and lighted torches which they slowly lowered and touched to the sheets.

Agnes never left my side, she was always there, applying cooling compresses, bathing my fiery skin, murmuring soothing words, and cajoling me to drink potions. And Edward kept vigil by my bed, every time I kicked the covers off he was there to draw them right back up again. He was so distraught that he summoned Dr. Bromtoft, the best medical man in the North. When he opined that if my fever rose any higher it would be necessary to shave my head Edward became hysterical, threw the Doctor's bag out the window, gave him two pounds as recompense, and shoved him out the door, leaving me entirely to Agnes's care. Of course, I am *very* grateful to him; I would not have liked to regain my senses only to find myself shorn. I daresay there are grounds for calling me vain after all, yet, I beg leave to remind you, I *never* said I wasn't!

Soon afterwards my fever broke. Edward was ecstatic and fell upon my weakened body, covering me with kisses until Agnes pulled him off by the tail of his tunic and put him from the room. I was in no condition to be subjected to that sort of thing, she pointedly informed him, she would ask him what he was thinking behaving like that, she continued, only she had known him long enough to know that he seldom bothered to think at all! And if he wanted to make himself useful he could go down to the kitchen and fetch up some chicken broth! Even as Edward uttered an indignant reminder that he was no lackey but King of England by the Grace of God, Agnes slammed the door in his face. I laughed until tears rolled down my face.

For days afterwards I lay weak and helpless as a newborn kitten. But the dream of the dreadful hourglass stayed with me, indeed, it has never left me.

One night when Edward had been persuaded that the danger was past and he could safely retire to his own bed, I was jolted awake by the vivid intensity of the dream. The shattering crunch as the sword severed the two halves of the hourglass, the tinkling of the glass shards as they fell, and the burbling of the sands turned to blood still echoed in my ears. I lay there trembling, freezing cold, despite the fur coverlet I hugged tight about me. My teeth chattered and an icy sweat layered my skin.

"The dream again, my sweet?" Agnes asked, leaving her chair by the fire and coming to cluck over me, bringing a basin of warm water to wash away the sweat then bundling me back into my blankets again.

"Will you get in bed with me?" I asked.

"Aye, of course I will, Child!" She climbed in beside me and I laid my head upon her shoulder.

"I am dying," I said softly.

"Now, Child, you mustn't say such things! You've been very ill, that's true, but you'll soon be yourself again!"

"*No, I do not want to!*" I said emphatically. "I no longer know *who* I am, only who people *think* I am, and I like that person no better than they do! Edward says: 'They love me not who hate my Gaveston!' but the truth is that even *I* hate

Edward's Gaveston! It's all gone *so* wrong, as if somewhere along the way a thread was pulled, causing my whole life to unravel, and leaving me with nothing but a bundle of gaudy threads!"

"Aye, Child," she nodded, "I know! This is *not* the life you should have had! Be patient only a little while longer and let your body heal and regain its strength. There *must* be a way for us to get out of England, and we shall find it, then we will start a new life."

"There is only a little time left to me," I said quietly. "It is what the dream means to tell me."

"Not all dreams are omens, Child," Agnes reminded me.

"I pray this one is not!" I sighed.

"As do I!" Agnes drew me closer and kissed my brow.

I was awakened at dawn by Edward's screams. He had tiptoed in to see how I fared and was horrified to find me sleeping soundly with my head on Agnes' shoulder. The way he carried on one would have thought he had found me murdered in my bed! His screams brought the whole guard rushing in with their swords drawn.

A few days later, when I was finally well enough to descend the stairs and sit by the fire in the Great Hall, a messenger burst in. Lancaster's army was at the city gates!

Edward was instantly at my side, grasping my hands, pulling me to my feet. There was not a moment to lose, we must flee, to Scarborough Castle; there I would be safe! It was impregnable, perched high upon the cliffs with the sea crashing beneath.

"But what of me?" Isabelle cried, following Edward around with a hand upon her belly to remind him of the child. But Edward had not a word or a care to spare for her, and I could do no more than glance back as Edward dragged me up the stairs.

"Forgive me for all the wrongs I have done you!" I implored. But I do not know whether she did; Edward chose that moment to give my hand an impatient tug and I never saw her face again.

We lingered only long enough for each of us to thrust a few things into a leather satchel. As I was leaving my chamber I impulsively turned back and, flinging open the chest at the foot of my bed, snatched up this book and thrust it deep inside my satchel. Something told me I had *one* chance left. I could not save my life, but I could leave the truth about it behind.

As soon as I stepped out my door Edward was there to grab my hand and drag me outside.

There was a rowboat waiting, rocking in the surf. My stomach lurched at the sight of it. I felt faint, my head throbbed, and stars danced before my eyes. I was on my feet and moving now only through sheer force of will.

"*Wait!*" I ordered, wresting my hand from Edward's bone-crushing grasp, and before he could stop me, I ran back and threw my arms around Agnes.

"This is the end! When we meet next it will be on the Isle of Apples!" I cried, ignoring Edward jumping up and down at the water's edge screaming my name. Mark my words, if somebody doesn't murder him he is sure to die of apoplexy!

"Oh Child!" Tears prevented Agnes from saying more as she gathered me to her and, for the last time, I lay my head upon her shoulder.

"*Piers!*" Edward's voice blared, carried on the wind. "*Get in the boat this instant! Piers! Do you hear me? Piers!*" With an impatient gesture he ordered the few guards who would accompany us to man their boats.

"Here!" I quickly unpinned my mother's brooch, the silver crescent moon paved with diamond chips. I pressed it into her hand and kissed her swiftly. "*I love you!*" I whispered fervently and we embraced one last time. Then Edward was there, demanding to know if I had suddenly gone deaf, tearing me from Agnes' arms, and dragging me back to the boat even as I would linger and look back.

"*Get in!*" He pushed me, and before I had time to settle myself he gave the boat a mighty shove, leapt in, and began to row.

I heard a dog bark and turned to see Blanche splashing through the surf, her ruby collar glinting in the sun.

"*Stop!* If you do not I shall jump out!"

"I believe you would!" Edward grumbled as he let the oars fall idle.

Blanche swam out to us, it was but a little distance yet I feared that at her age she would not make it. Edward divined my thoughts and leaned forward, poised to pounce; he knew I would not hesitate to go to her rescue. At last she reached us and I helped her clamber into the boat. Edward began to row as if his life depended on it while I dried her with my cloak.

Edward scowled when I kissed the top of her head. "I did not know she was capable of such exertion at her age. Yet lately I have learned that age is not always a deterrent where certain activities are concerned!"

I began to laugh then; it was *too* absurd! Here we were, fleeing for our lives in a rickety old rowboat with nothing but the clothes on our backs, the contents of our hastily packed satchels, and a white greyhound, who had just proven herself still spry at the age of twelve, and he was accusing me of being the lover of my lifelong nurse!

"Laugh if you like ..."

"Thank you, Your Most Gracious Majesty, I shall! After all, it *is* the usual response when someone says something absurd!"

"I *know* what I saw!" Edward shot back at me. "You kissed that woman! And oh how you clung to her! I was beginning to think that wild horses could not tear you apart!"

"Oh be silent, Edward! *You* have torn us apart and I shall *never* forgive you for it! This shall be the first time since I was born that Agnes and I have ever been parted for more than a few hours, she has even followed the army to be with me! And if you *truly* love me you will order one of those boats," I pointed to the two rowboats full of guards following us, "to turn back and bring her with us!"

"*Never!* For a dozen years I have endured the unnatural affection between you and your nurse! It is over now, Piers; you have no choice but to accept it!"

"*How dare you? How do you dare?* You accuse me of lying with the only person, besides my mother, who has ever truly loved me for myself, and never regarded me as an object of lust, ridicule, or contempt? Very well then, Edward, have it *your* way as you *always* do! I already stand accused of treason, sodomy, seduction, sorcery, nepotism, corruption, irreverence, and theft, and have been excommunicated twice, so why not incest as well? For that is how both Agnes and I would regard such a charge! And as you say," I smiled, "age is no deterrent; I once lay with a woman who was three years past eighty!"

Edward dropped his oars and had to go scrambling for them before the current carried them beyond his reach.

"*How could you do such a thing?*"

"Hold tight to your oars, Edward. The answer is a simple one, though I do not expect *you* to understand—I needed the money! *What?*" I sneered at his astonished stare. "*Surely* you did not think you were the *first* to have me?"

"Well ... I ..." Edward's face was all confusion. "I naturally assumed that when we lay together for the first time you were a virgin just like me!"

"Oh Nedikins!" I laughed. "You *are* naïve!"

"Was I the second then?" he asked hopefully.

Gleefully, I shook my head.

"The third?" he tried again. And again I shook my head. "The fourth? Fifth? Sixth? Seventh? Eighth? Ninth? Tenth? *Piers!* You were only *sixteen* when we met! Just how many lovers have you had?"

I smiled then and it gave me *great* pleasure to announce: "*Too many to count!*"

He let go of the oars then and lunged at me with an anguished scream, jerking me from my seat, his hands going straight for my throat. The boat dipped dangerously and water, salty and icy cold, came rushing in over me. It all happened so quickly that I did not have time to catch my breath, and oh how the water burned as it poured into my nose and throat and stung my eyes. Edward's grip slackened and I gasped, coughing and spluttering, retching, as I slowly sat up. My ears were ringing and I was dimly aware of Blanche barking.

Edward returned to his seat and resumed rowing. Shaking his head dejectedly, he asked with a plaintive wail: *"How could you do this to me?"*

"If you are referring to those who came before you, very easily, I did not even know you."

"That is no excuse!" Edward cried, whisking a sleeve across his eyes to wipe away the angry tears.

"On the contrary, I think it is the best excuse I ever gave you."

"I don't think either of us should say anymore," he said quietly and thus we continued our journey in silence.

SCARBOROUGH CASTLE

Scarborough Castle was a dismal sight, though majestic from a distance, perched high upon the cliffs above an angry sea, it was actually cold, dank, and ill-equipped to withstand even a short siege. My paltry band of supporters, including the faithful Dragon and my brother Guillaume, boastful and drunk and eager to protect the family's greatest asset lest he have to go back to soldiering for a living, were awaiting us when we disembarked from that accursed rowboat.

My other brothers, Arnaud and Raimond had gone scurrying back to Gascony the moment it was announced that I was banished from all English dominions before they too could be banned from their homeland. My star had fallen, so of what further use could I possibly be to them? Only Guillaume was willing to gamble on me. He said I was beautiful and clever, and that no one had ever starved possessing what I did. And if I lost the King, then maybe I could find a nice, amiable, and generous wine merchant to keep me.

The moment I stepped out of the boat my knees buckled and I collapsed, fainting, in the frigid surf.

My mind is a blur regarding the days that followed. All I know is that I was put to bed and Edward was far too busy being frantic, and jealous because I repeatedly called for Agnes, to dwell upon the revelations I had so recently made. And Edward has always excelled at forgetting that which he does not wish to remember. He rained kisses down upon my fevered brow and begged me to get well because he could not live without me.

Poor Edward, if you ever read these words I will be but a memory and you *will* be living without me. Believe me when I say that a year from now my features will have already begun to blur and dim in your memory's eye and a day *will* come when you realize that you cannot remember my voice. You will strive with all your might to recapture its essence, to hold onto it, but you cannot fight Time, for He is the greatest thief of all. And He *will* rob your emotions of their intensity, dry up your tears, and suture your broken heart until it is whole again though it will forever wear a bittersweet scar that, like an arrow-pierced limb though healed will ache whenever it rains, will feel a pang of wistful sorrow or regret whenever my ghost flits unbidden, forever beautiful, forever young, across your mind. Edward, you *can*, and you *will*, live without me!

The first day I was able, I left my room and went out into the salty air and sunshine. There was a spring on the castle grounds and there I washed the sea salt and fever sweat from my hair and skin and donned fresh clothing.

Edward came upon me as I stood in my white linen shirt, black hose, and leather boots, eyes closed, chin tilted up to the sky, breathing in the clean sea air, before I slipped my red wool tunic over my head. I was fastening my belt when I became aware of his presence.

"We come full circle," he observed. "You were dressed in a similar fashion the day we met."

"Red and black have always been my favorite colors," I reminded him.

"I remember how I sat there, so bored and languid, my eyelids drooping, and then …" As he looked back twelve years to that fateful day his smile was brighter than a summer's day, and his eyes … his eyes *were* love! "And then I saw *you!* I felt as if I had been shot through the heart, only it was no earthly arrow that pierced me, and not painful at all! I loved you then and I always will. Though I suppose it was naïve of me to have thought you felt the same. Did you ever *really* love me, Piers?"

"Yes," I answered, "if I have ever been in love it was with you. I will not lie to you, Edward; I did look to you to improve my circumstances, but I *did* love you; indeed, I loved you *so much* that I began to die a little inside each time you would reward me. I wanted something *more* from you than worldly goods and riches, Edward, and in the beginning I thought I had found it, but then my beauty got in the way, it dazzled your eyes and blinded you and made you forget all about *me* and my hopes and dreams. Loving me is expensive, Edward, and many men and women have paid dearly for my favors; lives, fortunes, and reputations have all been squandered for lust of me, but you alone made me feel cheap, and often even worse than cheap—*worthless!* All those jewels pinned upon my pillow and charters on my breakfast tray, it is richer, grander, but payment left upon my pillow is something I was accustomed to long before I met you. Did you never wonder how I lived so well on the pittance the army and your father paid me without any lands or inheritance from my family?"

"No," Edward admitted, "I feel very foolish now for not ... it was obvious you lived beyond your means—*you wore diamonds and ermine when you were sixteen!*—but you were *so* beautiful, I ... I was distracted!"

"I know, Edward," I said gently, "as the Lords Ordainers rightfully say, I have always been a distraction to you. And though I wanted something *meaningful*, something *useful*, to do, I *never* meant to interfere with the workings of the realm. I wanted to make your private hours, your pleasures, pleasanter still; I meant only to be your friend and lover, *not* the power behind the throne. Oh what I would not give to emerge from the shadow of Gaveston, The King's Catamite, The Gascon Upstart, The Devil's Minion, The Witch's Brat!" I said fervently. "I always meant to be *so much more* before I died, but now it is too late!"

"*No!*" Edward cried with the desperate gleam of madness in his eyes. "Do not say that! Tomorrow I leave for York! I will bring back reinforcements! We *will* win! You *must* believe that, Piers!" He grasped my shoulders and shook me hard. "You *must!* I love you! And when victory is ours, you shall sit beside me on the throne and wear a crown of rubies! You can design it yourself if you like; you have a flair for such things! And you will look *so* beautiful all the angels in Heaven will weep with envy! Or would you rather I gave up my throne? Ask and it shall be done! I *never* wanted to be King, so to give it up is no sacrifice! You mean more to me than *any* crown! Yes, that is what I will do! I shall give it all up and be free to spend the rest of my life with you! A wandering laborer I shall be, traveling the countryside with a pack of tools slung over my shoulder, taking work as I find it! And I shall skip, and prance, and sing as we go on our way, and at night we will sleep together beneath the stars, and we will be *so happy!*"

I shut my eyes and wished I could shut my ears to these insane ramblings.

"Edward," I said, irritable and tart, "I do not sleep beneath the stars unless they are painted on the ceiling or embroidered on the canopy above the bed!"

Undaunted, Edward smiled and clutched me tighter. "Then we shall carry a tent of blue satin embroidered with silver stars! Or would you prefer gold stars, my love? Whatever pleases you best! But, Piers," he said, the hysteria in his voice mounting, "you *must* believe, victory will be ours! You shall see, when I return from York I shall be at the head of a mighty army and we will vanquish them! You shall have the heads of Warwick and Lancaster on a golden platter! We will have them preserved and you can mount them on your wall, they will be your trophies! I love you, Piers, and you can have anything, or do anything, you want, you need only ask and it is yours! I would snatch the moon from the sky and present it to you on a velvet pillow if you asked me to!"

"*Then set me free!*" I shouted, shoving him as hard as I could, away from me.

"Anything but *that*, my love," he smiled as he shook his head and reached for me. "You belong *to me* and *with me*; I will *never* let you go!"

"Edward," I sighed, shaking my head in weary resignation. "*Oh, it is no use!*" I threw up my hands, and, shrugging free of his grasp, I called to Blanche and went back inside the castle. Granted it was a dreary place, but it matched my mood.

That night, our last together, I sat on the fur rug beside the hearth while Edward made ready for bed. He was leaving for York at first light, and I knew in my heart that we would never meet again, and I was both sorry and glad for it.

Love and hate, I think, are not so dissimilar. I often think of them as a circle, the two stand back to back and begin their respective journeys in opposite directions, hate traveling to the left, love to the right, but it is inevitable that they meet face to face. I have loved Edward, and I have hated him, I have despaired of him, and desired him. I have found him endearing and exasperating, often at the same time. We could live without each other, but only one of us will have that chance, and I hope Edward will make the most of it.

Edward came to kneel beside me. "When I return I will bring you a beautiful dressing gown trimmed with ermine!"

All my robes had been left behind at Newcastle; I had room in my satchel for only two changes of clothes, a few necessaries, some coins, jewels, and this book. I was thankful my black leather boots, though beautiful, were sturdy and newly made as they were the only shoes I had.

"I had much rather you brought Agnes; I can live without a robe, but I have need of her healing skill."

"*Only* her healing skill?" Edward asked dubiously.

"I cannot shake this fever, Edward! It is *always* with me! I am better for a day or two then I am back in bed again! My fever rises and falls, but never departs! I sleep only fitfully, I am plagued by nightmares, I have no appetite, my ears hurt, and my head aches constantly!"

"You just want to be coddled, and not by me!" he snapped petulantly.

"Believe what you like, Edward!" I sighed. "I know I shall never see Agnes, an ermine dressing gown, or you ever again so let us not quarrel about them now! And I have probably lost my health as well, not that it matters since I shall soon be killed; my life snuffed out like a candle, it is folly to think otherwise!"

"Piers, I promise you, if you do as I say no one will harm you!" Edward insisted irritably. "It is perfectly simple: just stay inside the castle until I come back with my army and I will bring you many fine things, including, if you insist, your wretched Agnes!"

"If I stayed in this castle until you returned with an army you would not even find my skeleton as my bones would already have crumbled into dust! You should have let me go when I had the chance! Now even if I swore upon my mother's ashes that I would depart this realm forever nary a soul in England would believe me!"

"You want to leave me!" Edward, on the verge of tears, accused.

"Dearest Edward, I am weary of this life!" I took his hand in mine and very patiently explained. "I have lived too fast in too brief a span. Though I am but seven-and-twenty I feel ancient and decrepit inside. You who have so much life can never understand, but my strength, my vitality, is gone. I would have liked to have lived, to start anew and travel far away, perhaps to some exotic land of sunshine and spices, where the scent of cinnamon hangs in the air. I still have my mind, and in time I might have regained my health enough to compete in tournaments again. And there are many beds in the world, and when I saw my reflection in the spring today it told me, though thin and pale and wan, I still have what it takes to bring the coins in. Edward, *I implore you*, as you love me, send for the Earl of Pembroke, though he despises me he is also a man of honor and integrity. I will humbly beseech his pardon for any offense I have given him. And you will renounce me and swear that you will have nothing more to do with me, and England shall evermore come first and foremost in your mind and heart. We will say goodbye and *mean it* and have *nothing* to do with each other *ever* again! This too may end in failure; Pembroke may refuse to intercede, but, if you *truly* love me, Edward, you will love me enough to try, and make an earnest attempt to save my life."

"But my darling, I *will* save you!" Edward insisted. "At dawn I leave for York, and soon I will return at the head of a mighty army ..."

"*Edward,*" my eyes filled with tears. "*Please, I beg you, let me live!*"

"Piers," he grasped my shoulders and shook me hard. "*Listen* to me! You *shall* live, I *promise*, you *shall!*"

"No, Edward," I shook my head resignedly, "not in any *real* sense, only in your heart, and as an infamous legend; I have already ceased to exist as anything else. And very soon now, not only the world, but I too, shall be free of the hated Gaveston." I stood up and walked over to the bed. "You can make love to me if you like," I offered with an indifferent shrug. "I think that is how you would prefer to remember me; it is how you have always thought of me, and it *is* our last night."

Never one to quibble about the spirit in which such an invitation is made, Edward tackled me in a breathless rush and together we fell onto the bed, sinking into the soft feather mattress in a tangle of naked limbs. Not even our sorry plight or my despair could dampen Edward's ardor. He was as passionate as I have ever known him to be.

I did not sleep at all that night. While Edward slumbered blissfully with his head upon my shoulder and a contented smile upon his lips, I lay awake with a river of tears running down my face.

I wept because this last night of love should have been poignant, both bitter and sweet, and yet I felt *nothing*, nothing at all. No pleasure or pain, love or hate, anger or desire. We had indeed come full circle and I had found myself back where I started from, merely going through the motions to satisfy a lover, pretending a passion I did not feel to disguise the emptiness inside. I am sorry, Edward, *I am so sorry!* But we have dragged this out far too long; it really is time to say goodbye, in truth, we should have said it some time ago! The truth is you fell in love with a fantasy, an illusion; we both did. Neither of us could in reality be what the other expected. I failed you, Edward, and you failed me.

In the gold-tinged gray light of dawn, Edward stood beside the bed buckling on his sword.

"I shall not say goodbye as I shall be back before you have even begun to miss me!"

I did not speak because, in truth, there was nothing to say; to disagree would only lead to more futile arguments.

Edward stroked my hair and lovingly arranged the fur coverlet to keep the morning chill at bay.

"You are my treasure and I swear no man or woman shall ever harm or take you from me!" Then he kissed me and, grinning broadly and squaring his shoulders, took up his satchel, and stepped confidently out into the dawn.

"I shall love you till my dying day!" he declared before he shut the door.

I still remember how bright and sure his smile was. He *truly* believed he would save me when in truth he had no more power than a kitten tied in a sack and thrown into the river to drown. We were both doomed, but only I could see that; Edward was blissfully blind. Only when the truth comes crashing down upon his head will he at last confront it.

SURRENDER

May 18, 1312

For ten days we have been under siege. Ten days since Edward left me though it seems more like ten years. There are days when I take to my bed and my mind takes flight. I writhe and cry out in delirium, and a blood-filled hourglass and a menacing, glinting broadsword stalk my dreams. Time blurs and becomes meaningless and jumbled. Were it not for Dragon, who faithfully attends me, I would have no notion of how many days have actually passed. And he assures me that it has been ten days since Edward left for York.

He shall never return to me. Lancaster has maneuvered his army so that it stands, a formidable barrier, betwixt Scarborough Castle and York, while Pembroke's army lays direct siege to this castle, patiently awaiting the inevitable—my surrender.

We were ill-equipped to start with and time has not improved our position. Our provisions and morale are low. Guillaume constantly reminds me that Arnaud and Raimond ran away, while he has remained and hopes to be rewarded for it when I triumphantly resume my place at Edward's side. And every night a few more of my supporters slink away, like rats deserting a sinking ship. But I bear them no malice. I have known all along that I am not worth fighting for.

Every siege must come to an end, and I have decided that tomorrow this one shall end. I have sent word to the Earl of Pembroke that I am ready to discuss terms. Now I must return to my bed. My flesh is on fire with fever and my head is a throbbing agony. Dragon waits now to help me back to bed. Often if I rise too quickly the walls begin to dip and sway and the floor rises up to meet me. So now I will lay down my pen until after I have seen Pembroke.

May 19, 1312

It is over. Pembroke has just left me. I was unable to meet him on my feet as I intended. Instead, I lay upon a velvet chaise, listless and aching, in my red wool tunic and black hose. Still, it was better than receiving him unkempt, unclad, and unshaven in my sickbed, I consoled myself.

"My Lord, I thank you for coming. I apologize for the manner in which I receive you. It is not indolence, I assure you, only illness."

Pembroke eyed me warily. "Gaveston, these evasive tactics will avail you naught. You would do better to surrender now. You cannot last much longer; I know your provisions are nearly gone, your men are deserting you, and all the King's attempts to raise an army have failed. He has even besought Robert the Bruce to shelter you in Scotland and promised the King of France and the Pope that he will relinquish all English claims to Gascony and give it to them if they will come to your aid, but they both refused. *No one* will fight for you Gaveston; you are alone against the world!"

"Verily, I know it well!" I sighed. "That is why I asked you to come, My Lord, to discuss terms; I would be done with this! I have neither the strength nor the inclination to see this further drawn out. Will you treat fairly with me and guarantee my personal safety until the time comes for me to plead my case before Parliament?"

Pembroke took a step closer and gingerly laid a hand upon my brow. "*You really are ill!*"

"I would not feign illness, My Lord. Like you, I have no patience for evasions and delays. I ask only that you safeguard my person until the time comes for me to stand trial and that what supporters I have left be allowed to re-provision this castle and remain here until summer's end if they so desire it."

"Agreed," Pembroke nodded solemnly. "I swear no harm shall come to you while you are in my care."

"Thank you, My Lord. I know you are a man of honor, and I am content."

Pembroke stood over me, staring down at me for what seemed like a long time, and then he shook his head and sighed. "You look *so* young and vulnerable lying there; it is hard to believe you could be the cause of so much trouble!"

"I know you will not believe me," I said softly, bitterly, "but I never meant to be. Do you know why I came back this last time?"

"Because you cannot keep away; the lure of the King's bounty proved too strong for you to resist! *What? You laugh?*" he asked incredulously.

"Yes, My Lord," I nodded, "I laugh because I meant to have gone away again before Edward even knew I had returned! It is *over* between Edward and I, even if *he* cannot see it, and it has been for some time! I came back only because I promised my wife I would be with her when our child was born. She is so young and sweet and good and deserves a husband far better than I, but she thinks she loves me! It was only by mischance that Edward and I met again. I told him that I meant to go away again, that I had *not* come back to him, but he didn't believe me, he ignored me, and the next morning there was that proclamation on my breakfast tray, and I was trapped! Had I set foot outside the King's protection I would have been set upon and killed! I sought the Earl of Richmond's aid, but he would not help me! All I wanted was to leave! I want no more of Edward or his bounty! He can take it all and stuff a Christmas goose with it!"

Pembroke stared at me long and hard then nodded slowly. "I believe you. I never thought the day would come when I would say this, but I believe you. I can make you no promises, Gaveston, but I will recommend that you be allowed to depart the realm, but ..."

"I know, My Lord, I have come and gone so many times that my words no longer ring true, but I thank you just the same. It means much to me to know that you believe me." Using my elbows, I levered myself up into a sitting position. "Shall I come with you now?"

Pembroke shook his head and gestured for me to lie back. "Rest now, and try to recover your strength, you will have great need of it in the days to come. But you need have no fears regarding your safety. I give you my word that I shall protect you; I swear upon my honor, my life, and all that I possess."

"Thank you, My Lord, truly it is more than I deserve!"

"I am a fair man, Gaveston, but not a cruel one," he said and then apprised me of his intentions. He would convey me to Wallingford and there place me under heavy guard until the time arrived for Parliament to adjudge my fate. My men must either remain in this castle or go their own way as none of them would be allowed to accompany me. "But you may bring your dog," he offered, nodding to Blanche napping at my feet. "We shall leave tomorrow if you are able. Have you sufficient provisions to afford you a proper dinner? Very well," he nodded when I answered in the affirmative, "I shall bid you good evening then."

He lingered for a moment, gazing down at me, his brow furrowed thoughtfully, quizzically, then he sighed, shook his head once more, and left me.

Truly the terms are more generous than I ever hoped or expected! Perhaps there is a small glimmer of hope left for me after all! Pembroke's wisdom and integrity are greatly respected, and if *he* believes me ... but I dare not let my hopes ascend too high, for if nothing should come of them then the harder and greater the fall. Until then I must go on as best I can. I am thankful it is ended. I am tired of running, it is time for me to go out and meet my destiny. I must face life, even if it means death!

In The Dungeon Of Warwick Castle

I keep hearing Blanche's whimper and the sickening snap of her delicate bones when The Black Dog broke her neck, grasping it viciously and twisting it, savagely, a smile upon his lips and his eyes upon me all the while.

I know, I have strayed too far afield. Forgive me; it is not my intention to confuse. But there is so little time left, and my mind and body are in torment! If I ramble, or my thoughts appear disordered, there *are* reasons, and, as so many have before, I hope you will indulge me.

Warwick has just had the supreme pleasure of informing me that today, the 19th of June, 1312, will be my last. I die tonight on Blacklow Hill. My head shall be stricken from my body. The Welshman delegated to perform the task has powerful arms, the broadsword is newly sharpened, and I have a little neck, so no one afterwards will be able to say that I suffered unduly. This is about Justice, after all, *not* revenge!

No beam of sunlight reaches me here in the dank, dark bowels of Warwick Castle. I am sorry for that; I would have liked to see the sun one last time. But now I must tell how I came to be here in The Black Dog's dungeon, for when last I wrote I was bound for Wallingford in the protective and courteous custody of the Earl of Pembroke.

I left Scarborough Castle in a litter. Pembroke had seen for himself that though I felt better at times I was never truly well. As we descended the stairs from my bedchamber I became lightheaded. Pembroke himself reached out to steady me and sat down beside me on the stairs and waited patiently for my faintness to pass.

I must say this *now*, Edward, lest Warwick's eagerness for my death brings this chronicle to an abrupt end. Do not hold the Earl of Pembroke accountable for what has befallen me, and though he pledged all upon my safety, do not punish him. He was *kind* to me, Edward, and treated me far better than I had any right to expect from a man who is my sworn enemy. Make a friend of him, Edward; trust in his advice, he will not fail you. And *please* tell him, for me, that I am grateful beyond words for the countless little kindnesses he showed me while I was in his care. I hope you will honor my request; after all, it *is* my last.

We traveled slowly, over the course of many days. Some days I was too ill to travel at all, even in the litter, and we lingered at various abbeys and castles along the way. Some days I was well enough to sit a horse, though Pembroke always kept me close and a sharp eye upon me lest I become faint and fall. But mostly I lay hidden behind the velvet curtains of the litter with Blanche beside me.

She was such a comfort to me, Edward! If only I could go back to the day I departed Scarborough and entrust her to Dragon's care! My selfishness has wrought the death of one whose love and loyalty I never for an instant doubted! Of all the gifts you ever gave me, Edward, none ever meant more to me than Blanche. And she is the only one that cannot be replaced. Twice I have had my earldom taken and restored to me, but it is not in your power, O Gracious Majesty, to give me back my dog!

At the little village of Deddington we stopped for the night. Pembroke reined his horse in alongside mine and, laying a hand upon my shoulder, said: "You are weary and need rest. There is a little village near here, Deddington, it is called, it is a pleasant place, and you will be comfortable."

He saw me settled at the rectory. We dined together. Then, as it was but a short jaunt to Bampton where his wife was staying, he decided to go and pass the night with her. And he bid me good night, never knowing that it was actually goodbye.

I know how your mind works, Edward, so I'll say it plain, lest you spend the rest of your life wondering. He was never my lover. But *never* think for a moment that I did not want him to be! We had conversations, Edward, *real* conversations! Not endless musings and delighted exclamations about my beauty, or suspicious scoldings and ranting rages about my infidelities and affection for my nursemaid, wife, and dog! No, Edward, music, art, poetry, philosophy, medicine, nature, religion, statecraft, finance, war, and history were the things that occupied our minds and tongues, not lust and lascivious kisses! He was surprised to find me so well read. And I made him laugh! He did not want to, but first a small smile betrayed him and then a chuckle escaped him! I did it; I made him laugh and smile *at me!*

He often sat with me when I was ill. He talked to me and placed cold compresses upon my brow even though the Earl of Warenne urged him to "let the fever take him; it will save us all a great deal of bother!" And on nights when I was well but sleep still eluded me, he came to me and we talked and played chess or cards.

I was never put into a dungeon. I was always given a proper bedchamber, comfortable but secure, with a pair of guards outside the door and below the window, and Pembroke's own valet was ordered to attend me. At the abbeys and castles where we lodged Pembroke often sat or walked with me in the gardens; it would calm me, he thought, and could not fail to do me good. And he would let no one, not soldiers, servants, or the commonfolk, mistreat or disrespect me. And though I was his prisoner, he would not suffer me to be chained, no matter how much others insisted upon it.

I will not lie to you, Edward, not now when I feel Death looking over my shoulder. I *wanted* him, as sick, wretched, and weary of life as I am, *I wanted him; I wanted him to love me!*

I've had *so many* lovers, Edward. The wine merchant who adored me beyond measure until the first tiny curls began to sprout from my crotch. The furrier who liked to take me upon a blanket of his finest sable, then afterwards, so ashamed of his lust was he, that he would fling a handful of coins at me and order me out even though we both knew that scarcely a week would pass before he would have me back again. The lawyer who had me serve as clerk in his four-poster bed, taking dictation while using his back as a desk. The randy Scottish widow who liked to bathe me, kneeling on the hearth with a lost look in her eyes as she reminisced about her dead son, who, had he survived the fever, would have been exactly my age, while her hand dipped beneath the water, upon which crushed lavender bobbed. Amerigo dei Frescobaldi, the Florentine banker, classed as a nefarious foreign moneylender by the Lords Ordainers, we coupled on the coin-strewn floor of his counting house. The lord and lady who brought me into their bed to amuse them both then ended up quarreling like cats, rolling on the floor and pulling each other's hair, because each thought I enjoyed pleasuring the other more, when in truth I disliked them both in equal measure. The bishop who decided it was time to be rid of me because the fear of discovery made his knees tremble. I found being his "guilty pleasure," as he called me, so profitable that I leaned back in my chair and pouted: "I am jealous of this fear; *I* used to be the only one who could make your knees tremble!" And, slipping off my shoe, I eased my foot beneath his cassock and made him smile. The amiable and elegant earl who spanked "the practiced tart of seventeen" yet sought his favors six years later when he reigned as Regent and Royal Favorite. I thought his affection genuine, yet he abandoned me when I needed him most of all. The King who loved me more than life itself, yet never truly knew or understood me; he was too blinded by my beauty to actually *see* me. And all the gullible fools who bought my virginity; so many times I've gasped in feigned delight: "*Oh!* I've *never* done *this* before!" And the women who vied to be the one to wean me from masculine caresses; they never understood that it was only the coins, not the caresser, I cared for. And all the lovers whose savage, single-minded thrusts left me sore and made me bleed, and the hours I spent afterwards lying on my stomach waiting for sleep while Agnes massaged me and a clyster made from her special recipe nestled inside me, slowly melting from my body's warmth, soothing the irritation, and bringing me blessed relief.

And there have been so many others, countless others, so many whom I could name, but I will not. My time grows short, and I am weary of this game. So look for the rest of your life at every man and woman who crosses your path, Edward, and wonder if they had me; that is my gift to you!

But do not punish or despise Pembroke because I desired him. Blame *me*, Edward, as beautiful as I am, blame *me!* Realize for the first time in your life that beauty is not grounds for absolution; it does not stand as a surety for love, truth, honesty, constancy, or anything at all. It is just one more roll of Destiny's dice that determines whether we come into this world beautiful, grotesque, or simply plain, and we never know until it is too late whether we have won or lost the game; whether our appearance is a blessing or a curse. Which is worse, I have often wondered, to go through life never being wanted at all, or to be wanted for all the wrong reasons? Well the time to ponder philosophy has passed, and I have let my thoughts stray from my story when I need to tell how I came to be in this wretched place.

After Pembroke left me at Deddington Rectory I lay upon my bed. When sleep finally came it was fitful and filled with terrors—the hourglass and broadsword, the stake in the heart of the crackling orange flames, the priest's voice thundering "*Thou shall not suffer a witch to live!*", Warwick's snarling face, a low growl issuing from deep within his throat, and Lancaster's malevolent glare of soul-devouring hate. And then I realized that I was *not* dreaming. Exhaustion and fever had lulled me into a peculiar state where my mind seemed to float just beneath the waters of sleep, bobbing to the surface one moment and below the next. But these were no dream figures standing at the foot of my bed! They were *real!* And it was not Warwick who growled, but Blanche, crouched protectively at my feet, teeth bared.

"*Traitor!*" Warwick roared. "*Get up! You are taken!*"

Blanche began to bark and it was then that he took hold of her neck. It all happened so quickly, that savage, sickening snap of bones and the single shrill yelp abruptly become a whimper. He left her lying dead, white and limp, across my feet.

"*The Black Dog has come to keep his promise that you shall feel his bite!*" Warwick barked as he motioned for two of his men to seize me and drag me naked from my bed.

"*I told you to get up!*" Warwick snarled, sweeping disdainful eyes over my body. Suddenly he stepped forward and drove his fist hard into my stomach. I fell to my knees, gasping, bent double and breathless with pain.

"You try my patience, Gaveston! Did you not hear me tell you to get up? Make haste, man, and dress yourself or we shall take you as you are! Perhaps the good people of England would like to see the charms that have enslaved their foolish King?"

I staggered over to the chair where my satchel sat with the clothes I had worn that day draped over it. I had barely slipped my linen shirt over my head before Warwick grumbled: "No doubt you are accustomed to this leisurely manner of dressing, Gaveston, but we have neither the time nor the patience for it! *Take him!*" No sooner had the words left his lips than there was a guard on either side of me, gripping my arms.

"My Lord, I protest, I am the Earl of Pembroke's prisoner not yours!" But my words fell on deaf ears; Warwick simply turned his back and strode from the room with the gloating, jubilant Lancaster trailing after him.

As I was hustled out into the night, barefoot and wearing nothing but my shirt, I noticed another guard—Geoffrey, I later learned his name was—stuff my clothes and boots into my satchel and swing it over his shoulder. For this I have much cause to be grateful. Today my possessions were restored to me so that I may die decently clad. And, since this book was inside, I am able to finish what I began. Geoffrey has promised to deliver it to Agnes and ask her to see it safely into Edward's hands. And if he keeps his promise, Edward, for better or worse, you shall read these words. And perhaps in death you shall come to understand me as you never did in life, for this body you love so shall rot, ripen with a noxious stink, and no longer dazzle your eyes!

They loaded me with such a surfeit of chains it would have been a hard burden for a broader built man in the full bloom of health to bear. "Just as His Majesty loaded you with jewels," they chortled. "Imagine them gold, Gaveston, it will help you bear the weight better!"

I was not allowed to mount a horse but made to walk instead. Soon the sun rose, blazing hot and scorching bright. And the curious came to throng the roadside to see the King's Favorite scantily clad, walking barefoot and in chains behind Warwick and Lancaster, sitting tall and proud, haughty and triumphant, in their saddles, their silver armor shining in the hot June sun. The people cheered them, blessed them and threw flowers, while they cursed, spat, and laughed at me.

Once Lancaster looked back and cautioned: "Stay on your feet, Gaveston; if you fall we will not stop for you!" And I knew he spoke the truth.

The hard dirt road was so hot it burned my feet, and it was badly strewn with ruts and rocks. Again and again, I stumbled and gasped as sharp stones stabbed the soles of my feet. When I looked back over my shoulder I saw the footprints I left behind me were red.

As we traveled, word spread and the crowds swelled. They made up songs to "let the glorious news be spread! The land, sea, stars, and all mankind rejoice in his fall! There will be peace and rejoicing throughout the realm when evil Piers, with all his charms, is dead!" Others blew their hunting horns and raised their tankards in toasts "now that the peacock has lost his splendor!"

One bold matron darted forward and lifted my shirt, saying she wanted to see the cock and balls that were the King's favorite toys. And, not satisfied with this glimpse, she tore a long, ragged strip from the hem to keep as a souvenir. I was powerless to stop her, and the others who followed her, as my hands were chained behind my back.

At last the procession halted and a pitiful little white donkey was brought for me. "An ass for an ass!" those about me quipped. It was not an act of mercy, but of expediency; all games grow tiresome after a time. There was no saddle and the donkey's hide chafed my flesh and brought me fresh agony. And it was such a dainty beast that my feet scraped the ground. I tried to draw up my knees and at the same time struggled not to fall with my hands still bound behind my back.

When we reached Warwick Castle they took off my chains and I was cast into the dungeon. Exhausted and aching, I lay upon the cold stone floor, welcoming its chill against my burning flesh. But they were not done with me yet. Some of Warwick's men elected to sample "The Favorite," to see what all the fuss was about. Their actions were not born of lust but of a desire to hurt and humiliate.

They were brutal and coarse, peppering my body with blows and kicks, ramming their cocks into me, tearing my skin, and making me bleed. But through it all they took special care to leave my face unmarked, "so the King will be sure and recognize his minion when we send your head back to him!" It would have been futile to resist, I was weary and weak, and there were too many of them, so I lay submissive and still, and bit my fist to suppress my screams. I was thankful for the darkness that hid my tears. Then it was over. Chuckling heartily and clapping each other upon the back, they filed out to reward themselves with a flagon of ale. And I was left alone in darkness.

I lay on my stomach, striving to stay still, for each movement, no matter how slight, brought fire-tipped arrows of pain. Even if by some miracle my life were spared, I think I would die anyway. I think their blows and kicks may have broken or burst something inside me, there is such pain in my stomach, sides, and back, and when I must ease my bladder there is yet more pain and blood. And the soles of my feet fester and throb in a way that reminds me of the day my hands were burned.

Here in this dungeon there is no bed or blankets for me, not even straw, only hard stone floors and walls that ooze with dampness and stink, and a pair of torches mounted in iron sconces too high to afford much light or offer even a vestige of warmth. The cold no longer feels good against my skin. I never realized how difficult it is to remain still.

As I lay there, my body broken and shivering, I endeavored to stave off the pain with my mind. I thought of my daughters, Amy and Joan. It brought me a measure of bittersweet comfort to remember holding them. Amy used to try to teethe on "La Cerise," she was like a little magpie, her bright eyes and eager little hands always going straight for my jewelry. I shut my eyes and tried to imagine both my daughters as women grown. Joan, delicate-boned and slight, with an air of fragility and milk-pale skin, and a wealth of red-gold hair cascading down her back. And Amy, with her black hair and eyes; Agnes says she is the image of me and my mother combined. I hope she will grow up a loyal daughter of the Goddess, and that Grunella will teach her about the Isle of Apples and how to heal with herbs, so that my mother's beliefs, and my own, will live on and the circle will not be broken. And, on a more frivolous note, when she is of an age to take an interest in such things, I hope she will favor gowns of red and black and love rubies just like me.

And then my thoughts turned to Meg, almost eighteen, and so soon to be a widow. She will look *beautiful* in black! Forgive me, I know I should not be flippant at a time like this; but my wit is the only weapon that is left to me. Do not cry for me, my sweet, I am not worth your tears. You have a good heart, Meg; you should find someone worthy to share it with, someone who *knows* how to love and will never take you for granted. You *deserve* to be the cherished center of someone's world! Do not be like some widows and consecrate your life to the memory of your dead husband. Forget me, and, if you can, forgive me!

I longed to be tended by Agnes, to have my wounds dressed and to be given a potion to dull the pain. I wanted to be bathed, to be cleansed of all the blood, dirt, filth, spit, semen, and sweat. And, most of all, I *longed* to lay my head upon her shoulder one last time. Agnes is the only one who will truly mourn me because she is the only one who really *knows* me. She knows *why* I am what I am, and she knew me long before I became notorious. Her hands brought me into this world; she *knows* I am not evil.

And, though I would much rather forget, I thought of John, Earl of Richmond. Rarely have I ever felt so hurt and betrayed. Indeed, Edward, no one but you has ever wounded and disillusioned me more! But I will not let the veil of pain prevent me from seeing the truth and telling it plain. We were lovers, but we were never *in* love. We were comfortable together, our affection, I thought, was warm and deep. I was *furious* when he spanked me, but later I thanked him for it. With this gesture he showed that he thought more of me than I did of myself. And in the years that followed, although we did often comport ourselves like randy beasts, there were talks, and walks, and so much laughter, and always, when we were apart, long letters. He never belittled me or dismissed some issue of statecraft or a scientific or philosophical concept as being too complex for my untutored mind to grasp. I always thought we would go on forever. I thought we were happy together. Verily, I have searched my mind and there was nothing to suggest it would end as it did! Did he ever, I wonder, truly care for me? Was I just another conquest? Or was I just a joke? Did he secretly laugh at me? *I'm so tired of all these games!* The players take their masks off and no one is really who or what they pretend to be! Were I to go on living, never again would I believe in anyone's sincerity. If it happened once, it *can* happen again! Trust no one, lock up your heart and throw away the key! The pain of loneliness is sharp, but the pain that comes with losing someone you love and trust is sharper, especially when you discover that it was all a lie. Trust and Love, they are a Fool's game, and I'm glad to be dealt out, even if it is by Death. I don't want to play anymore. I'm tired.

And yes, Edward, I thought of you. I know by now you must be wondering if I had a thought left to spare for you. In truth, I thought of you a great deal. And

I have tried hard not to be bitter and resentful at the end. But I have failed, so I will take my thoughts with me to the grave.

From the length of the stubble bearding my face some days must have passed before the guard Geoffrey came to me. I lay motionless and taut as he knelt beside me and laid a hand upon my back. Throughout my life I have been touched by a great many men and women, and at interpreting their desires I have become adept. This man would have me, whether I wished it or not, and I needed an ally in this place. I had two desires left—to die clean and decently clad and to ensure the delivery of this book—so I did what was required.

I took a deep breath and forced myself to concentrate, to see myself as I was before I came to this sorry fate. In my mind's eye I saw myself standing before my silver mirror, freshly bathed, my face clean-shaven and my hair newly washed and combed sleek, my body healthy and strong, slender and seductively arrayed in emerald brocade, glistening with golden threads, with a belt of gold roses with diamond centers about my waist, rings on my fingers, and jeweled chains about my neck. I held this picture in my mind and willed myself to roll over onto my back.

Pain flashed like lightning along my spine and I nearly fainted, but then I remembered the secret for enduring pain. Agnes had taught it to me when I was seven, when she maneuvered my shoulder back into its socket and tended my burned hands. As I remembered her words it was as if I heard her dear voice speaking to me out of the darkness: "Pain is like an ocean, Child, wild and roiling. You *cannot* fight it! When you try to swim against the current it only tires you, and in the end it will drag you down! You must go *with* it, Piers, swim *with* the pain!" I pictured the pain as a stormy, churning ocean and myself as a lone swimmer, flowing with the current, letting it carry me. Then, reverting to the vision of myself, elegant in all my former glory, I looked up at Geoffrey and laid my hand upon his chest.

"Pleasure," I said with a knowing smile and a look of invitation in my eyes, "can be taken by force or given freely."

Geoffrey smiled and called me "a little slut" as I drew him down to me and kissed him, nipping his bottom lip playfully between my teeth.

I have been a whore since I was nine, Edward; I know *all* the tricks of the trade. I made him think I desired him. But when he rolled me over and I lay upon my stomach while he had his way with me I bit my fist until I tasted blood and tears coursed down my face. And I thought of *you*, Edward; *make of that what you will!*

Soon afterwards I was dragged up to the Great Hall to face my judges. I stood before them with the tattered remnants of my shirt tied round my waist, filthy, naked, bearded, and bruised. To combat the shame, I did as I had done with Geoffrey and imagined myself in peacock splendor. I held my head up high; I would not grovel or give way to tears! I would not beg for my life! Indeed, I did not account it worth begging for!

"I have no help, every remedy is in vain, so let the will of the earls be done!" I said tartly and let them prattle on about my alleged treason while I yawned and rolled my eyes.

I shall not dwell upon the charges; they have all been stated before. The verdict was a bygone conclusion, and I was quickly condemned to die.

"From being just a tiny spark of light you became a blazing star outshining all the rest! Now we shall put out that light forever!" Lancaster proclaimed.

A little while later, Warwick descended into the dungeon. "This is your last day, Gaveston," he announced, "use it well; you've a rendezvous with the headsman tonight on Blacklow Hill, so prepare your soul. Shall I send you my priest?"

"*I want no priest of yours!*" I said hotly.

"Well pray to the Devil then," he shrugged.

After Warwick left me, Geoffrey brought my satchel and warm water. I was surprised to find my gem-encrusted book and some coins still inside, but as he pointedly informed me: "We are men bent on seeing Justice done, not thieves and scavengers like you, Gaveston!"

It was a laborious process, I was in so much pain, but he helped me bathe and dress then shaved my face for me. I chose a simple but fine black cloth tunic, black silk hose, and a leather belt decorated with silver filigree in a pattern of crescent moons and lilies. And since I would not be needing it again, and the collar would only impede the sword, I tore my spare shirt into bandages and wrapped them round my feet before drawing on my boots. Thus arrayed for death, I sat down to finish this memoir, content with the knowledge that I die worthy of the portrait painter.

I will never disillusion or disappoint you, Edward, by growing ugly or old. I will remain frozen in time, like a dragonfly caught in amber, perpetually on the threshold of eight-and-twenty and keep forever my place in your heart.

There is the rattle of locks and chains. The heavy door swings open with a shrill squeak. There are footsteps on the stairs, the purposeful tread of boots, and the clank of armor. They have come for me!

I am determined to make a good death since I could not make a good life!

Au revoir, my dearest, I go to eat of the magic apples and become eternal, live long and prosper, and be well and happy! And know that when your time to live is past, and the boat that bears you to the Isle of Apples arrives, I will be waiting for you!

Come Death, and with thy fingers close my eyes,
Or if I live, let me forget myself.

—from *Edward II* by Christopher Marlowe

Postscript

Written by Aymer de Valence, Earl of Pembroke,
June 22nd in the year of Our Lord 1324

All has come to nothing! England teeters on the brink of war and I am dying! The ship creaks and sways upon the waves that carry me to France. Pray that I arrive in time so that, just *once* more, I may pull Edward back from the brink of disaster; like The Fool in a deck of Tarot cards, he is about to stride smiling blithely off the precipice! But I fear both my body and my will shall fail me. There are moments when I cannot draw air into my lungs and a sharp pain pierces my chest and flashes like lightning along my arm.

The Despensers, father and son, rule the realm, and Edward frivols and fawns on Hugh the younger and fancies himself both loved and in love, while Isabelle consoles herself in the arms of Roger Mortimer.

For love of Hugh, Edward has flouted the King of France and war portends unless I can soothe the sovereign's injured pride.

Warwick and Lancaster are dead. The first by cancer of the stomach or poison depending on who tells the tale, and the other by the axe two years ago, beheaded per Edward's pleasure upon a hill to remind him of how Gaveston died.

But now I must tell of Gaveston, it is for him that I have taken up my pen. I owe him that, for, like Edward, I also failed him. And I have already delayed too long although it was years ago that this book came into my hands when Edward left it lying singed and battered with its spine broken upon the hearth while, with the royal physician's aid, he grappled against rage, grief, and madness. Isabelle picked it up and threw it into the fire again then followed the physician into Edward's bedchamber. But I snatched it out, I couldn't let it burn, I wanted to know, I *had* to know, what he had written. That was twelve years ago. I kept it and it has been with me ever since. I could not destroy it. Piers taught me something vital—never judge a man by the mask he wears.

I saw him in my dreams last night, laughing, young, and carefree, dressed all in white, spinning in a shower of apple blossoms. And he spoke to me: "Just because it's a dream doesn't mean it's not real." Is there an Isle of Apples after all as he believed or is Heaven what we make it? Lord forgive me if by wondering I do blaspheme!

Now I must turn back to that fateful June of 1312 and the day, the night, June 9th, for which I shall always reproach myself.

Piers had been well enough to sit a horse that day, but as the afternoon progressed his strength began to falter. I decided to stop at Deddington. My castle of Bampton was nearby and I knew my lady-wife to be in residence, so I thought I might go and pass a pleasant night with her. I should have taken Piers with me, but he seemed so weary. It was a grave misjudgment on my part. But I thought he would be safe; Deddington is such a quiet, secluded little place!

I saw Piers settled comfortably at the rectory and we dined together. While I made arrangements for my departure he sat upon the window-seat. A previous guest had left a lute behind and he took it up and played a mournful air. I did not understand the words; they were in a language unknown to me. Spanish, he told me afterwards, taught to him by a nobleman who had briefly been his lover. And then, as God is my witness, I do not know what possessed me! It happened so quickly; impulsively! I said to him, half-jestingly: "I had no idea before this misfortune brought us together that you were so accomplished! If you were a woman His Majesty would have a serious rival in me to have you for a mistress!"

When I spoke these words his arms went round my neck and ... *he kissed me!* I gasped and pulled away. It all happened so suddenly! Yet when I looked into his eyes there was no seduction there, no teasing or coquetry, only longing, naked and deep. But it was not of the lustful kind, no; it was a yearning of the soul that went too deep to measure. When I close my eyes I can still see those eyes, and his lips, slightly parted, hopeful and atremble. And in that instant my anger fled. I could not reproach him.

Piers divined my thoughts and saw the rejection in my eyes. Eyes downcast, he nodded to show that he understood, and drew away from me and bent to retrieve the lute from where it had fallen on the floor. And despite all the years that have passed I still cannot account for what I did next. I took his face between my hands, tilted it so he would look at me, and then I kissed his brow most tenderly.

Through the open window I saw that the sky was all aglow in hues of orange and rose and I knew if I were to reach Bampton before nightfall I must depart.

"Sleep well, Piers," I said softly, "and I shall see you in the morning." And he in turn bid me good night and asked that I convey his greetings to my lady-wife.

As I mounted my horse, I looked up at the window and saw him leaning there, framed in ivy, watching me, a slender, wistful figure dressed in red and black. I've never forgotten. That was the last time I saw him alive.

And all that night, though I enjoyed the embraces of my lady-wife, it was those eyes I thought of. Like some unquiet spirit they haunted me, and still do.

When I arrived back at Deddington in the gray light of dawn I found him gone. The men I had left to guard him had remained at their posts, indifferent to his fate, and let Warwick and Lancaster take him. The beautiful white greyhound lay dead across the bed with her neck broken. I nearly sank down and wept in outrage and despair, but I did not. Instead, I rode forth to seek help.

I sought aid in Oxford, from the University, lawyers, and justices, and also from the Earl of Gloucester, the brother of Gaveston's wife. "Let him die as he deserves!" they all said. "While Gaveston lives England will never know peace!" So I rode on to Warwick Castle where I argued long and vigorously with Warwick and Lancaster. Gaveston was my prisoner and they had no right to remove him from my custody, I railed, furthermore, I had pledged everything I possessed upon his safety. They laughed in my face, called me a fool, and told me to "learn to negotiate more cautiously." They would not let me see him either, so I never knew until I read his words that he did not blame me, for in the days and years that followed many rumors flourished that I betrayed him into their hands. I am glad to know that he never doubted me or felt any anger or bitterness towards me. Had he desired to, Piers could have destroyed me with but a few strokes of his pen.

Had he known of it, Edward would never have forgiven me for that kiss. I myself was present as he read and saw him summon the Earl of Richmond and chase him all around the room and beat him savagely about the head with the book, the pearls popping free and the emeralds cutting into his scalp, before Edward collapsed weeping on the floor and banished him to Scotland. But about that kiss Piers kept silent and protected me. From beyond the grave, he commanded Edward not to punish me. Had he not done so, I fear I might have gone the way of Lancaster; blinded by the madness of grief, Edward was determined to punish all who had played a part in Gaveston's demise. And I was counted among his enemies. But Edward did not hold me to my pledge, he did not take my lands and titles away, and until two years past, when the cunning Despensers stepped fully into prominence, I was his chief advisor. "Pembroke the Peacemaker" they called me and it was my steady hand that kept the ship of state from floundering.

It was Gaveston's misfortune that I, being a man of honor, expected to find the same honor in others, when in truth they had none. And so they killed him.

I have had the details of his execution from several who witnessed it.

Piers met them boldly at the foot of the stairs, confident, nonchalant, and smiling. Anyone who says he fell on his knees and wept and begged for mercy is either misinformed or a liar.

"My Lord of Lancaster, Edward shall be *very* angry with you if you spoil my looks by striking off my head!" he chided saucily.

But Lancaster was not amused. "It is my greatest hope that the day will come when my royal cousin shall thank me for what I am about to do," he said solemnly. "I have spent many hours upon my knees praying that one day, when all his grief and anger are spent, he will understand that what I do now I do for the good of Edward and England alike. You cannot be allowed to live, Gaveston; you do not *deserve* to live!"

"My Lord of Lancaster, even if you live to be a hundred you shall *never* match all the hours I have spent upon my knees!" Piers boasted with that famous Gascon swagger. "Why if I had a gold coin for every time I have gone down upon my knees ... Oh, come to think of it, I do!" He threw back his head and his laughter rang throughout the dungeon.

And then, with nimble grace, he darted up the stairs.

"Come along then, I would be done with this!" he called back over his shoulder as the guards rushed to surround him.

It was accounted witchcraft by those who had seen the bruised and battered body beneath his clothes that he was able to move at all, let alone with such ease and grace.

At the top of the stairs he turned and looked down at Lancaster.

"The Lady gave me life, My Lord, *so who are you to take it away?* Do no harm lest it come back to you threefold! Remember that, Tom of Lancaster, *and what you do to me someone may someday do to you!*"

Lancaster shivered under Gaveston's piercing gaze.

"*Take him away! In God's name, take him away!*" he ordered and brusquely shooed the other guards to go on ahead of him. When he thought no one was looking, he surreptitiously crossed himself.

Some weeks later, when the hour was late and he was far into his cups, Lancaster confided to me that when Gaveston spoke these words and looked at him thus, the hairs on the back of his neck stood on end. "The Gascon had unnatural powers," he slurred as he drank himself into oblivion, "I'm glad I sent him to Hell where he belongs!"

And I, knowing what came later and how Lancaster died, have to wonder, was it some kind of divine retribution or mere coincidence? Or was it another of Gaveston's games? Did he only *seem* to foretell the future? After all, Piers knew Edward better than anyone. Lancaster murdered the object of Edward's grand obsession, and it doesn't take the Oracle of Delphi to predict that Edward would seek vengeance. Then again, standing on the threshold of Death, maybe Piers truly did catch a glimpse of the future.

I only know that on the 22nd day of March in the year 1322, Thomas, Earl of Lancaster, his head and feet bare, and clad in the coarse robe of a penitent, ascended St. Thomas's Hill, just outside the walls of his own castle, to die a traitor's death. He was mounted on a worthless, flea-bitten, bag-of-bones white donkey and accompanied by a cheering, jeering mob of peasants who pelted him with offal. It took three strokes of the axe to sever his head. But I digress, and now, I must return to Gaveston.

At the top of Blacklow Hill two soldiers guided him to stand before a large flat-topped stone that seemed to glow an eerie white in the moonlight. There was a sizable crowd present despite the late hour; men, women, and children, they had all come to watch The Gascon die.

All was still as Piers gazed down upon the stone. No breeze was stirring nor did anyone make a sound. Many expected him to break then and beg for mercy. Instead, he looked up at the moon, and, spreading his arms in a gesture of entreaty, began to speak in a voice clear and steady: "Lady, Mother of us all, hear my plea! Send a boat to convey me quickly to the Isle of Apples!"

Suddenly, from out of nowhere, a breeze stirred the trees, causing the rustling branches to incline towards Piers as if they were nodding.

All around, guards and peasants crossed themselves and backed away from him with fear in their eyes. Some clasped rosaries or crucifixes if they had them or made signs with their hands against witchcraft and the evil eye. Others fled.

But Piers, appearing completely confident and serene, merely bowed his head and fervently uttered "Thank you!"

Was it some sort of chicanery? Gaveston—and his old nurse Agnes too—had an uncanny knack for predicting the weather; did he read some sign and know a breeze was about to blow? Or did some higher power answer his prayer? I do not know.

There was a priest present, for none would have it said that they had denied him this consolation in his final hours, but Piers disdained his offer of confession.

"*I am done with games!*" he declared, his eyes and voice hot and adamant.

And though the priest besought him earnestly to think of his immortal soul and repent his evil ways, Piers would not hear him. He silenced him with a look and waved him away. Then Lancaster, flanked by the Earls of Hereford and Arundel, read the sentence, but Piers interrupted to ask the whereabouts of Warwick.

"As you can see, he is not here!" Lancaster snapped.

"Ah, so The Black Dog prefers to keep to his kennel!" Piers exclaimed. "He has the courage to send me to my death but it doesn't extend to seeing the deed done!"

Lancaster glared furiously at Piers for a long moment then continued reading.

"And may God have mercy on your soul for no one else will!" he finished sharply. "Piers Gaveston, have you any last words?"

With an impish sparkle in his eyes, and a nod of mock solemnity, Piers answered: "Yes, My Lords." And after a lingering pause to further madden Lancaster, flippantly announced: "My feet hurt!"

Lancaster and the others were appalled. A condemned man's dying speech should be solemn and repentant!

"The Gascon seemed to laugh right in the face of Death!" Geoffrey the guard averred. "God's teeth, he was an audacious rascal!"

"*Well sit down then!*" Lancaster shouted, waving his arm in the prearranged signal.

It happened then, quicker than it takes time to tell. A powerfully built Welsh soldier stepped forward and, without an instant's hesitation, thrust his dagger into Gaveston's heart.

He gasped softly, all the color draining from his face, as he sank to his knees, gracefully, like a flower wilting. Then a second Welshman leaned over, grasped his hair, and pulled him forward so that his head lay upon the stone. He rested his head there, as if it were a pillow, his eyes closed, his lips murmuring softly, and then the broadsword fell, severing his slender neck in a single, swift stroke, and the warm redness of his blood gushed out to forever stain the white stone. So ended the life of Piers Gaveston.

Only in death would any show pity for the despised Gascon Favorite. When both Lancaster and Warwick refused to take responsibility for his remains, some shoemakers reunited head and body with a strong steel needle and black thread, and, with a ladder serving as a makeshift bier, bore his body away to the Dominican Friars at Oxford where it was embalmed most skillfully. But since Gaveston had died excommunicate Christian burial was denied him.

Dressed in an elaborate gold brocade robe liberally spangled with diamonds and pearls to symbolize Edward's tears, with a skullcap of delicate gold mesh embellished with seed pearls covering his dark hair, Piers lay in state in the chapel at Langley for two years while everyone with any influence tried to persuade Edward to allow the funeral to take place. Even in death, Edward could not let Piers go. Preserved with balsam and spices, as beautiful as he was in life, and looking as though he was but sleeping, Piers had in death truly become the dragonfly in amber.

In the end, upon Edward's orders, a magnificent tomb was constructed. He was so grateful to the Dominican Friars for preserving Piers' beauty that a new monastery was built for them adjoining the sepulcher. At all hours, day and night, the clock around, he charged, twelve monks must be in the chapel praying for the soul of Piers Gaveston, and for this service each would receive the sum of 100 marks per annum. And to this day, when Edward can spare the time from dancing attendance on chaste and cold Hugh Despenser, and trying to connive and lure him into bed, to Langley he hastens to weep and lavish kisses upon the life-like alabaster effigy that crowns Gaveston's tomb. With one hand upon a cold, unyielding alabaster thigh, he sits and dreams of the past and vows "I will love you till my dying day!" then weeps floods of guilty tears because he has fallen in love with Hugh Despenser. And he has grown a beard, short, gold, and curling, which he proclaims is a testament to his grief. Of this book he never speaks; he has forgotten what he has no wish to remember, so his illusions will never perish, and reality need never intrude upon his memories.

In his grief for Piers, which would forever run the gauntlet betwixt lust, sentiment, melancholy, and anger, Edward and Isabelle drew closer—for a time at least—and produced four children, a pair each of sons and daughters, before Edward's passion for Hugh Despenser permanently estranged them.

For the entire two years Piers lay in state, Agnes sat nigh constantly in the chapel beside his coffin. Slowly she wasted away. On the day Piers was finally entombed and the alabaster effigy set in place she stood beside Edward and was among the last to look upon his face. Then she turned to Edward and hissed one word "*Murderer!*" The next morning a maidservant found her dead. Of old age or a broken heart; who can rightly say?

I do not know what became of Dragon, he simply disappeared. Perhaps he took to the roads and wanders still a vagabond once again?

For six years Meg wore widow's weeds and grieved for Piers, faithful to his memory, preserving tenderly all his possessions at Wallingford, and cherishing the daughter, parrot, and spaniel he gave her. All the suitors who came calling she turned away, vowing that she would never take another husband. Edward tried to wed her to his new Favorite, but, in the end, it was her sister Eleanor who stood with Hugh Despenser before the church doors and was showered with silver coins by a jubilant and smiling Edward.

Then Grunella the midwife died and Meg was prevailed upon to take the child Amy into her household as Guillaume Gaveston, her reputed father, had perished in the same year as Piers in the aftermath of a drunken fall in which he tragically mistook a window for a door.

One day, while Meg, Joan, and Amy sat embroidering in the rose garden, Meg asked the precocious dark-haired child if she had any memories of her parents. Of her mother she had none, Sarah having died giving birth to her, but she remembered her father quite well. And in the child's words Meg recognized her husband; no one, not even a child, could confuse Piers and Guillaume. And she remembered that he always wore a sparkling brooch shaped like a crescent moon and a ring set with a red stone that was big and round like an enormous cherry.

The truth nearly destroyed Meg, and, for a time, madness seemed to claim her. All of Piers' possessions were brought together in the courtyard in an enormous bonfire, Joan and Amy were sent to separate convents, and even the parrot and the spaniel were dispatched to the marketplace and sold and the money given to the Church. Meg knelt in the courtyard and wept as her love for Piers went up in smoke and flames. Then she dried her tears, put aside her widow's weeds, and married the most persistent of her suitors—Hugh Audley. They have a daughter now, named Margaret after her mother. To the details of their married life I am not privy, though to Hugh Audley's love I can attest; it is there in his eyes every time he looks at Meg, he worships and adores her. Piers hoped that she would forget him, and I pray that she will also forgive him someday.

Sequestered behind the convent walls at Amesbury, Joan died of a fever at the start of this year. As for Amy, over the years I have watched her grow from child to woman. Every year I find some excuse to visit the convent though I find it so disquieting that afterwards I leave shivering in a cold sweat with my knees wobbling, swearing that this time is the last, yet I always go back. The sensuous curves of her body show through the shapeless novice's habit and a ringlet of black hair always manages to escape from the modest white coif. Though I have never spoken a word to her, when I am there her eyes follow me everywhere, quizzical, mischievous, and inviting. They are Gaveston's eyes, and her smile is Gaveston's smile.

Edward now entirely relies on Hugh "The Indispensable Despenser." He will not make a single decision without the approval of the man they call "the King's right eye." He is an able man, honesty compels me to admit, but a colder, more ruthless one I have never met. He might do much good if his ambitions were for England and its people and not himself alone. He uses his power to take everything he can, he bullies, threatens, and intimidates people until they agree to sell him their lands at greatly reduced prices, and if these tactics fail he is not above resorting to violence, devious and cunning manipulations of the Law, or even blatant and outright fraud. He will do *anything* to get what he wants and will let *no one* stand in his way; anyone who tries to thwart him faces ruin, imprisonment, and disgrace. But Edward is blind to his beloved's vicious streak; anyone he loves can do no wrong, he just smiles and says to his darling: "Do what thou wilt; my heart and kingdom are yours to command!" And Hugh takes him at his word. He and his father rule the realm and leave Edward free to dig ditches, thatch roofs, trim the hedges, and dream of Piers Gaveston.

But hatred more venomous than the poison from a serpent's fangs is the greatest of the rewards Hugh Despenser has reaped from Edward's favor. And by the memory of Piers Gaveston he *is* cursed. In England now it is often declared that Despenser is "thrice worse than Gaveston was ever!" And all wait now with bated breaths to see how Edward's second great passion will end. I cannot think it will end happily for any.

At the time I write this I am summoned by Edward's wringing hands and anxious tears from the shadows of disgrace where the Despensers banished me. Fealty was due to the King of France for England's dominions across the sea. Edward would not travel without Hugh, nor would the French King welcome the man who has made Isabelle's life "a greater Hell and torment than The Gascon ever did," so Edward, famous for his radiant health, claimed sickness and cancelled his voyage. This was taken as an insult, and now across the sea is sent "Pembroke the Peacemaker." Whether Death will spare me long enough to render this one last service to England I can only pray!

Addendum

Writ by John, valet to the Earl of Pembroke

On this day, the 23rd of June in the year of Our Lord 1324, my master, the Earl of Pembroke, arrived in Paris. While at table dining, he went suddenly statue-still and sat with his eyes agog, staring intently at the open doorway. Slowly, he stood up, his body all atremble.

"Is it really you?" he asked, but neither I nor the other servants saw anything but an empty door.

With quivering limbs he walked unsteadily round the table, bracing himself against the backs of the other chairs. As he approached the threshold, he smiled and reached out his hand as if to welcome a newly arrived guest, and in that instant the years and infirmity seemed to peel away from him. And then, upon the threshold, he collapsed.

I ran to him and knelt and supported his head in my lap while the others went to summon help—a doctor and a priest—but he died before either could arrive. May he rest in peace!

978-0-595-45523
0-595-45523-9

Printed in the United States
108225LV00003B/9/A